# MATEFINDER

MATEFINDER BOOK ONE

LEIA STONE

Copyright © 2014 by Leia Stone. All rights reserved.
Matefinder characters, names and related items are trademarks owned by Leia Stone.
No part of this publication may be reproduced. Stored in a retrieval system, or transmitted in any form or by any means, electronic, mechanical, photocopying, recording, or otherwise, without written permission of the author.
This is a work of fiction. Names, characters, places, and incidents either are the product of the author's imagination or are used fictitiously. Any resemblance to actual persons, live or dead are purely coincidental.
Stone, Leia
Matefinder
Gilbert, Arizona 85297
1. Fantasy Fiction

For information on reproducing sections of this book or sales of this book go to www.facebook.com/leia.stone
leiastonebooks@gmail.com

 Created with Vellum

## DEDICATION

*For every woman who has ever had to fight to be who they were destined to be, this book is for yo*

## 1
## CHANGED

My black Jetta's headlights lit up the dark night as I crept my car up the winding road that led to Mount Hood. My roommate had convinced me to take a break from my hectic life, and go stay at her parents' vacation home on the mountain. As I pulled into a gas station to grab a coffee, the dash clock said it was near midnight. The hour drive to Mount Hood from Portland was making me fall asleep.

Stepping out, I silently cursed at the light falling of rain. I was still wearing the yoga pants and tight crop top that I had on from teaching my women's self-defense class. My rain jacket was shoved in the bottom of my duffle bag in the trunk. I jogged across the parking lot, clutching my credit card and keys, jumped up on the curb and tripped, dropping my keys. Luckily, I caught myself before face-planting onto the cement.

*Real smooth, Aurora.* I bent down to grab my keys just as the glass door opened. Afraid of getting stepped on, I stood quickly and came face-to-face with a gorgeous guy in his mid-twenties. *Hello there.* He was a mere breath away and locked me in an intense stare. He had medium-dark East Indian skin with wild chocolate-colored hair that hung in loose wisps around his strong jaw. Standing over six feet tall, he was made from rock-hard muscle. My eyes drifted down his body as I took in his shirtless torso and chiseled abs. He wore cut off sweatpants, and no shoes. *Odd.* I tried my hardest not to completely check him out—but was that an eight-pack? I blushed as he caught me looking.

"Hi." He flashed a gorgeous smile full of white teeth and dimples. His voice was a deep baritone that made my stomach warm.

I swallowed hard. "Hi." The air was heavy with some sort of tangible connection. I felt like I had met him before, although I was sure I would have remembered a guy like him.

A dirty-blond, equally gorgeous man stepped up behind him and clapped him on the shoulder. "Shall we get back to our *run?*" the friend asked.

Snapped from my trance, I smiled weakly and brushed past the tall, dark, and gorgeous man. As his arm brushed against mine, I felt my stomach warm again. Damn, how long had it been since I'd been on a date? My hormones were going crazy on me. *Down girl.* The guy could have been an axe murderer for all I knew.

The door shut behind me and I poured my coffee, relishing the smell of a fresh cup of Joe. It reminded me of the two things I loved most in the morning, coffee and the thump of my fist hitting my punching bag. One woke me up, the other made me feel safe. Both equally important for getting through the day. After paying for the coffee, I walked back out to my car just in time to see the two guys walking into the thick woods.

Not many people roamed the mountain after midnight ... barefoot.

Hmm, definitely an axe murderer. The hot guys were always twisted.

Sipping my hot coffee, I sighed. Thirty more minutes and I would be snuggled up in my mountain retreat, hopefully drinking wine and not coffee. I sooo needed this relaxing weekend.

I pulled back out onto the main road, single-lane and winding. A thick fog had settled on the ground, leaving me low visibility. Typical Oregon weather. My mind drifted to that guy from the gas station; he seemed different. All jokes of being an axe murderer aside, I couldn't shake the feeling I knew him from somewhere—like déjà vu. Maybe I should have stayed and talked to him.

As the road curved up ahead, I glanced at the clock on my dash for a split second. When I looked back up, I spotted a mother deer with her two babies right in front of me. *Shit!* I didn't think—slamming my foot on the brakes, I swerved hard to the left, plowing through a flimsy rusted guardrail and then my car was airborne, flying off the mountain.

Car accidents were so weird; they took seconds to

the observer, but when you were in them they feel felt really long and drawn out. My car went airborne and I knew it was bad. It was going to be a horrible accident and there was nothing I could do. Oh God, why the hell did I have to be a vegetarian? A meat-eater might have taken those deer out no problem. As I sailed over the treetops and down the embankment, all I could do was hold my breath and brace for impact.

My car hit the ground with such force that my head cracked into the dash and then all went black.

---

As I came to, I realized I was hanging halfway out of the open car door. Oh shit ... the accident. I tried to move, but a whimper escaped my throat as pain flared in my body. A warm, wet sensation trickled from my abdomen, and as much as I didn't want to, I looked down. A scream ripped from me when I saw a thick tree branch protruding from my belly.

Oh God. *No.* Adrenaline pulsed through my body as panic flooded my system. I was going to die.

The crunch of footsteps caught my attention, and I looked up to see someone approaching. My vision was blurry, but as the footsteps drew nearer I saw that it was that guy from the gas station. His eyes were wide and ... *yellow?* The buzzing in my head was getting louder and I was starting to feel faint and cold. My body shook and I couldn't speak as the fear gripped me. I was totally going to die, right here in the woods, in front of the hot axe murderer from the gas station. There was nothing I could do—what an awful feeling, this helplessness. I hated it and I swore I'd never feel that way again.

Suddenly the man dropped his pants, standing completely naked before me. *What the hell?* Before I could process his nakedness, fur rippled up his arms; the sound of bones cracking drowned out the buzzing in my head, and then he shrank down on all fours as muscle bulked into the form of an animal. All of a sudden, he was a huge, black wolf, staring at me with piercing, coppery eyes.

I was hallucinating; this was what happened before you died. Too much blood loss made you visualize human wolf-monsters. You entered some insane dream world. *Yes, that explained it.* The dreamy wolf padded over to me with those yellow eyes and bared his razor-sharp teeth.

Oh shit, bad dream.

"No, please," I whimpered, because as he got closer, the glistening saliva on his teeth looked way too real, and I could smell the animal on him. I thought of all the things I had yet to do with my life. There was so much I wanted to do. I wasn't ready to die. As he lunged at me, a startled shriek escaped me, and pain exploded in my body as his teeth clamped down deep into my flesh.

'Mine.' His voice echoed inside my head, and took hold before I collapsed again into a dreamy state where I couldn't tell reality from vision.

---

Pain everywhere. Every cell in my body ached and I felt on the verge of losing consciousness again. *'Stay with me. Please survive,'* his voice said, the man from the gas station, and I felt a hand cup my face. The last thing I thought of before going unconscious again was the memory of my body lying by the winding road that led to Mount Hood. And the tall, dark man that changed into a wolf and bite me.

---

I jerked awake sometime later and sat up, fully expecting to be sore or to have stitches all over my body —bandages, a cast, something. Looking down at my smooth pale arms, I saw no injuries. What the hell? The fresh memory of my nightmare was still playing in my head and I was having a hard time remembering what was real. I had on an oversized t-shirt and it smelled like *him*. Frantically, I pulled it up and traced my fingers along the small, white, teeth-shaped scar that marked my belly. That's where he'd bit me first. Oh my God, he *bit* me. It all came back to me now, like getting hit in the gut with a baseball bat, the memory of last night slammed into me. Other than that bite mark, my skin was flawless, which wasn't possible. I looked around. I was in a regular room with hardwood floors, a small bed, and a dresser. I tried to control my breathing to keep from hyperventilating.

My mind flashed back to the scene, to last night. The dark-skinned man that turned into a ... a wolf, and attacked me. Well, that wasn't quite right. I had been in an accident. Oh God, it was so bad. Remembering it, I grabbed my head and tried not to think of the pain I had felt. My leg had been twisted at an odd angle—blood pouring freely from my abdomen—I had been waiting to die. If I hadn't tried to swerve and miss those damn deer, I wouldn't have crashed my Jetta. What do they tell you? Swerve into the mountain? Away from the mountain? Don't swerve? Hit the deer? I couldn't remember. I was a vegetarian, so I had gone on instinct. My instinct said not to hit the cute baby deer, and it got me killed.

Well ... I *would* have died, but then *he* attacked me, he *changed* me. No matter how much I tried to deny it, I knew it—I could feel it. It was an awful crawling feeling under my skin, this drum beating rapidly in my chest, an anxiety attack waiting to hit and bring me to my knees. I was ... I was ... a shapeshifter?

'You're a werewolf,' the man's voice said in my mind, I jumped up, startled, and looked around the room. Oh God. This wasn't happening. His voice ... was inside my head. That word ... he said...

*Werewolf.*

The panic roared inside of my body so strongly that I suddenly felt nauseated. Thinking quickly, I grabbed an empty flower vase next to the bed and vomited inside. I hadn't had a full-blown panic attack since I was a kid, but considering the circumstances I wasn't surprised. My heart was racing as I looked down at my body once more. How was this possible? I'd healed, like in the movies, like Hollywood werewolves did. No, no, this wasn't happening—it wasn't real, I told myself. I wanted to believe that it was all a hallucination, but I couldn't deny the facts. I had been near death, horribly injured and bleeding, and then he ... bit me. Now, here I stood, fully healed and having an existential crisis, a man speaking inside my head. I bit my lip as tears rolled down my cheeks.

A soft knock came at the door, I set the vase down on the floor and jumped back into the bed, covering my legs, which were bare. Reaching over, I grabbed a pen from the nightstand and gripped it under the covers.

"Come in?" I said, unsure—it wasn't like it was my room. The door creaked open and a girl who looked to be about twenty years old poked her head in. She had bright red hair that was cut in a short pixie style and spiked up all over, with long bangs in front. Her heart-shaped face and green eyes gave her an innocent girl-next-door look.

*Pack,* I thought, and shivered at the new feelings. That voice. It was my voice but different. Oh shit, I was losing it for sure. Full-blown psychosis.

"Hi," she said tentatively, as she came in and softly closed the door behind her. In her delicate hand was a plastic bag.

"Hi," I croaked back, unsure of what to say and suddenly realizing how thirsty I was. *Where the hell am I and what the hell happened to me?* That's what I really wanted to say. My gaze fell to the window, which didn't seem to be barred. Had I been kidnapped?

She tossed the bag onto the bed and then her eyes flicked to the vase full of vomit, but she quickly looked away and didn't mention it. "We seem to be the same size, so I hope they fit."

I opened the bag, and saw clean clothes and a pair of flip-flops.

"Thanks." I was naked under this shirt. *Oh my God. Who dressed me?* My cheeks went red.

"Kai sent me to check on you. To help you get accustomed. I can't believe you survived." She sat at the edge of the bed and gave me a warm smile.

"Kai?" I swallowed nervously. Somehow the name resonated deep inside me; a warm tingly feeling spread throughout my body, settling my nerves.

"The guy who saved your life. Our alpha." She seemed unsure of what to say next, peering at me with those big green eyes.

My voice shook. "Alpha?"

Don't say it—don't you dare say it.

"Alpha werewolf," she said softly, gauging my reaction.

That's when the second panic attack hit. Breathing rapidly, the room spun as I leaned back on the bed and stared at the ceiling. Holy shit, this wasn't happening—no, no, no. An alpha? A dominating asshat telling me what to do? No way. Sitting up, I lifted my shirt again to see the scarred bite mark there.

*Oh God, this is happening—this* has *happened.*

The girl sat there patiently while I had my freak-out. Hottie eight-pack gas station guy was my new alpha? My stomach dropped. Everything I had ever heard or read about alphas in books was not good.

"Does he own us?"

I shuddered at the thought. I had worked very hard to get my college degree, start my own business, and become an independent woman. The last thing I needed, on top of becoming a flesh-eating monster, was to have some psycho hopped-on steroids bossing me around.

The girl barked out a laugh. "Well, that's funny. I hadn't thought of it that way. He protects us, keeps us safe from rival packs. Keeps us fed, happy, and takes care of all of our needs. He keeps peace within the pack. He's a good alpha, the strongest man in the pack, and we're lucky to have him."

I noticed she didn't exactly answer my question straightforwardly. Like, did he own us? Yes or no. When I didn't say anything more, she spoke again.

"My name is Emma."

She held out her hand to me and I shook it. "I'm Aurora. You will have to excuse me but ... twenty-four hours ago werewolves didn't exist to me."

She looked at me with pity. "I'm sure it's hard to believe. Want me to shift and prove it?"

My eyes went wide. "No, I'm good."

Seeing it once was enough for now, and I hated to admit that I felt something lurking just beneath the surface of my skin. My wolf, I assumed. It was a knowing that needed no proof. I was different and there was no going back.

She held up her hand. "How about a partial shift?" The sound of a snapping twig made my back go rigid before I realized it wasn't a twig—it was her bone. Right before my eyes, her fingers turned to claws, fur covering them completely, until it became small reddish wolf paw.

My mouth gaped open for a full minute and I had nothing intelligible to say.

"Werewolves are real," I said stupidly.

She grinned and her hand popped again, shrinking and losing its fur until it was a pale slender human hand. "You need the vase again?" She tipped her head to where the vase stood and I smirked. "Maybe."

We sat there in companionable silence for a few long moments.

"How old are you?" she inquired.

"Twenty-two. How old are you?" I enjoyed the normalcy of the question.

"Nineteen." She sat there in silence for another few minutes, biting her lip. "Look, I'm sorry about your accident. This must be really overwhelming. I can take you out to meet the others, but first we should go over some things. Kind of like Werewolf 101."

"Werewolf 101?" Sadly, that class wasn't offered at my college.

"Yeah, let's start with the rules. When you're around Kai, you don't look him directly in the eyes for more than a few seconds. You actually wouldn't be able to hold a staring contest with him. It's physically impossible for less dominant wolves. You don't want him to think you're challenging his strength to lead us."

Well, that confirmed my fears. He was a dominating, controlling alpha male. Everything about those men grated on my every nerve.

"How're you doing? You okay?" Emma asked.

I picked this odd moment to suddenly think of my roommate and my mother. How worried they must be that they hadn't heard from me. "When can I go home?" I asked shakily.

Emma's face fell. "Aurora, you're pack now." She rested her hand on my knee and it felt oddly comforting.

*Pack,* a small voice inside me said, and I tried not to jump. It was my voice again.

"You can't leave. Kai wouldn't let you. If he cut ties with you, then you wouldn't last a week as a lone wolf before another pack found you. Female werewolves are *rare*. Most of them don't survive the change, and only a handful are born to werewolf couples. If another pack claimed you, they might not treat you properly. Kai's pack is respectful of females. They cherish us, protect us. Not all packs are like that." Something dark crossed her face, but before I could figure it out, it was gone.

Great. I was stuck here. For now.

"I can't go home, can't stare the alpha in the eye. Okay, keep going." I took a deep breath. Werewolves existed and I was one of them. I would have been dead if Kai hadn't changed me, yet I couldn't go home. Just breathe, I told myself.

Emma nodded. "That small voice you are probably hearing, that's letting you know that I'm pack, or that you're safe, that's your wolf, your instinct. She will barely speak to you now, but as you get to know her better and trust her more, you and she will become one."

I could only nod and try not to feel revulsion at the thought. *There is a monster inside of me.*

Emma smiled. "You're doing great. Now that big booming voice in your head, that's Kai. He can pick up on your thoughts and emotions, and he can speak directly into your mind. You'll get used to it."

No, I wouldn't. I never would, I thought, but I just nodded because Emma was turning out to be a really sweet person, who only seemed to be doing her job. She was like the pack's HR representative, welcoming me to my new job.

She returned my smile and continued: "In a moment, I want you to change into the clothes I brought you. Then I'm going to take you out to meet everyone, and we can establish your place in the pack. The sooner we do that, the better off everyone will feel."

"My place?" I could feel something inside me thrumming with excitement. My inner wolf, I recognized.

Emma nodded, sending red spiky hair fluttering around her face. "Every pack functions smoothly because we all have a place in it. There's no need for me to get into a dominance battle with Sadie because I know she's ninth in the pack of dominants. I'm twenty-sixth, the last and most submissive wolf. Everyone protects me and that's my place, that's where I feel most comfortable. That's why Kai sent me in here, so that there was no chance that your inner wolf would feel threatened."

I nodded. Something about what she said felt right. I would go out there, establish my place, and then talk to this alpha about my old life. I needed to at least call my mother ... and my roommate, Lexi.

"How do I establish my place?" I stared into Emma's green eyes. I was envisioning some type of fight or weird interview with the alpha.

She quickly lowered her gaze after a few seconds and swallowed hard. "A staring contest," she muttered. "You will start with me. If I lower my eyes first, then you are more dominant than I am and you move to the next person in the pack, so on and so forth. You do this until you lower your eyes, then we all know your place. No fights. Kai runs a clean pack."

Seemed pretty straightforward. I nodded.

She elbowed me. "I can already tell you are more dominant than me. For a human female to survive the change, you have to at least be in the middle. You might even be higher than Sadie." She grinned like that would bring her immense joy.

Nausea churned in my belly. "Well, you survived, so you must be pretty strong, too."

Shock colored her features. "Oh, Aurora, I wasn't changed, I was born this way. Both of my parents are wolves."

"Oh. Well, how many females do you have in the pack that have survived the change?" My heart raced in anticipation.

She fiddled with her hands. "Just you."

Before I could even process that, Emma cocked her head to the side. "Kai says everyone is waiting, so go get dressed, okay?" She smiled sweetly and left me alone in the room, closing the door behind her.

I stared at the bag of new clothes in shock. This reminded me of how after staying at a hotel, you can't wait to get back to your own bed. It felt like I was on some weird vacation, and I wanted my own bed and clothes, but I had a sick feeling that wasn't going to happen. What else could I do but go have a staring contest and then try to get my life back.

When I walked out of the room, all changed and ready, Emma was waiting for me. Her face was taut with anxiety. Was she nervous ... for me? My stomach suddenly tightened with unease. As she led me through the beautiful home, I realized we were in a huge house that overlooked Mount Hood. The ceilings were vaulted, with exposed wood beams, and one of the living room's walls was entirely made of glass. Peering through the glass, I could see a large gathering of people stood outside; they were all lined up in a row and talking. As we came closer, Emma led me through the front door and they became silent.

*Pack. Pack. Pack,* my inner wolf chanted, and I tried not to freak out at the foreign feeling.

As I scanned the faces of the group, some smiled at me but others scowled. Then my eyes rested on *him*. Kai. I glanced at his chestnut eyes and then quickly looked down toward his full lips, remembering Emma's advice not to meet his gaze. If I wasn't feeling like I had been abducted by aliens and taken to a new werewolf planet, I might actually admit that my new *alpha* was extremely sexy.

His eyes hooded as his lips quirked up to a smile, and I remembered the other thing Emma had said, that he could read my emotions, my thoughts. *Oh God, kill me now.* His smirk disappeared as he stepped forward, placing a warm, possessive hand on my shoulder that sent my pulse skyrocketing. I wasn't sure whether I wanted to break his hand or be turned on by the dominating gesture. Emma smiled at me before taking her place at the end of the line.

"Brothers and sisters, a new pup has joined our ranks!" Kai's voice commanded attention and oozed with so much power the hairs on the back of my neck stood up. "This strong female survived a horrific accident and the change. I feel your anxiety about her. Is she submissive, should I protect her? Is she dominant, more dominant than me? Could she be my mate? I think it's best to establish her place, before we have celebrations to welcome her. This will ease your minds and your wolves."

I balked inside when he said *mate*, but kept my

face a mask of calm. Werewolves could smell fear, right? Well, I wouldn't give them the satisfaction.

Kai walked me toward the end of the line to where Emma stood and she smiled sweetly.

"Emma, you have explained how this will go?" Kai spoke to her as if she was a cherished little sister, somebody to protect.

She nodded. "You can start with Sammy. I already know she's more dom than me."

Kai let go of my shoulder and Sammy stepped forward. He looked about fourteen years old, had sandy-blond hair and kind brown eyes. I stared into his eyes, heart pounding, not out of fear but out of nerves. Where would I fall in the pack? What would it mean? If I was low, did that make me weak? If I was high, did that make me more of a monster than I already thought I was? After about five seconds, Sammy looked down. Sweat beaded on his forehead and I wondered if that was from me. I glanced nervously at Kai and he nodded as I moved along to the next person, a tall and lanky man with caring eyes. After a few seconds, he too looked down, sweat showing on his brow as well. So I kept moving up the line. Once I got to the middle, the pack began to murmur.

*'Silence,'* Kai commanded. It was so alien to hear someone speak in my mind that I nearly jumped, startled. I looked back at Kai, unsure now if I should proceed.

"Keep going, Aurora. You're doing exactly what Emma and I told you. Don't worry."

Don't worry! I was pretty sure I was a monster and I was being made to provoke other monsters by glaring at them. But yeah, don't worry! Again, he smirked. *Ugh, get out of my head!* I just wanted to get this over with! Turning, I faced the next person and then the next; each time something within me rattled like it was stuck in a cage. I walked to the next person, who I assumed to be Sadie. She was ninth from the top of the pack and had long, ink-black hair, and medium-dark skin. She looked Native American, maybe mixed; she was beautiful, exotic, and intimidating as hell. As we stared, her glare cut right into me and I felt my pulse pick up the longer we locked eyes. A bit of sweat beaded on my upper lip and heat flushed throughout my body, but before I was bothered too much by the feeling, Sadie looked down. She was panting as she cursed under her breath and shot me a death look. I assumed she wasn't happy about my place in the pack being above hers. Swallowing hard, I moved on.

It began to be more of a challenge to hold their gazes, but I was able to. Three pack members from the top, whispers started again. Kai had to quiet everyone multiple times, and he kept reassuring me that I was doing fine and needed to continue. So I did, until I was standing in front of the last man. A man I recognized— the guy who had been with Kai at the gas station. Tall, broad-shouldered, arms littered with scars. What would be so bad that it would scar a werewolf? His ice-blue eyes met mine and he stepped forward, puffing up his chest in dominance.

"My name is Max and I have been Kai's second-in-command for forty-six years." His voice could cut steel. It was full of anger and jealousy. I swallowed hard. Forty-six years? He didn't look a day over twenty-five and neither did Kai. Kai put his hand on Max's shoulder to comfort him.

"Yes, you have, and a great second you have been. I know this is a bit of a shock to all of us, to have a newly-changed female so high up in the pack. But as you know, nothing will feel settled with you about Aurora until we know how dominant she is. Your wolf will wonder if you could take her in a fight and I can't have that. Not in my pack. Max, Aurora ... continue."

Shit. I was already sweating because the last two staredowns had been extremely difficult. I had felt like looking down multiple times, but didn't, not before they did. But with Max I was scared; I was genuinely afraid of what this would mean. If I was more dominant than him, would I become the second-in-command of some new pack I knew nothing about? Some life I didn't ask for? Maybe I should just look down halfway through so I didn't have to deal with this...?

*'If you do that, his wolf will always wonder where you stand, and a fight will break out eventually.'*

Kai, in my head ... great.

I stepped forward, so close that I could feel the heat of Max's body against my exposed skin. We locked eyes and I didn't blink. I barely breathed. After about thirty seconds he started panting and I felt weak in the knees. I had the strongest urge to bow my head in submission, to give up, but I pushed the urge back. I *was* strong.

I had been through a lot in my short twenty-two years on this planet, enough to give me a thick skin—through things that still gave me nightmares, things no person should ever have to endure. I didn't know what this meant for my future, didn't know what being a werewolf meant for what I had planned for my life, but it was better than being dead, and if Kai hadn't saved me, I would be. If being this high up in the pack was where I was meant to be, then screw this guy. I wouldn't give in to any man, wouldn't bow my head ever, if I could help it. I stared. He stared. A growl rumbled in his throat; sweat broke out on my forehead, and on his as well. Then ... he bit his lip, and with a grunt dropped his eyes, bowing his head down low.

Taking a step back, I wiped my forehead, startled, and tried to catch my breath. Max looked at Kai and something unspoken seemed to pass between them. Anger was coming off of Max in waves. Kai nodded slightly, and Max scowled at me with burning yellow eyes, then took off running into the woods. He shed his shirt and slowly changed into his wolf form, his body contorting and cracking as he ran off. I sucked in a breath at the sight of him changing his human form for a wolf. I'd seen Kai change last night, and Emma had shifted her arm into a paw, but I didn't think I would ever get used to it.

Kai turned and opened his arms wide. "Brothers

and sisters, I welcome Aurora into my pack as my second-in-command."

*Holy shit.* I stood straight, clenching my muscles so I wouldn't shake like a leaf.

There was murmuring among the wolves. *Pack,* they told me, as they looked me up and down.

Kai's warm body pushed up against me as he whispered in my ear, "You have their inner wolves' respect. Any one of them would die in a fight for you, but now you need to get their human sides' respect. That's a whole other ball game, as you Americans like to say." His breath against my neck made my stomach drop, but his words flushed cold water through my veins.

"Let's eat! Steaks are on the grill out back," Kai announced, and motioned for us to move to the back of the house. My inner wolf was pleased with our new place in the pack, but I was scared shitless.

# 2
## SECOND

"Wow, SECOND," Emma squeaked behind me. Turning to her voice, she cast her eyes down slightly toward my nose, and I wondered if I would ever get used to people having to think before they made eye contact with me.

Now that I had time to look around, I realized we were in a heavily wooded area on Mount Hood. There were cabins dotting the property, but Kai's was by far the biggest. There were no fences, just open space and beautiful large cedar and fir trees.

"Yeah, who knew?" I shrugged, not sure what to say to Emma. I still wasn't completely convinced that this wasn't some kind of paranoid delusion. I was still in shock over making second in the pack and what that really meant. Emma and I walked together around to the back of the house toward the smell of cooking food.

She smiled and grabbed my hand. "Come on, I'll introduce you to my mate."

That word again. Kai had said some of the men here were wondering if I was their mate.

"Your mate ...?" I left the sentence open.

"Yeah, Devon. We just had our mating ceremony a few months ago. You missed it."

"So, that's like a wedding?"

I was hoping that mating wasn't something the women were forced into. Most of these people seemed nice but my guard was up. Glancing around, I saw that the backyard was a large green space with four large rectangular tables and a few grills. I wondered if they had any veggie burgers. Yeah, right. I was assuming there was no such thing as a vegetarian werewolf.

Even thinking that word, *werewolf*, made me feel positively insane.

"Kind of like a wedding, except mates are extremely rare, and once a werewolf finds theirs, they mate for life. And instead of exchanging rings, like I've seen humans do on TV, you exchange blood."

My eyes must have bulged out of my head. *Blood.*

"Not like drinking blood! Just a little nip, a marking." Emma pulled up her long shirt sleeve to reveal a bite mark on her wrist. "It's infused with magic. Devon and I are mated for life and now we can have children." She smiled.

"Talking about me, I hope?" A tall guy with sandy-blond hair and blue eyes came up behind us, wrapping his arms around Emma.

She blushed. "Aurora, this is Devon. My mate and husband."

Devon grasped my hand and bowed slightly. "A pleasure. Welcome to the pack. We are all really excited to have you—most of us anyway." He gestured to Sadie and a few other guys that sat at one of the tables, scowling in my direction. Emma smacked him on the arm and he kissed her cheek before heading over to tend to one of the grills. I remembered Devon being toward the middle of the pack.

"So it's not a problem that you're submissive and Devon's..."

"Dominant?" Emma threw the word out there, like it was nothing. "It's actually the best combination for mates. Two wolves that are too close within pack rank could either be very powerful together or have underlying tension. If you have two highly dominant wolves and danger comes, who protects who? If the less dominant tries to protect the more dominant, it's like saying they can't protect themselves. It could start a fight."

Jeez. So many rules and things to be aware of.

"With Devon and I, we know our place. If something ever happened and he was hurt, I would protect him with my last breath, but generally I let him take the lead." She smiled. "Enough Wolf 101, let's mingle. We'll have plenty of time to talk in the coming centuries. Did I forget to tell you? Unless killed, werewolves pretty much live forever." She walked toward the crowd, leaving me with my jaw dropped open.

*What did she just say?* I was immortal? Holy crap! I should have hit the deer.

I slowly walked over to an empty table, feeling like the new girl in high school with one friend. A young Indian boy, who looked to be the spitting image of Kai, set a large bloody steak in front of me. I remembered him from the staring contest. "For you, my lady." He grinned. He looked about sixteen but who knew what his real age was. I covered my nose; the smell of meat made me nauseated.

"Thank you, but actually I'm a vegetarian," I told him.

The boy's face fell. Werewolves must have really good hearing, because every voice stopped and all heads turned toward me. The boy began laughing then, a deep throaty laugh. "My brother's new second-in-command, a vegetarian?"

Was he making fun of me? I smirked at him. "Yes. Key words, second-in-command." Power radiated out of my voice but I hadn't meant it like that. The boy immediately stopped laughing and dropped his gaze and everyone went back to talking. Whoops. I wasn't sure what I had just done but I felt bad. Kai walked over with a plate of corn on the cob and mashed potatoes and set it in front of me, then he ruffled his brother's hair.

"That will teach you to mess with a dominant vegetarian," Kai joked.

His brother sulked, then turned to me. "I'm Akash. Welcome to the pack," he grumbled.

I smiled at him, feeling really bad now. "Thank you. I will try to remember all of these names but remind me if I can't. Thanks for bringing me the steak. It was very sweet of you."

Akash blushed from head to toe ... and was that a low growl I heard from Kai? Akash looked at his brother, grinning, then ran off to get his food.

"What part of India are you from?" I asked Kai.

"Are you assuming because I have dark skin I'm from India?" His face was blank.

"Oh. I'm sorry, I..." I didn't know what to say.

He grinned. "I'm from Delhi, and so is Akash."

*Jerk.* I wanted to smack him but thought better of it. "I've been to Delhi. Amazing food and wonderful people," I told him. I didn't like that I was sitting and he was towering over me with his massive form. I also didn't like the way his scent made my stomach warm.

It was his turn to look shocked with nothing to say. I took the time to study his features. Five o'clock shadow dotted his strong jaw and I couldn't help but think again of how attractive he was. He was that rugged mountain man fantasy that every woman secretly had. Like at any moment he might start chopping wood.

"You've been to Delhi?"

"Yep. Six months ago, volunteering. I set up a domestic violence shelter there. God, I miss the food." I thought then about all the cold nights I spent sleeping on a cot at the women's shelter with my mom. Snippets from my childhood rushed through my mind but I tried to suppress them. I tried not to go to that dark place if I could help it. Looking up, I saw Kai's jaw clench; his eyes turned from black to golden yellow. I jerked my head back in fear, but he recovered quickly and forced a smile.

"That's nice of you to do that kind of work." His voice was raw as if he was angry. Had he picked up on my thoughts? My very private thoughts? Anger took hold of me and I grabbed my plate and stood.

"I think I'm going to mingle, then you and I need to talk about my old life and what to do with it." My voice was clipped as I stalked off. How dare he read my mind when I was thinking of my painful past! That was private.

Two words came through our bond and into my head. *'I'm sorry.'*

Whatever.

I shook off the conversation with Kai and sat down with Emma and Devon. I spent the next two hours talking and getting to know the other wolves. I found that I could immediately tell who was submissive and who was more dominant. My inner wolf could sense it and I fell into easy conversations, letting my inner wolf instinctually guide me. As much as all of this was completely weird to me, I felt like this was *my pack*, my family, and I felt more protective over the submissive wolves. But one thing was for sure, Sadie was shooting me daggers all night. I reminded myself to ask Emma about that later. While I was in the middle of telling Luke, a mid-pack wolf, about my favorite hiking spot on Mount Hood, Kai placed his hand on my shoulder.

"We need to talk," he whispered in my ear, stepping fully into my personal space and dominating. I glanced at him, and nodded curtly.

"Luke." He nodded.

Luke smiled. "Kai."

We walked toward the house together, and as I passed Sadie I couldn't help but envy her straight black hair and muscular body. She was very pretty—and the complete opposite of me. I had fair skin and pale blond hair. I felt plain compared to her exotic beauty.

'*You look like an angel,*' Kai said as we reached the door to his home.

I tried to contain the blush that was no doubt hitting my cheeks, but recovered quickly. "Okay, first thing on the agenda, you need to get out of my head. Like NOW." I seriously was torn between smacking this guy in the face and...

His sexy hooded gaze met mine as if he'd heard that thought too, and was daring me to finish it. When I didn't, he just smirked and opened the door to the house, leading me to his office. After closing the door behind us, I stood there unsure of what to do. My eyes roamed over the nicely decorated room with modern masculine colors, dark blue and gray, and I decided to sit on the brown leather couch. Kai sat on the edge of the large wooden desk. He towered over me. Again.

"I will teach you how to keep me from reading your every thought. But I will *never* fully be out of your head. What's the next thing on your agenda?" He smiled and his eyes twinkled, as if me having an agenda caused him great delight.

Okay, he was willing to teach me to keep my thoughts to myself. That was a start.

"I need to call my mother." That was non-negotiable.

Kai sighed and ran his large palms across his tight worn jeans. "It's best that after a wolf goes through the change, they fake their death. I took your car deeper into the woods, away from the road and hid it under some fallen trees. One call to the police saying I found it while jogging will do the trick. Your blood ... is all over it. They will think animals took your body."

My mind was reeling. If this jerk thought I was going to fake my death, he was in for a big surprise. "Animals did take my body!" I roared, and his eyes flared yellow. I didn't care about pissing him off anymore. This was not okay. "And I'm not faking my death!" I stood, stepping closer to him. "I am all my mother has." Then I willingly let images of my childhood filter through our mental link, images of my mother being beaten, trying to keep *him* from hitting me—images of me being smacked around for the smallest thing. Then I stopped them. "She's all I have, too." My jaw was clenched so tight I thought my teeth would break.

Kai closed the distance between us in a second; his jaw tightened and he looked murderous. '*Who hurt you?'* he asked, making me regret ever showing him such personal things.

At this close proximity I could smell him. His unique scent had the beast inside of me rattling the cage again, just as warmth pooled south of my navel. "Don't," I told him fiercely, and tried to sidestep him, but he moved in front of me.

'*Let me in,*' he pleaded, and for once looked vulnerable as he stared into my eyes.

'*No.*' I pushed back into his mind and glared back, not looking down like I should, showing him that he couldn't force me; he didn't own me. Alpha or not, I had a say and I could take care of myself. He stared back, unwavering. *Challenge,* my inner wolf said. Shit, what was I doing? My forehead broke out in sweat and my knees went suddenly weak. Why was I doing this? The smell of him was intoxicating and I couldn't make myself look away. I knew it was wrong, bad, and awful to be challenging the alpha, but there was a survivor inside of me that would never give up. Ever. And he'd just pulled her into this. I needed to stand my ground or he would walk all over me.

He leaned in slowly, keeping his eyes locked on mine. Pleasure pulsed inside my gut as his body pressed against mine, and when I felt his breath on my lips I closed my eyes in submission.

*Screw it.*

His hands came up and grabbed my hair, slowly tilting my neck back as he pressed his soft, warm lips onto mine. A shock went through me at their touch.

'*I win,*' he taunted playfully in my mind as electricity sped down my body from head to toe, and suddenly I didn't care about being right anymore. I only cared about kissing him. It felt like I was taking a breath for the first time; I was starved for him. He deepened the kiss then, opening his mouth and sliding his tongue against mine. I matched it for few more seconds, but then he pulled away.

I stood there, stunned and in complete and utter shock. I did *not* do things like that. How the hell did that even happen? We were arguing one second, and then the next ... I felt like I had been waiting to kiss him since the moment I first saw him at the gas station. He looked as dumbfounded as I felt. We were both panting heavily and just staring at each other. This was crazy. I just met this guy. What the hell was I doing? Before I had time to think of something to say, the hairs on the back of my neck stood.

*Foreign wolf,* my inner wolf said, and I frowned. I didn't know what that was, but something smelled off, something bad.

"Shit," Kai said, and bolted outside.

I ran after him and noticed the other wolves beginning to perk up. Some of them shifted into their wolf forms and some stayed human.

Kai stood on one of the picnic tables and closed his eyes, taking a deep breath in through his nose.

"Portland pack just crossed our border. Seven wolves about twenty miles away." He growled and looked at me. "Where were you born?" he barked.

I jerked back at the power in his voice. "Portland," I answered.

A rumble went through the pack, and one of the wolves that had shifted howled, causing chills to run the length of my arms.

"What's wrong?" I felt completely lost. My mind was still recovering from that kiss in his office.

Kai's eyes took a possessive inventory of my body. "When someone is changed, the alpha of that pack who changed them becomes that person's pack. That's why you're *mine*. But there is an old magic law that states that the alpha from the pack of the changed human's birthplace can fight to claim him or her if they can reach that person in twenty-four hours. It's been sixteen hours since I changed you."

What? My breath came out in rasps. "So ... the alpha from the Portland pack is coming to claim me?"

Kai's eyes blazed yellow, like tiny pools of fire were contained in them. "No." There was power behind that one single word. "He's coming to try. I was hoping you were born in Michigan, or some place a bit farther away."

Emma stood next to me looking angry. "If it was a submissive male, he wouldn't even try!"

Females were rare, she had told me. I guess I didn't understand how rare until now.

*Foreign wolf.* My pack sense was tingling now, as I was becoming more aware of my newfound senses. They were in *our* territory and there was nothing we could do because of the rules. I could feel the irritation coming off of Kai—my own wolf was annoyed by this invasion.

As Kai barked orders to the other wolves to take up positions at the perimeter, I leaned into Emma. "I think it might be a good time for you to tell me about killing a Werewolf 101," I whispered. If this Portland alpha was going to fight me, I needed to know how to protect myself.

Emma swallowed, her bright green eyes looking fearful. "Two ways. Extreme blood loss or silver poisoning. Our power to heal is in our blood. If you decapitate, or tear into a wolf enough, they will die before they can regenerate."

I nodded fiercely. "Okay, so keep my head on. Don't touch silver. Got it."

Emma looked at me shocked. "*You* don't fight the Portland alpha, Kai does."

"Oh."

"You're the prize," Emma told me. "And there's something you should know about changed wolves. The Portland alpha is a changed wolf. He wasn't born that way and so he has a ... *gift*. He is immune to silver."

"A gift." I let that sink in. "So all changed wolves have a gift?"

Emma nodded. "You will too. Once you shift for the first time it will begin to manifest. The lycanthrope virus binds to the human DNA and then it activates in some mutated form."

Mutated. DNA. Lycanthrope. Whoa. Way over my head.

"Okay, so Kai has to fight another alpha who only has one way of being killed, because of his gift..."

"Yes, he can only be killed by blood loss. But Kai is a changed wolf, too." Emma's eyes gleamed with pride. I wondered what his gift was, but before I could even fathom what these different gifts might be, Kai screamed my name.

"Aurora!" Kai barked, and I quickly ran to his side. He gently took my hand and pulled me to the side yard, where we could talk in private. I stood there, suddenly nervous for him.

"I will fight for you because you're *mine*. But I pride myself on doing things differently in my pack. I won't keep you here against your will."

Those words were magic to my ears. I detested men who were too pushy with me. Kai seemed to be this raging alpha male on the outside but a soft teddy bear inside.

"I know you haven't had time to learn what being a werewolf is all about." He continued. "When I saw you lying in the road on the verge of death, I knew I had to at least try to give you life. Females that survive the change are rare, and Dane will try to take you at all costs. So, if you think you would like the chance to switch packs, tell me now."

There was a vulnerability in his look that made my heart hurt. He was an alpha, the most dominant of wolves, and he was asking me to stay—maybe not with his words but with his look. The way he said *mine* was possessive in an endearing way. Did I want to leave Emma, Kai, and the others that I had begun friendships with? Did I want to leave without exploring what was behind that kiss in his office? My inner wolf howled in pain at the thought. I wanted to go home. I wouldn't lie about that, but if I had to be a werewolf then I wanted to be one with him.

"This is *my* pack. I'm not going anywhere," I told him firmly.

The corners of his lips curled. "Good. Now, if I die, the pack transfers to you as my second. That could be a disaster because you know nothing about being a wolf or leading a pack."

"Then don't die, for that reason and others." I reached out and quickly squeezed his hand. Was I flirting with the alpha before he was about to go into a fight to the death for me? He smirked and turned to leave.

"They're coming," he told his wolves. "Emma, don't shift. I need you to be able to communicate with Aurora."

I smelled something then. Whisky and cigarettes, rain and wood. *Portland pack. Foreign wolves.*

I followed Kai back around to the front of the house, and saw three large men walking through the clearing behind a thicket of trees, followed by four wolves. One of the men smiled and his teeth shone in the setting sun. They were capped in silver, all of them. *Oh, shit.* That must be Dane. Silver immunity. He wore rugged jeans and a loose-fitting t-shirt, his dark hair slicked back with what looked like grease. I wondered when the last time was that he showered.

"Excuse the intrusion, Kai, but I believe you have something that belongs to me." His eyes roamed over my body and Kai let loose a growl.

"She's *mine*," Kai said, barely retaining his humanity, and I could see patches of black fur rippling over his body.

Dane flashed his silver-pointed teeth. "I was hoping you would say that."

The pack began circling them, opening up an area for them to fight. My wolf was itching to come out. I felt the need to shift, to fight instead of Kai, to protect him. I didn't even know how to shift, but I wanted to. No one should die for me. It was against everything I taught as a self-defense instructor. I taught women to take care of themselves.

Dane stood in the center of the circle and bowed. "I enact the right to fight the Mount Hood alpha for *my* wolf, a human that was born in *my* territory. A female. According to rules, this fight ends in death or forfeit." I didn't like the way the word "female" sounded dirty in his mouth.

The words barely left Kai's mouth before he began shifting. "I accept."

In a blur of motion, Kai was human one second and wolf the next. His clothes tore as he shifted from a large human male to an even larger black wolf. He lunged at Dane, who was mid-shift, and sank his teeth into the meat of Dane's thigh, coming away with a chunk of flesh. Something between a howl and a human wail cut through the night. Kai was *fast*, really fast. That must be his gift. Not only could he shift as fast as I could blink, he ran faster than I could track. He had the most beautiful markings too, all black with a white star on his forehead and white socks on his paws. The vegetarian in me wanted to close my eyes; there was blood and flesh flying everywhere, but the wolf in me stared. My hands were clenched, my breath coming out short, the tension killing me.

Compared to Dane, Kai was a blur of motion. Dane had just finished fully shifting and Kai had already torn off most of his leg meat.

I leaned into Emma. "So is that Kai's gift? He's fast?"

Emma nodded and kept her voice low. "He can shift instantly, and he can move faster than anyone's ever seen."

I watched as Kai dodged Dane's silver jaws and ran from left to right in a blur of motion. Then, once he was close enough, Kai swiped a claw at Dane's belly and Dane used the close proximity to bite Kai in the shoulder. It was quick, but I heard the crunch of bone from where I stood. A howl ripped from Kai's throat as he darted to the other side of the clearing. He was still fast, but slower than before, and now with a slight limp. The silver must be affecting him. Emma let out a low growl beside me and I got a sinking feeling in my gut.

Dane's wolf grinned, and I saw Kai's blood glistening on his metallic teeth.

In a blur of motion, Kai came closer to Dane and lunged, biting into the side of his neck. He planted his paws firmly in the ground and shook Dane like a ragdoll, until his body stilled. I felt sick watching such violence but I couldn't tear my gaze away, and I couldn't deny the excitement I felt that Kai had the upper hand. The pack roared in exhilaration and Kai's wolf relaxed for just a second. Dane used that moment to jerk violently, loosening himself, and grabbed Kai's left front paw in his mouth. Those silver-capped teeth bit down hard, and for the second time we all heard the crunch of bone. Oh God, I couldn't bear this. I stepped forward, ready to run into the circle, unsure what I was going to do, but someone grabbed my arms from behind.

"Easy there." It was Devon, Emma's mate, holding my arms tightly behind my back. Kai was limping away, getting slower by the moment, and Dane stalked after him. Dane's leg, I could see, was already healing, and so was his neck.

"Why isn't Kai healing like Dane?" I asked Emma as Devon loosened his grip on me, satisfied I wouldn't do anything.

"The silver. One more bite and he will probably be poisoned beyond repair," Emma informed me.

Tears lined her eyes, and that's when I realized I could stop this fight. I just needed to tell Dane I would transfer to his pack and stop this. Kai said he wouldn't keep me against my will. I opened my mouth to speak, and just then two yellow eyes caught my attention, and I stared into them.

"*Mine*," Kai said and lunged at Dane with more speed and strength than he had before. Dane was slow, too slow, and Kai landed on top of him. They both rolled. Kai's black wolf had Dane's neck in his jaws and he was chewing. Oh God. I was going to see someone decapitated! I wanted to look away but I couldn't.

The muzzle of Dane's wolf began shifting into human lips. "I forfeit!" he croaked in a half-human voice that would haunt my dreams forever.

Kai held his jaws over Dane's throat, not backing down until a man stepped forward from the Portland pack. "The rules say you can forfeit and still walk away with your life," he reminded Kai firmly. My wolf instantly recognized that this man was Dane's second. Kai let his yellow wolf eyes linger one more moment on the alpha's second before he released Dane's head from his strong jaws.

My inner wolf, the thing that had been rattling at the cage inside of me, finally broke free. I felt rage flood my body and pushed myself to step forward. "A foreign alpha who trespasses on *our* land, picks a fight with *my* alpha, and then forfeits, is a coward. As second-in-command, I will tell you this once—get off our land and don't come back without permission!" My inner wolf had fully taken over. I could feel the power radiating off of me.

Confidence flooded my system, chasing away all

fear. The dominant wolves in my pack howled their agreement, their cries echoing into the night. Devon, Luke, and a few others stepped up behind me as Dane's wolf took one last appraising look at me before limping away. I scowled as I watched his pack leave through the trees, taking their foreign smell with them. If there was one thing my wolf and human side agreed on, it was that we hated bullies.

## 3
## CHALLENGE

Dane and his men had retreated, but Kai still lay where he was, his yellow eyes boring into me. He was panting, and hadn't moved, which made me think he was hurt more than he let on. I started toward him but his voice stopped me. *'Don't let the pack see me weak,'* he told me in a strained voice, and I stopped where I stood.

"Fight's over. Go home." I pushed power into my words to the rest of the pack. The submissive wolves whined, and Sadie growled and stared at me. I don't think she liked my giving orders so soon, but I didn't care. This dominating power was new to me, but it came as naturally as breathing.

"Go home," I told Sadie again, harsher than I meant to, and this time she stormed off. Reaching out, I caught Emma's hand as she was moving to leave, indicating I needed her to stay. I had no idea what I was doing; all I knew was that Kai had saved me from my accident. He'd kissed me like I was the last female on earth, and he'd just fought to keep me in his pack. I was finding that I didn't know much about being a werewolf but my inner wolf did. Kai was hurt and I needed to help him. The more I let my wolf bubble to the surface, and the more I ran on instinct, the easier it felt to fall into this new role. Somehow, I knew that keeping Emma back with me was good because she was submissive and wouldn't be a threat to my injured alpha.

Kai stood then, shifting into human form, favoring his injured hand, as he gazed around at the retreating pack, looking strong. *'I protect what's mine. Remember that.'* I could tell by the looks on the others' faces that he had sent that to everyone. When the last person had left through the trees, Kai shifted back into wolf form and collapsed, unconscious.

Emma turned beside me and looked at me with fearful eyes.

"Help me get him inside," I told her. Why was Kai afraid of the pack seeing him weak? Would they ... do something to hurt him further? It sounded crazy, but they were half wild animal so ... I wasn't ruling anything out. I bent over and hooked both arms under Kai's bleeding shoulder as Emma grabbed his hind legs. On three we hoisted him up with surprising strength.

Who knew two petite girls could lift a 250-pound, bleeding, and halfway unconscious werewolf into the house? I had strength I couldn't even dream of before, and I was barely winded after getting him to his bedroom. Running into the adjoining bathroom, I ripped the plastic shower curtain down and lay it on the bed to protect the sheets from getting bloody. Then Emma and I placed Kai on the bed and waited.

I stroked his fur, unsure of what to do, until his voice spoke inside my head.

*'When an alpha is weakened like I am, a dominant member could take this chance to challenge me for the pack. Two of my highest are considering it: Max and Jake. I can sense their thoughts. They are torn between being my friend and respecting me, and their wolves' inner urges to be alpha.'* Kai's words sent chills down my spine.

*'What do I do?'* I asked him.

He was fading in and out. It took him a few moments to respond.

*'Don't let them get a single word out. If they say the word challenge, I'm gone. A fight for alpha status ends in death. There is no forfeit.'* And with that, he collapsed.

Shit, shit, shit! I had to think—I had to think fast. "Emma!" I screamed, and she ran in from the living room. "Jake and Max might try to challenge Kai. Who do you trust? Who would Kai trust to guard him and not challenge him?"

Emma paled. "Sadie, and Devon. Akash is too young."

"Sadie?" I questioned, unsure of that choice.

Emma swallowed. "They dated for a long time.

She still loves him. She would do anything for him, I'm sure of it."

I didn't even want to process that right now. My inner wolf was going into possessive-jealous-rage mode and I had to push her down. I barely knew this guy, he wasn't mine to be jealous over. For a small moment I pondered running away. Kai was down and this could be my chance to get away and leave this whole nightmare behind me. But I shoved that thought deep down and focused on the bleeding wolf before me. I didn't want this life but it was mine nonetheless. I had spent my lifetime trying to protect the weak. I taught the defenseless how to protect themselves, and I couldn't leave Kai now to fend for himself.

"Get them for me. Now," I urged Emma.

She ran out of the house and I could hear the cracking of bones as she shifted. Bouncing my foot nervously, I realized I had one hand still on Kai's fur. I had to force myself to let go. I stood and began tearing apart the room trying to find what I was looking for. If I were an alpha and I knew silver injured werewolves, I would keep some around. I would keep it somewhere safe, so it wouldn't hurt me, but I would have it on the off chance I needed to subdue my own kind. Five minutes later the room was in shambles, and I was no closer to finding what I was looking for, when Sadie walked in looking feral at the sight of Kai bleeding on the bed, not healing.

"He's hurt worse than he let on," she said softly, her wide brown eyes roaming over his wolf form.

I didn't waste time crossing the room to meet her head-on. "Can I trust you to protect him? Not to challenge him?" My voice was flat as I tried to keep emotion out of it.

She looked right into my eyes and something passed between us, between our wolves. We both wanted to protect him. This we could do together.

She nodded, lowering her eyes.

"I need silver," I told her.

"The basement."

The second the words left her lips I bolted downstairs, leaving her with Kai. I would just have to trust her. As I passed the living room, I caught sight of Emma and Devon, both in wolf form, outside protecting the perimeter. I had a plan. A sloppily-put-together, fast plan, but a plan nonetheless.

Flicking on the basement lights, I saw three iron cages bolted to the far wall. There was also a gym set up with free weights and mats. My eyes scanned further and I found what I was looking for, a toolbox. Crossing the room quickly, I ripped the lid off and smiled. Silver. I grabbed a handful of thin chains, and two pillows from the couch on my way out of the room.

Making quick strides, I ran outside just in time to see Max stalking toward the house in human form with a predatory look on his face. His fists were balled and his eyes glowed a hot yellow. Good. He was in human form.

Plan A. Before he could open his mouth, I ran toward him and, spinning, delivered a perfect roundhouse kick to his jaw. He dropped to the ground, out cold. Emma's wolf gasped behind me and I had to suppress a small grin. Maybe I should have mentioned that I ran women's defense classes on the weekends and I was a black belt in karate.

Another time. I liked being underestimated.

The sound of cracking bones pulled my attention to Emma shifting into human form behind me. She was stark naked and didn't seem to be embarrassed, didn't try to cover up.

"You can touch it? Without pain or gloves?" she said, shocked, looking down at my hands holding the silver chains.

I didn't have time to process that comment. Kneeling down, hunching over Max's unconscious figure, I grabbed the chains and began tying him up by the wrists and ankles. Then I ripped the pillow to shreds and stuffed huge gobs of fluff into his mouth, before tying a strip of cloth around his face to hold the stuffing in. Red blisters were popping up where the silver touched and I nearly gagged at the smell of burning flesh. He was still unconscious, so I sat back, panting in relief. If it killed him, then so be it, but I didn't want to kill him if I didn't have to. Devon came over from the side of the house and shifted as well. Apparently, modesty was lost in the pack, because he stood naked and gestured Emma toward the house.

"Let's get him in a cage," he barked.

As they hoisted him up, Max began waking. "Rahheng, raahenge!" Max roared, his eyes burning like the glowing sun—luckily the cotton in his mouth made it hard to understand him. It sounded an awful lot like "challenge," but I ignored it. He could have been saying "revenge." Emma and Devon shared a tense look and then took him to the basement as I stood guard outside.

I sat in the front yard for the next three hours as the night crept on, while Emma staked out the back and Devon roamed the perimeter. Either Jake was waiting until we weakened or he had thought better of challenging. My eyelids began drooping, and before I could stop it, I fell asleep.

---

I AWOKE to the sound of footsteps and bolted upright, my body tense and ready for a fight.

Sadie walked over to me, padding across the grass barefooted. "He's asking for you. It was touch and go throughout the night but he's healing fine now."

I didn't know what to say; the thick heavy blanket of sleep still clung to me, but the thought of seeing him, making sure he was okay, made my heart pick up.

"Go, I'll take watch," she said, with some bitterness in her voice. Emma's words came back to me then, about Sadie still being in love with Kai. I didn't blame her.

I gave a curt nod and looked down at myself. I was covered in dirt and Kai's blood, I had sleep in my eyes, and my hair probably looked like two birds had mated in it. Taking a deep breath, I entered the house and made my way back to Kai's bedroom. The door was left cracked open, so I pushed it wide and stepped through. Kai was in his human form, lying in his bed wearing low-slung sweatpants and a tight t-shirt. The thought of him shifting in front of Sadie made my inner wolf seethe in jealousy. I quickly tamped it down so he wouldn't pick up on it as he gestured for me to sit near him.

"You did well. It's an honor to call you my second," he told me with a sandpapery voice. A voice that made heat pulse in my core. I could see his bite marks were oozing pink fluid but, incredibly, they were healing.

"I did the best I could. Max is bound by silver chains and gagged in a cage in your basement," I told him. The past twenty-four hours made me feel like I had been run over by a train. I needed a Hawaiian vacation and a margarita, STAT.

Kai looked sad for a moment. "Max as a human, as a friend, would *never* challenge me, would never want me dead. Max as a dominant wolf, well ... it's a part of this life."

He tried to sit up and groaned. I reached out and stopped him with a soft hand on his chest.

"You're not moving until you're fully healed," I told him. "That's an order," I playfully added. I wasn't sure how much power a second–in-command had over an alpha, but I planned on testing those limits.

He gave me a sultry look, eyeing my hand on his chest, then flashed his bright white teeth in a full-blown smile. They were in stark contrast to his olive skin, and his canines were more pronounced. *God, he was good looking.* The place where my hand rested felt hot, and I was tempted to rub lower and feel how hard his abs were. I removed my hand quickly and placed it in my lap.

"Yes, ma'am. Well, if you won't let me get up, then I'm going to have to ask my vegetarian second to fix me three rare steaks. I will heal faster with meat in my system."

I gulped. *Gross.* "Coming right up." I faked enthusiasm and stood. I wanted to prove to Kai I was a part of the team here. It was the only way I would get him on my side when I asked him to let me go back to work, to go home. I could still be a part of this "pack," but have my old life. I would make it work. Besides, he'd nearly died last night trying to protect me and had since earned my loyalty.

After gagging my way through the kitchen getting a meal ready for Kai and silently apologizing to the cute cows that had given their lives for his breakfast, I went to the guest bathroom and showered the grime off of my skin.

Padding out of the bathroom in my towel, I made it back to the bedroom I was staying in and found a stack of clothes on the bed. I smiled. Emma. She was quickly growing on me, a thoughtful and kind friend. I changed into the skinny jeans, teal cotton V-neck, and black ballet flats. Then I quickly dried my long hair and went in search of Kai. Standing outside of his bedroom door,

I was unsure of whether or not to go in. We still had so much to go over. It was Sunday and I had a job, an important job waiting for me on Monday. My roommate and my mother would be beside themselves with worry if I didn't call soon. I couldn't deny that Kai and I had something growing between us, more than that kiss. I was confused, and my emotions were raw. He clearly had something with Sadie from the past, and maybe this new werewolf side of me was messing with my hormones. Then a horrifying thought struck me—what if my human side fell in love with him but my wolf was mated to someone else?

The door creaked open and Kai peeked his head out.

I blushed. Crap! This stupid bond!

"Want to talk?" he asked graciously, not bringing any of my thoughts up.

I nodded and noticed he looked my body up and down before letting me in the room. That heat that had pulsed before was an inferno now, but I stuffed it down, trying to ignore it. Looking around the room, I scolded myself for picking his bedroom of all places to have a chat. I sat on the edge of the bed, which had been stripped clean and dressed with new sheets, and straightened my back, trying to look strong.

"I own an organization called Safe Haven. It's a domestic violence shelter and women's defense class studio. Being that it's a non-profit, I don't exactly have the money to hire a lot of people to take over my job. I can't leave it—I *won't* leave. We run on volunteers only, and a lot of families depend on Safe Haven for support, for survival." I couldn't look him in the eye. I knew he was thinking about the thoughts he had picked up from me earlier, from my own domestic violence situation as a child. I just kept my eyes on the white baseboard below until I saw him moving closer to the bed. The last forty-eight hours had been bat-shit crazy, and I needed this guy to say I could keep my old life or I was going to lose my mind. I'd run.

He sat next to me and placed a gentle hand on my leg. It was possessive and tender at the same time. "Is this Safe Haven located in Portland?"

I nodded, finally looking up from the baseboard, and he sighed. "We can't go to Portland without the Portland pack's permission. After last night, I highly doubt that is going to happen anytime soon. I own the territory from east of the 205, near Gresham and all of Mount Hood to the 97. Portland pack owns west of the 205 all the way to Forest Grove and down to Corvallis."

"Oh." My heart broke. Giving up my life's work because of a territory dispute was heart-wrenching.

His hand squeezed my leg lightly. "But ... we can open a second location in Gresham, and I can get the pack to volunteer there. We can pay some humans to head up the Portland location and stay in contact with them through videophone. I will fund the entire venture. That's the best I can do."

My mouth dropped open as shock ripped through me. He wasn't saying no, he was offering to fund a second location for Safe Haven? I couldn't ask that of him—I wouldn't. I'd worked so hard to get Safe Haven up and running all on my own.

*'Let me take care of you,'* he said into my mind.

"I take care of myself," I said defiantly.

I didn't like the idea of having to depend on a man for money.

"Not anymore." His words were possessive yet endearing.

I felt something then, something from him through the pack bond, something I couldn't explain—a feeling I had never felt from a man before and it shook me to my core. This feeling was of complete and total safety. Family. Pack. Support. I had to bite the inside of my cheek to keep from getting too emotional. I didn't trust people easily, so these new feelings were overwhelming.

"Let me do this," he said, and his voice held a vulnerability. He was asking, not telling me, and I thought of all the women and children we could help with a second location, with more volunteers. After a long pause, I nodded.

"Thank you." I would swallow my pride if it meant helping more women.

He stood, towering over me. "Then it's settled. Now I need to deal with Max. He won't challenge me now that I'm fully healed. His crazed wolf will be gone and my best friend will be back in place. Thanks to you, I have my life."

I stood as well and met his eyes. "Consider us even. You saved my life first."

He wasn't leaving, and now that I'd stood we were six inches from each other and I could feel the heat from his body, smell the soap on his skin from his shower. I expected him to move, but he just stood there staring into my eyes. I allowed my gaze to lower and rest on his lips. Swallowing hard, I recalled our kiss in his office. If I was being honest, it had been the best kiss of my life. Primal, carefree.

He grinned then from ear to ear, assaulting me with a dimple-filled smile, and grabbed me in one quick motion, pressing his body against mine. The breath went out of me as he reached up and rubbed small circles on my neck with his thumb, and cupped my face. I didn't resist as his lips met mine and electricity jolted through me down to my toes. I opened my mouth, deepening the kiss and matching his passion with my own. The heat below my navel exploded and I moaned. My hands roamed over his tight muscular back and I had a thought. Maybe this was what it was like to kiss a werewolf. Maybe Kai wasn't special, and if I kissed one of the other wolves it would feel the same as this?

He pulled away with a soft growl, eyes fiercely yellow. Oops.

"I really need to get around to teaching you how to shut me out of your personal thoughts." His buttery yellow eyes bore into me. His wolf.

"Sorry," I squeaked. "This is new to me."

He motioned between the two of us. "This is new to me too." He reached into his pocket and tossed me a cell phone. "It's yours now. Call your mom. Tell her you met a guy online and you're moving in with him. She can visit anytime you like. Just give us notice so we don't have any abnormally large wolves running around." Then he left.

I sighed. *This is new to me too*, he had said. What did that mean? Catching my breath, I took a deep lungful of air and dialed my mother.

"You what!" my mother screamed for the second time.

"I'm moving in with him," I told her.

"How long have you known this guy? Honey, this isn't like you. What about Safe Haven? Mount Hood is a long commute." Her voice was high-pitched and full of panic. I was the perfect only child and I never did rash things like this.

"We met online three months ago," I lied. "I actually have more exciting news. I got a really big donation to Safe Haven too. I'm opening a second location in Gresham. I will have the money to hire someone to run the Portland location."

"Honey, that's great news about Safe Haven. You've known him three months? How come you never told me?" There was hurt in her voice. I hated this.

"I wasn't sure it was serious, but it is. Say you're happy for me? That you will visit?" I tried to pull on her heartstrings.

"Of course I'll visit. You're my daughter. It's just ...

you know I didn't get to know your father very well, I jumped in without thinking and look where that got us."

Now it was her turn to pull on my heartstrings.

"Mom, he's not like that. He would never hurt me." Okay, the line between making up a story and the truth was getting blurry. I wasn't really moving in with Kai, was I? What the hell was happening to my life?

"What does he do?" my mom probed, and my stomach tightened with nerves. I had no flipping clue what he did for a living and I had already kissed him twice. What was wrong with me?

"He ... he comes from a wealthy family and he has a community up here. A ... treatment center. For .... recovering alcoholics." What the hell was I saying? I was always a horrible liar, but I had a wild imagination —quite the combo.

"Oh, well, he sounds a lot like you. A do-gooder. Except for the wealthy family part," she joked. I thought of her in her bright teal trailer on Ash Lane near downtown Portland. I wish I could give her more. She deserved the best.

"Thanks for understanding. I'll call you tomorrow, okay, Mom?" I couldn't talk to her anymore without blurting out the truth.

"Okay, sweetie. The only thing I have ever wanted was to see you happy. You sound happy," she admitted.

Did I? Was I? God, if she only knew.

*Mom, I got in a horrific accident. My back was broken, I was gushing blood, and this new boyfriend of mine—the one I said would never hurt me—he bit me—'cause he's a werewolf and now I am too.*

I wanted to tell her.

"Thanks, Mom. Love you."

"Love you too, Aurora."

So that was it. I was a werewolf and I was moving in with my alpha that I had kissed twice, and I was lying to my mom. My life was officially complicated.

you know I didn't get to know your father very well, I jumped in without thinking and look where that got us."

Now it was her turn to pull on my heartstrings.

"Mom, he's not like that. He would never hurt me." Okay, the line between making up a story and the truth was getting blurry. I wasn't really moving in with Kai, was I? What the hell was happening to my life?

"What does he do?" my mom probed, and my stomach tightened with nerves. I had no flipping clue what he did for a living and I had already kissed him twice. What was wrong with me?

"He ... he comes from a wealthy family and he has a community up here. A ... treatment center. For .... recovering alcoholics." What the hell was I saying? I was always a horrible liar, but I had a wild imagination —quite the combo.

"Oh, well, he sounds a lot like you. A do-gooder. Except for the wealthy family part," she joked. I thought of her in her bright teal trailer on Ash Lane near downtown Portland. I wish I could give her more. She deserved the best.

"Thanks for understanding. I'll call you tomorrow, okay, Mom?" I couldn't talk to her anymore without blurting out the truth.

"Okay, sweetie. The only thing I have ever wanted was to see you happy. You sound happy," she admitted.

Did I? Was I? God, if she only knew.

*Mom, I got in a horrific accident. My back was broken, I was gushing blood, and this new boyfriend of mine—the one I said would never hurt me—he bit me —'cause he's a werewolf and now I am too.*

I wanted to tell her.

"Thanks, Mom. Love you."

"Love you too, Aurora."

So that was it. I was a werewolf and I was moving in with my alpha that I had kissed twice, and I was lying to my mom. My life was officially complicated.

## 4

## RUN

After getting off the phone with my mom, I sat on the edge of the bed in silence for a moment until my pack sense began to tingle. *Alpha. Alpha. Alpha.* I got up and made my way outside, where I could see the pack gathering in the yard around Kai.

"Glad to see you fully healed," Sadie purred at Kai as her fingers trailed over the spot where his wound had been. He nodded coldly to her and then turned as if sensing me, I had to mask the jealousy on my face. Again, his eyes trailed over my body and I felt heat pooling in my belly.

"I think it's time we go for a run! To welcome Aurora properly, and introduce all of us to her wolf. We leave in five minutes," Kai barked to the pack, and then beckoned me toward the side of the house, where we could talk in private.

I followed him wordlessly, trying to contain my fear. I was a werewolf, and up until now it hadn't been real. Shifting into a wolf, that shit was real. Would it hurt? Would I hate it? What if I liked it? I was a mess of emotion, and now I was standing before Kai. Alone. He turned to face me, tucking a piece of hair gently behind my ear, letting his fingers brush my neck on the way down.

"Wolves need to live in packs to be fully healthy and feel whole, but as far as lovers go, most of us can only hope to be lucky enough to find our mate, to be blessed with children and a life of love. We prepare for a life of fleeting relationships. We have distractions, but the one thing we are all really waiting for is our mate."

My heart was beating in my head. I wasn't expecting this topic of conversation; it took me completely off guard. "As you can imagine," he said, "with a shortage of female wolves, most males spend their life alone, romantically. Your arrival has every unmated male in the pack in a frenzy. I feel it fair to warn you that no matter what has started between you and I, if your mate is out there among the pack..." He didn't finish.

"And how will I recognize my mate?" I asked him, pressing my body against his and staring into his eyes, watching them go yellow. I always had restraint when it came to men, but not him. He was different, magnetic, alluring. His hands found their way to my hips and squeezed them slightly.

"Have you seen my wolf? Its markings?" he asked with a gravelly voice.

I nodded and lowered my eyes to his lips.

"Well, my mate's markings will be the exact opposite of mine. Instead of a black coat with a white star, she will have a white coat with a black star. Mates were made for each other, a union blessed by Spirit. When mates meet for the first time in wolf form, it's said to be indescribable. Your mate might not even be on this continent, but I wanted to warn you in case he is." Kai's voice had finality in it, and I stepped back from him. I didn't want to be someone else's mate because our stupid markings matched—I wanted to choose for myself.

"Let's get this over with, then." I pulled fully out of his grasp, afraid of getting too close. One thing was certain: I wouldn't be anyone's mate unless I wanted to be. I didn't care what *Spirit* thought. As I turned to leave, I could feel his eyes burning into the back of my head.

The entire pack was assembled and I noticed some of the men staring at me with longing.

"The first shift is painful, and it takes a while," Kai told me. "Since you're a changed wolf, you will have a gift. We may not know what it is right away, so just be patient."

"How do I shift?" I felt stupid for asking.

I heard Akash chuckle behind me. "You let your wolf out. No pun intended. Let her bubble to the surface, then push with everything you are and it just happens. I threw up during my first shift, so don't feel bad if you do too."

I laughed. "Okay, just don't get too close to me. I

might throw up on you." He smiled and then ran to be with his friends, as Kai turned and walked a few feet away, leaving me standing there alone.

Okay, I was about to shift into a werewolf, no big deal, right? *Holy shit.* I felt sick with nerves and was in the grips of a serious, impending panic attack, when something tingled down my spine and caused me to look up. Kai. His gorgeous dark chestnut eyes were burning into me, and somehow I drew strength from them. I wanted to prove to him and everyone else that I was strong enough to do this. I had run from a lot of things in my life, but I wouldn't run from this. I couldn't. The mere thought of shifting into my wolf form and running had an excited thrill coursing through my body, right alongside my anxiety. At that thought, Kai nodded and dropped his eyes.

The pack began undressing around me, including Kai, but I noticed everyone kept their eyes on the ground. *Here goes nothing,* I thought, and began peeling off my clothes. Clearly no one gave a crap about nudity here so I might as well embrace it. I wasn't ashamed of my body. When I was about to unclip my bra, I looked up by instinct. Kai was staring into my eyes and I blushed. He shifted in seconds right before my eyes while the rest of the pack started slowly. I heard cracking bones all around me and took a deep breath, calling to my inner wolf.

*Pack. Run.*

*I can do this.* Closing my eyes, I took a deep breath and let my wolf take the lead. Once I felt her at the surface, I pushed and then let go. It was like screaming with no sound. As the blood rushed to my face it felt like it was carbonated; I was sure I might explode—my skin suddenly felt like JELL-O. I heard a loud crack, and then it felt like someone had taken a knife and filleted me in half. One second I was standing on two legs and then suddenly I was standing on four paws. Panting, I let the burning on my skin settle as nausea rolled through me. The other wolves hadn't finished shifting yet but all eyes were on me. They went from me, to Kai, then back to me. I thought they must be staring at us because we had the same gift, the gift of shifting instantly, being super-fast ... but then I heard it.

His deep, passionate, possessive voice in my head. 'Mate.'

I looked up at Kai in his wolf form and gasped as a thousand images passed between us. It was like a mental projector movie screen going on in my head. I saw him as a little boy in India hanging clothes on a clothesline with his mother. Then me as a little girl being rocked back and forth to sleep by my mother. Him as a young man being attacked by a rogue wolf, being changed. Me around twelve years old covering my ears as my father screamed at my mother and raised his hand to hit her for the hundredth time. Him as a young wolf fighting for dominance. I felt every bite, every broken bone. I *felt* his pain. Then me as a teenager standing over my father in the kitchen, a knife dripping blood in my hand. My father's dead body on the tile next to my unconscious mother. Kai happy as an alpha of his first pack. Me happy when my mom and I moved into our first place. It was like a review of what we had missed in each other's lives until now, it was both absolutely terrifying and incredible. All of my walls broke down in that instant.

He crossed the space between us lightning-quick and pounced on my wolf, rolling me down the grassy hill and nipping at my neck playfully. I breathed him in. Cedar, mint, and home.

'*Mate,*' my wolf said.

'*You're mine,*' Kai said, and my inner wolf howled in agreement.

'*I wanted it to be true from the first time I saw you. Your markings are beautiful, white with a black star and black socks,*' he told me.

Holy crap, Kai was my mate. I could feel it now, the rightness of it. My wolf was pleased and my human side didn't even have time to process it. I heard a painful howl behind me and turned to see a wolf with glaring black eyes. My wolf recognized her. Sadie. She took one long look at Kai and I before running off through the woods without waiting for the pack, and I suddenly felt sorry for her. Kai nipped my leg playfully and I jumped over him and began to run. There would be no way to describe the feeling of blazing through the woods on four paws to any of my human friends. It was ... freeing. The wind rushed past me, so fast I felt as if I were flying. My agile paws leapt over fallen logs and branches without problem.

'*Chase,*' my wolf said.

Kai took off after me, grinning. The rest of the pack was at our heels. I could feel them. *Pack. Run.* I pushed myself faster, harder. Kai was right next to me.

'*You're fast like me,*' he said. I pushed faster, delighting in the feeling of the wind on my fur. Then I circled around to meet up with the pack.

A small, reddish wolf with two white spots on her back pounced on me playfully, yipping. Emma. My wolf nuzzled her and then I noticed Devon circling Kai. They seemed to be talking. Devon's markings were the exact opposite of Emma's. He was stark white with two reddish spots on his back.

'*You found your mate!*' Emma's voice said, and I froze, startled. '*The pack can communicate through the pack bond while in wolf form.*'

'*Oh, cool,*' I tried.

Emma gave me a wolfish grin, but then her eyes sharpened as she tracked something behind me.

I felt movement at my back, a gust of wind, and spun around to see Sadie's wolf growling with a feral look in her eye.

'*First you land yourself as second in the pack and now you take him!*' she roared in my head, and lunged for my wolf, knocking me back.

One second I was falling back, and the next I was slammed with a vision, like a movie playing in my head. I could no longer see Sadie or the trees before me. I saw Sadie in human form, in a grove with the downtown Seattle Space Needle peeking out of the skyline behind her. Then she changed into a large, female wolf with brown and reddish markings. An entire wolf pack came out of the clearing, and one of them had the exact opposite markings to Sadie. Her mate. He howled in joy sprinting toward her, and they nipped each other, running in circles. Then I was shown Sadie in human form looking back at Kai. He nodded. She was saying goodbye, leaving our pack.

Then the vision was gone. Akash and Kai were in front of me whining in anxiety. Sadie was nowhere to be seen; she must have run off.

*'I said, Are you okay? Can you hear me, Aurora?'* Kai asked.

*'Maybe she's having a seizure? I read about staring seizures once,'* Akash added.

I shook my head to clear it. *'Not a seizure, a vision.'* That's the only word I had to describe what I had experienced. I padded over to Kai, to reassure his wolf I was okay because he seemed tense and distraught. If we shared some mental bond, I wondered if I could show him what I saw. I nudged his muzzle and then replayed my vision for him in my thoughts. His wolf's eyes suddenly glowed with a fiery heat; his muzzle opened as he began panting. A shockwave of distress rippled through the pack as Kai let his emotions leak out into all of us.

I backed up in fear. *'What's wrong?'*

*'I know what you are. There are stories about your kind,'* he said ominously.

*My kind?* I thought, as the pack closed in around me in a protective formation.

'You're the Matefinder. The most sought after, the most ... hunted.' At this, his wolf tipped his head back and howled. My fur rose up and my ears went stiff while I fought the panic rising up inside of me.

The other wolves circled him now to see what was wrong. I could feel their concern pressing down on me like a hundred pound weight. Jake brushed my shoulder as he passed me and it happened again! *No, no, no!*

I no longer saw the pack in front of me. I was pulled into another vision. This time I saw Jake, then I was shown a hospital sign. *Mayo Clinic Cancer Center, Scottsdale, AZ.* Then the room #314 flashed in my mind. It was like I was walking into the room. Lying upon the bed was a frail, skinny female hooked up to an I.V. and some machines. She was sleeping.

A nurse walked in with a doctor and they whispered.

"Her white blood cell count is not good. She will be dead in two days. Call the family," the doctor told the nurse.

The nurse frowned. "She doesn't have family. I'll call a priest."

She was Jake's mate. I didn't know how I knew it; it was just there in my mind, a knowing. Then I flashed to months later. There was snow on the ground. Jake and the girl from the hospital were having a mating ceremony, and Emma was sitting in the front row, her belly swollen with pregnancy.

The pack came into focus in front of me. Furry faces all pressing in on me with worry. Kai was in human form, shaking my shoulders gently. I opened my mouth to speak or try to send him the images of my second vision, but I hit a blank wall and blacked out.

---

SUDDENLY, I became aware of breathing on my face. Cracking open my eyes, I saw a human Kai inches from my nose, his eyes glowing yellow.

"Jesus!" I shrieked, pressing my head deeper into the pillow. "You scared me."

My throat felt dry and my body slightly weak. Kai didn't move but he sighed in relief, leaning his forehead against mine. "You scared me, too. I couldn't get Brother Wolf to calm down." Finally he backed up and I could see his eyes fading back to brown.

"I'm fine. I just ... when did I change back to human?" I looked down at my body. Someone had clothed me. I blushed.

"A little while ago. You passed out. After you ... discovered your gift," he said awkwardly.

I exhaled. My gift, some freaking gift. "Do they know? The pack?"

"They picked up on your thoughts. When we're in wolf form we can communicate with the entire pack. It makes us better hunters. Instead of communicating with just me, you sent your vision to the whole pack. I have to teach you to close your mind, but Sadie and Jake are waiting outside the room. They're grinning from ear to ear. If it's true, Aurora, if you can find mates"—he cleared his throat, eyes gleaming yellow again—"well, that makes you very valuable to other wolves, to all wolves. You could be in danger."

I placed my hand on his. The touch seemed to reassure him, and to be honest, my body ached to touch him. I was still processing this whole mate thing, but one thing I was sure about was that I felt better near him.

He went on: "Our race has been slowly dying out. Not many can survive the change, and children can only be born to mates. Finding our mates has become harder and harder. Take you and me, for example. If I hadn't saved you from that accident, you would have died a human and I never would have known. I would have lived out my life alone, with no family." His voice became a whisper. He lowered his head, and for one brief second he looked like a small child. I sat up slowly and wrapped my legs around his waist. It was like I had no control over my body. It was pulled to him in every way.

"About this mate thing," I began, and his face went slack; the Mount Hood alpha looked nervous. He placed his hands possessively around my waist, keeping me close to him as I instinctively placed my hands around his large, tan biceps. "When we're in wolf form, I feel like your mate. But as humans ... I need us to start slow." For Christ's sake, I just got turned into a werewolf and now I find out I'm "mated" to this hot domineering alpha. I needed to pump the brakes big time.

"Slow?" He looked confused.

Clearly he didn't understand the concept. I brushed my fingers through his thick hair, unable to keep myself from touching him.

"Slow, like, when we're human ... you're my boyfriend. I'm not ready to jump into some mating ceremony and have kids next month. Okay?" I smiled.

His laugh was deep and distinctive and it made me want to hear it over and over again. "Boyfriend. Okay. I can do that." He kissed me chastely. "... for now." His eyes scanned my body and my skin heated at his meaning. I let go of my hold on him and detangled my legs, clearing my throat. He grinned, clearly amused with my nervousness, and flashed his bright white canines.

"I'm the luckiest man alive," he said, kissing my forehead as he stood. I sat there frozen, not prepared for the comment he had just made. Holding out his hand, he pulled me into a standing position. "You're not used to being treated right, are you?" he asked, looking deep into my eyes. My breath began to come out in ragged gasps. This was intense. Yet, something inside me assured me he could be trusted with anything, even my past. He was my mate. *Mine*. Made for me. It was hard to explain. My human friends would say we were moving too fast, but there was this knowing, like I had known him for years, lifetimes even.

"No, I'm not," I told him, breaking his intense stare. "The only experience I have with men, is of them raising their fist at me or walking out the door never to return." My lip quivered at the admission, but I wouldn't cry. He needed to know, but he also needed to know I was strong. I had been through a lot, and it took more than some hot guy kissing my forehead to make me become whipped. I wouldn't be beneath him. I was his equal or nothing.

His face fell at my thoughts and his eyes took on a sad look. "I wouldn't have it any other way. Mates mean equals in the wolf world. Dominance aside, you are my other half, my equal."

I tucked a blond lock behind my ear and gave him a small smile. Okay, enough intense talk, I thought to myself as I grabbed his hand and led him out of the room.

The moment the door opened I saw Sadie was waiting for me, head bent low in shame. I let go of Kai's hand and indicated he give us privacy in the hallway. Reluctantly, he did.

Sadie looked up once we were alone. "I'm so sorry. I—" She sounded genuinely distressed.

I put a hand up to stop her. "Woman to woman, I get it. It's cool." Relief washed over her as she nodded. If I had dated Kai for a long time and then he met his mate right before my eyes, I would be pissed too.

Kai was at the end of the hallway calling us out

into the living room. Sadie and I shared one last small smile and then walked out into the large room to see that it was full of pack members.

Jake practically leapt on me, giving me a tight hug. "Are you okay? You scared us."

I was taken aback by all of the attention, the affection. Looking beyond Jake and Sadie, I saw the rest of the pack in the living room and trickling out onto the lawn. They were whispering. I heard one of them say, "Matefinder."

"I'm fine, thank you," I told him.

Jake cleared his throat. "So ... I think you know the location of someone I am very interested in finding." His eyes flashed a buttery yellow and he was grinning from ear to ear.

Sadie nodded. "And me as well."

A small growl came from Kai. "Give her some time before you bombard her. She doesn't even fully know what she is. She just had her first shift." Jake and Sadie lowered their heads and backed off a few steps as I placed an arm on Kai's shoulder.

"Actually, we need to get to Jake's mate immediately. She's..." I paused.

"She's what?" Jake stepped forward, reeking of fear. I could smell it, salty and acidic. "I didn't get the whole vision from your thoughts, just pieces, and then you passed out."

"She's dying of cancer in a hospital in Arizona." I tried to keep my voice calm, but the agony on his face made my eyes tear up. I could see now how important mates were to these wolves.

"She's human?" he stated as if to himself. "Wolves don't get cancer."

Sadie put a comforting hand on his shoulder. "And my mate? All we got from your thoughts was that you saw my mate too?"

I nodded. "Your mate is a wolf. I think he is a member of the Seattle pack," I told her.

Kai nodded. "Sadie, I'll call Shamus in Seattle to schedule a pack meeting to sort things out. Jake, I'll book our tickets to Arizona immediately."

Jake and Sadie nodded. Then Kai spoke into all of our minds. *'We tell no one of Aurora's ability. The only stories I have heard about Matefinders are that they have a history of being the most hunted wolves in history. Protect her with your last breath.'* The last part came with alpha-infused magic. I could feel it. That was an order. Every single one of the pack members' eyes glowed yellow as they nodded. I could feel the command pressing on everyone, as the entire pack bowed to one knee and lowered their heads.

After the wolves dispersed, Emma came over to talk to me. She bumped her hip with mine, causing me to lose balance for a second. "Matefinder, huh? First you make second in the pack, then we find out you're Kai's mate—now this ..." She smiled genuinely, and I realized she was becoming very dear to me. I could trust her, I knew it, I could sense it. Emma was a good person and I didn't trust easily. I returned the smile as best I could, given the overwhelming situation.

"Boyfriend," I said, smirking as Kai caught my eyes a few feet away where he was talking to Devon. "Kai's my boyfriend. We're taking it slowly."

I heard Kai growl and then discreetly cover it with a cough. Emma snorted with laughter. "Playing hard to get?" she whispered in my ear. I grabbed her hand to lead her away where we could have some girl talk. Once we were alone, I told her about my vision of Jake's mating ceremony.

I smiled. "You're going to be pregnant."

"When?" she asked, grinning and placed a hand on her belly as silent tears slid down her cheeks.

"I don't know. Time is hard to tell. There was snow on the ground."

Emma just stared at her belly in disbelief. I couldn't help but think of how young she was. Nineteen and married, about to have a baby, but in this society it seemed okay. She clearly wasn't forced, and the gift of having children seemed denied to ninety percent of their population, so it was understandable she would want to have them as soon as she could.

Emma looked up at me, so much emotion in her eyes. "Aurora, you have no idea what your gift means to our kind. You can literally save our race from extinction."

Her words slammed into me with all of their seriousness and I suddenly felt nervous. I didn't want that kind of responsibility. Before I could think more about it, Kai and Devon came to find us.

"I still don't know fully what a Matefinder is or what they are capable of, but I know someone who does," Kai told us.

I looked at him expectantly.

"Sylvia," Kai said with resignation.

Devon groaned. "I hate witches."

I jerked my head back so fast that I almost fell over.

"Witches! Wait. You're telling me witches are real too?"

Emma smirked. "And vampires."

Vampires! I swallowed hard. Okay, breathe. Just breathe. "And fairies?" I added. Everyone busted up laughing as Kai placed a hand on my shoulder. Okay, I guess that was a "no" on fairies. Wow, witches and vampires were real. I would need to tuck that information away in my special spot to mull over later, because it was too much right now.

"Why would a witch know about my ability?" I prodded.

Kai let me lean against him. "Because witches are the keepers of all supernatural knowledge. I only know rumors of the Matefinder, things I learned on my travels through packs. Stories my mother told me. But witches know everything."

I guess it was time to meet this witch.

## 5

## SYLVIA

Sylvia was tall, with long, thick, auburn hair, and bright green eyes. She appeared to be in her early forties, but she was a witch, so who knew what her real age was, right? She was beautiful and had long, slender fingers that traced the lines of my outstretched palm. Kai stood like a sentinel to my right, Devon to my left, while Emma stood outside the door keeping the pack out of earshot. With her werewolf hearing, I was pretty sure she could hear every word.

Sylvia's voice took on an airy quality. "Yes, it's all here. She can find mates, although not at will. Only Spirit can guide her visions, but there is dark magic that could force her abilities. She could be coerced to find mates for anyone. That is why she will be hunted."

Kai growled and his whole body went rigid; fear trickled down my spine.

Sylvia looked up at him. Her eyes, once a bright green, were silver. "Not by me, wolf. Stand down."

Kai's body relaxed, but only slightly.

The witch looked back down at my palm and sniffed long and deep. I fought the urge to pull back. "Yes. She has magic, too, from her grandmother." She paused, looking up at me, tilting her head to the side. "How odd. Your grandmother was a witch." Her brow crinkled and she took a deep breath again. "Your blood smells powerful, but there is a block. I can't see more. I don't know which clan you are from. Someone has shrouded you in protection magic."

She looked absolutely fascinated, and I wanted nothing more than to jump out the window and run for my life. I couldn't handle this; it was too much.

"How can she be part witch? That isn't possible," Devon said, stating what I was thinking.

Sylvia grabbed Kai's hand, holding it palm side up, and rested it next to mine. "It shouldn't be possible. Old lore states that the Matefinder can take on their mate's ability. She can do what Kai can do. It also states that the Matefinder is always female, always born in a set of twins."

I gasped and pulled my hand away, breaking the spell. Her eyes became green again as I choked on a sob.

"Drake ..." I couldn't speak. A rush of images bombarded my mind. My twin brother drowned at six years old ... pulling me from the raging creek. My father never forgave me for losing his precious son. That's when he began the drinking and abuse.

Kai picked up on my thoughts, giving me a look of

concern. Sylvia reached out slowly and grabbed my hand, looking into my eyes with compassion. "Like I said, Matefinders are born in a set of twins. The female always inherits the gift and the male is her protector."

My mind was still playing catch up. "Wait, my grandmother was a witch? That means my mother or father is half witch?"

"Men are called warlocks, dear." She winked, but then a sad look came over her face. "The story is written that the last Matefinder, your mother I presume, was half witch and half wolf. She gave you and your twin to a guardian for safekeeping, someone she trusted. Your mother, as you call her. That's what the legend says. Your biological mother was the only other Matefinder on record. You are the second, and it's believed to be a genetic gift."

My mind was reeling. My mom wasn't my real mom? I felt like throwing up. "My ... my biological mother. You said *was* ... she *was* half wolf and half witch. Is she...?"

Sylvia nodded. "She died. She was captured and forced with dark magic to use her abilities. They forced her to find mates before it was time. Wolves started changing humans, kids, anything to grow the werewolf race, but they were changing their mates before it was their time. Or their mates were already wolves but it wasn't yet the right time to meet. They had to force the mating ceremony with dark magic because it was not a union guided by Spirit, it was evil."

Spots were dancing at the edges of my vision as my

breathing turned into hyperventilation. Sylvia frowned. "From what I heard, your mother ... she killed herself. As far as how she was half witch and half wolf, we don't know. The legend stops. There is no information to suggest interspecies child bearing is even possible. It's a mystery. The harder I look into it, the more confusing it becomes, like someone has blocked it. So we call it a legend. Those that lived through it have only vague memories. Very powerful magic has been put into covering this up, but then ... you come along."

The silence was tangible. I let go of her hand and sat on the floor staring at a crack in the baseboard, completely numb.

"I think that will be all for today," Kai told Sylvia.

She nodded. "I understand. Then there is just the matter of my payment."

He held out his arm, and to my shock the witch produced a blade and sliced his arm, catching some blood in a jar. Once she was done, the wound healed before my eyes. Then she turned her gaze on me and held up the jar.

"Weres' blood makes for some powerful spellcraft. When you want more stories, come and find me. I'll be expecting an invitation to the mating ceremony." She smiled knowingly.

Kai knelt and cupped my face. "Tell me you're okay." His eyes were pulsing from brown to yellow. His wolf was close to the surface.

"I'm okay," I croaked, lying. "I just need to lie down. I'd like to take a nap."

He scooped me in his arms and carried me down the hall, ignoring the stares from others. I couldn't feel anything. I was completely numb. Learning that my mother wasn't my biological mother had broken me.

---

SOMETIME LATER I awoke to find a single yellow wildflower on my pillow, accompanied by a note. *You twitch your nose in your sleep. It's adorable. – Kai (Your boyfriend).*

I smiled, taking a deep inhalation of the flower's fragrant petals, which worked in lifting my mood a tiny bit. What Sylvia had told me, about my mother and Drake, I couldn't believe it ... but I also could. It made sense in a weird way.

I got up to get ready, and after showering and changing I made my way to the kitchen. Jake and Kai were talking in hushed voices, standing over the stove. A frying pan sizzled and I could smell grilled onions. Kai turned, facing me, as if he sensed me coming. He beamed, his smile reaching his eyes.

"Good afternoon! Are you vegan or just vegetarian? According to the internet there is a big difference!"

I laughed. "Vegetarian. I have milk and eggs. Free range, obviously."

"Obviously," Jake agreed, covering a smile with his hand.

"Good. Then enjoy this veggie omelet and Jake and I will be back from Arizona before you know it." He turned back around, tending to the skillet.

I scowled and put a hand on my hip. "Nice try, Kai. Really, well played. When do we leave? I am *not* staying here!"

Jake shuffled his feet uncomfortably. "You're not going," Kai said, putting the power of the alpha behind his words and turning around to face me.

I stepped forward, holding my head high. "I *am* going. I was in the vision and you are not leaving me here. This is *my* gift and I need to see this through."

Kai sighed. "You're safer here. I have already called and asked permission from the Scottsdale, Arizona alpha, to temporarily cross into his territory, but he is wary. He will send men to make sure we don't outstay our welcome."

"Do I have a sign on my forehead that says Matefinder?" I probed him.

Kai gave me an annoyed look. "No."

"Good, then it's settled. No one will know what I am." I popped a sautéed mushroom in my mouth and kissed him quickly on the cheek.

"Fine," he grumbled, "but there's one last piece of business you need to attend to before we leave. Finish your breakfast and meet me outside." He handed me a plate and stalked off with Jake.

"She doesn't exactly get the alpha orders thing yet, huh?" Jake mumbled to Kai.

I just rolled my eyes. He knew I could hear him. They were in for some amusement if they thought I was taking orders from anybody.

I ate quickly and made my way outside so I could see what this business involved. Max was standing against a tree looking down at his feet. Burn marks from the places I tied him up with silver marked his skin. Silver wounds took a long time to heal I was learning. I walked slower, treading carefully. Kai stood a few feet off, talking with Jake and Sadie, but motioned me toward Max, urging me along.

"Max..." When I reached the tall werewolf I simply nodded, unsure what to say. In all of the recent drama, I had forgotten about him completely.

He sighed for a second and then looked up at me with piercing blue eyes. "Kai's my best friend, my brother. I never could have lived with myself if I had challenged him. Brother Wolf was too close and I couldn't stop him. Thank you for what you did. You may be inexperienced but you are a worthy second. You acted on instinct and saved me from doing something horrible." He extended his hand as I stood there in shock.

"Friends?" he asked.

A slow scowl crept across my face. "So, I knock you out, tie you up with silver, cage you, and you're thanking me?" I didn't take his hand yet, pretending to look suspicious.

He laughed deeply. "I know, pretty stupid, right?"

I smiled genuinely then, and extended my hand. "Friends."

We shook, and I realized that I felt more at home here than anywhere else I had ever lived in my life. These were my wolves, as much mine as I was theirs. I felt Kai's approval at that thought.

## 6

## ANNA

On the flight to Arizona, Jake kept tapping his foot incessantly. He wiped his palms on his jeans for the fifth time as our plane prepared to land.

I squeezed his hand. "Jake, it's going to be fine."

He let out a deep breath. "My mate is dying of cancer. That's not fine. She's in pain. What if we don't make it in time?"

"Look at me," I commanded him.

His eyes locked on mine and I spoke with surety. "I have seen it. We get there in time. They give her two days left to live and we get there in time."

He swallowed. "Okay."

---

Room number 314. We all stood outside the door. The nurses were more than delighted to let us through after I explained I was college roommates with the patient in room 314. Jake looked at me expectantly and I shrugged. "This is as far as my vision goes."

Kai seemed to pick up on my apprehension. Looking at Jake, he placed a strong hand on his shoulder. "Go introduce yourself to your future mate while Aurora and I figure out a way to get her out of here without alerting the police or the Scottsdale pack."

Jake swallowed hard; he nodded and let himself into the room. After the door closed, Kai looked at me. "There are two ways I see this going down. We take her out of here by force and anyone in our way gets wolfed ... or we lie."

I snorted. "Wolfed?"

He smiled. "Your laugh is cute."

"Focus," I reminded him playfully, but my stomach fluttered at his compliment.

He stared at the nurses' station. "You go tell the nurses you would like to take her home to pass on in peace. I'll call the Scottsdale alpha and tell him we will be leaving shortly with a college friend of my new mate. What can go wrong?"

I took in a deep breath. "Let's find out."

After getting all of the necessary paperwork in order, the hospital staff was pleased to release Anna into our care. As an only child with deceased parents, she had no living relatives.

"You what?" I shouted, getting stares from the nurses in the hallway.

Jake rubbed the back of his head nervously. "I told

her we were from a private research group and we wanted to try a very risky gene therapy procedure to cure her cancer. Now she's willing to hop on the next flight to Oregon."

Kai groaned. "Well, it's not like we can change her here. Poor thing will be in for a scare when we tell her who we really are and what we have to do to save her life." A look passed over his face. I knew he was thinking of when he bit me to save my life. I could already see he was becoming protective over Anna. He was already accepting her as pack.

I introduced myself to Anna as vice president of the research company, and Kai as president, and she agreed to let us take her right then and there. As we made our way out of the hospital, Jake tenderly pushed Anna in her wheelchair.

"How did you hear of my case? Did Dr. Pasternick call you?" she asked in a frail, breathy voice.

"Yes, he called us. Like I said, we have a very high success rate," Jake said, and we all exchanged a look. "Once you get to our clinic in Oregon, we can tell you more about our methods."

"Well, I am surprised my case passed your approval—I had given up." The look on Jake's face was torture. Anna was slumped in her wheelchair and her skin was translucent. The very act of talking seemed to take the breath out of her. Her hair was gone, even her eyebrows, but her eyes were a deep hazel and there was so much life, so much fight left in her. I could see that she would survive the change; she had no fear of death.

Maybe that was the key. Even in her sickened state, she was beautiful. She was ready for a new beginning.

The Scottsdale alpha had sent two wolves to tail us from the airport, and as we exited the hospital they were leaning against our rental car. Jake let out a low growl and Kai motioned for Jake, Anna, and me to hang back. Hah. Not a chance. I approached the men with him, ignoring his gesture for me to stay back. He gave me one good glare over his shoulder before walking right up to the two men.

Kai stood tall, nodding to the men. "We are just retrieving our friend and we will be on the next plane back to Oregon. Give our thanks and respect to Steven for allowing us to spend the day in your territory."

One of the men, a tall, broad-shouldered, thirty-something guy with a scruffy beard, nodded his head and locked eyes with me. I inhaled deeply. Second-in-command, I could tell. He wasn't looking away and neither was I. I wasn't sure what the protocol was for meeting other packs, but I sure as hell wasn't going to look weak in front of a stranger.

*Threat*, my wolf told me. Should I look away? I didn't want to start a fight.

'*Stare for as long as you are able. Don't look weak,*' Kai told me. With that permission, I stood taller and took a step toward the man, lifting my chin. The man grinned and I could see tension creasing his forehead. My nostrils flared in anger. How dare he challenge me? I came with permission, with my alpha to retrieve a frail human. Who the hell did he think he was?

'*Stop it. Calm down. You're shifting,*' Kai told me.

Shit! I could feel my fingers turning to claws just as the man lowered his gaze. I took a shaky breath.

Kai stepped forward. "Now that we've had a little fun, I think we'll be going."

I stepped forward to get in the car when the second-in command took a deep breath. "She smells new and unmated. Mmmm." He grinned, licking his lips.

Kai's arm flew out faster than my eye could track, and grabbed the man by the back of the head. A second later, he slammed his head into the hood of the car, pressing down on the back of his neck.

"Did I give you permission to smell my mate? Do you want to start a war? We asked your alpha for approval and it was granted. Safe passage for the day. You were curious about my mate and how dominant she was, so I allowed you to have a little fun. Your fun stops here. If you want to fight, I would be happy to oblige that request." Kai released him and opened the door for me. Holy crap! This possessive mate thing was real. I stood there in shock for a second and then sank into the seat.

A few more *pleasantries* were exchanged outside the car and then the two men walked off. I turned around in my seat to see that Anna looked shaken after seeing the scuffle, but allowed Jake to hoist her into the car anyway. He tenderly buckled her next to me. When he was done, she leaned into me. "You're not cancer researchers, are you?" She whispered.

I gently held her hand. "You're going to be okay." An edited version of the truth was best.

"I'm too tired to care," she said a little louder, and leaned her head on my shoulder, falling fast asleep. Her hand was clammy but I didn't let go.

We flew back to Oregon in a private jet. I was going to have to ask Kai what he did for a living. Once we had Anna back at the house and asleep in my bed, Jake, Devon, Emma, Max, Sadie, Kai, and I all gathered in the kitchen whispering.

"How do we change her? Who should change her? What if she doesn't survive?" Max asked.

Jake stepped forward. "She is my mate. I am changing her!"

Kai nodded. "If you want to be the one, I will grant it."

"No." I spoke through the hushed voices and stared at Jake, holding his gaze. He opened his mouth to argue, but I spoke first: "Jake, this is the woman you will spend the rest of your life with. Have children with. Do you want her to remember you as a monster or a savior? Take it from me, being the one to change your mate isn't always a positive thing. Some images you can never get out of your head."

I heard Kai's breath leave him in a rush. The look of hurt that crossed his face was undeniable. Shit. I knew the comment might hurt him, but I wanted better for Anna. I didn't want her to see her lover with shreds of flesh in his mouth and yellow, murderous eyes.

I placed a hand on Kai's shoulder, but he brushed it

off. "I'll change her, then. I seem to have no problem being a monster."

Dammit. That didn't go as planned. Note to self: talk less.

We all agreed that a quick attack was best. We shouldn't tell her of our kind until after her change. No use in frightening her more. Kai had a few private words with Jake, ignored me, and then took a sleeping Anna, draped in his arms, to the basement.

We all waited anxiously upstairs. Jake was pacing back and forth as the rest of us stood around tensely, watching him. Maybe Kai would forget what I said and we could talk about when my mom could visit.

*'Do you think I enjoy this? Enjoy attacking a young, innocent girl? I'm doing this to give her life!'* Kai screamed into my head. Well, there goes that idea; he wasn't letting this go.

*'No, I don't think you enjoy it!'* I responded. *'I'm sorry. It was scary for me, and I didn't want that for Anna ... for her to see Jake like that.'*

No reply.

A few moments later, a hair-raising scream ripped through the house. *Anna.* Jake began changing into wolf form on instinct, and I changed instantly into my wolf as well. If this went wrong, if my vision was wrong and Anna didn't survive the change, then I had to protect Kai from Jake. I was already in full wolf form and in front of the basement door before Jake was even halfway changed. Sharing this fast-shifting gift with Kai was turning out to be useful. Jake bolted for the door with his hackles raised. More screams. I prepared to pounce, but Sadie stepped in front of me, facing Jake.

"Jake, you aren't thinking clearly. Kai isn't hurting her. Not in the long run. I know how you feel. I'm going mad sitting around while we get your mate changed, knowing my mate is a three-hour drive away in Seattle. He is so close! But I have to be patient. It has to be like Aurora's vision, and the timing needs to be right. You have to be patient and trust her. Anna will survive the change, and she will be your mate. You wouldn't even know that if Aurora hadn't told you. She's on our side."

Whoa. Sadie had my back?

Jake's yellow eyes were pinned on me, fur raised, but at Sadie's reassurance they slowly threaded back to their normal color. He whined and rolled over, exposing his belly. My inner wolf was pleased. I relaxed and approached Jake, giving his muzzle a nudge. Then he stood and we both began to change back.

We all decided it was best to wait outside for the reminder of her change. Once I had put on some clothes, I met everyone out back. After a couple of hours of idle chatting, Kai finally spoke into my mind. *'She will survive the change. Bring Jake and Emma.'*

A huge sense of relief washed over me. It was pitch dark out now and the day's events had worn me down. I was exhausted. I still wasn't even sure about being a werewolf, or if I felt confident being a Matefinder and having visions, but this was confirmation that my vision was correct, and it gave me chills.

"Jake, Emma, we are needed," I told them. Akash and a few others had joined our backyard party and now everyone looked at me expectantly. "She will survive the change," I said, grinning. Jake picked Sadie up and swung her around as she laughed. Happiness descended on the pack then and it made me smile.

We rushed into the house to see that Kai was waiting for us at the door to my bedroom. He had obviously just showered. His hair was still dripping wet and he wouldn't meet my eyes.

"Her wounds are already closing and her hair is growing back. Her blood tasted like poison. The chemotherapy, I assume." He scraped his tongue against his teeth. "Jake and Emma, would you keep watch by her side and get me when she is coherent?"

They nodded and went into the room quietly.

Kai met my eyes and I paled and stared at his chin. "Anna will be using your room for the night, so you can either sleep on the couch or with me. Let me be clear that sleeping is all I intend. And maybe some kissing." He winked. Relief crashed over me that all was forgotten from our earlier argument. I was also pleased to see that he was taking my request seriously for having things move more slowly. I hated to admit it, but my issues with my father always leaked into my relationships. I didn't trust easily.

I stepped closer to him, giving him a sexy, hooded

stare. "Well, I will only share your bed if there is a promise of kissing *and* snuggling."

Kai looked left and right down the hallway and then put his finger to my lips. "Shhhh! I have a reputation to uphold. Alphas don't snuggle."

I smiled, tilting my chin up and crossing my arms defiantly. "Then I'm not coming."

He scooped me up in his arms and I screamed in delight as he walked me into his room, setting me down at the foot of his bed. Looking at his soft blue sheets, I felt my stomach drop. I didn't want to go too fast, I had major trust issues, and as much as Kai felt like my mate, my home, I couldn't get past my deep-rooted fears.

"Just a kiss or two and then to bed. I'm tired, and I wouldn't do *that* until our wedding night anyway," he stated.

"Ugh! Get out of my head." I smirked while kicking off my shoes and jumped into his bed, wondering if he was serious about waiting until marriage. True to his word, three toe-curling kisses later he was snoring beside me with his arm tightly around my waist, snuggling.

As I looked at his sleeping face, I took a moment to reflect on all that had happened. I couldn't believe the transformation that had taken place within me. I really couldn't believe I was lying in bed with a man I'd just barely met—that he was my alpha ... and my mate. Normally I wouldn't rush into things so fast with a guy. I wouldn't trust so easily. I would have my guard up twenty-four/seven. Being a werewolf gave me new senses and instincts I never had before, and I could sense a deep connection to Kai, like I had been waiting my whole life for him. Like we had been created for each other. Oh man, I had it bad. I was falling in love for sure. With a sigh, I drifted off to sleep.

---

"MERI PYARI," a husky voice whispered in my ear before kissing my neck. I opened my eyes to see a sexy Kai with dark, tousled hair inches from my face.

"Is that Hindi?" I inquired.

"Yes, now get showered so we can take Sadie to Seattle before she bugs me to death." He stood, rubbing his head, and I swallowed hard at the sight of him shirtless and in gray, low-slung sweatpants. Jesus Christ, it looked like someone had draped skin over cement; his body was that rock hard. He gave me a knowing smile and I groaned. It was awfully convenient he hadn't taught me to get him out of my head yet.

Before he left the room, I felt the need to warn him of something from my vision with Sadie. "You know she is going to leave our pack and join his, right?" In my vision, the look she and Kai shared as she walked toward her mate was a look of goodbye.

He simply nodded.

"Will you miss her?" I added delicately.

He gave me a weak smile. "I'm happy for Sadie, and if she wants to join the Seattle pack I will grant it."

He left the room, shutting the door. Okay, that didn't exactly answer my question. I needed to find out more about Sadie from Emma. I was starting to recognize something else about my newly-changed self, something I never had before—jealousy.

# 7
## GOODBYE

God, being a werewolf was so political! Because we had pissed off the Portland pack recently, we were denied access to travel through Portland to Seattle, which meant we had to take some different freeways. It was annoying. Sadie was sitting in the back seat rubbing her hands on her legs nervously, and I was staring out the window at the beautiful green scenery, when I felt a tingling sensation in my head. I tried to ignore it, but Kai could sense something.

"Aurora?" he asked from the driver's seat next to me.

Before I could answer, a vision slammed into me. I saw Sylvia, that witch, standing over a large oak table littered with small bottles and crushed powders, a tall and very pale man in a gray silk suit beside her. The man's eyes glowed a deep violet hue.

"Tell me what you know of a person called the Matefinder. Where is she?" His voice was trancelike.

Sylvia shook her head and frowned. A fine mist leaked from her skin like a protective bubble.

"How dare you try to use compulsion on me! I'm a high priestess!" She clutched a medallion on her chest. "You are here to pay a blood debt. Pay and then be on your way!"

Anger flared on the man's face, but he extended his wrist to pay the debt.

Then I was kicked out of the vision, and suddenly became aware of Kai growling in front of my face. The car had been pulled over and Sadie was peeking from the back seat at me.

He shook me. "Aurora!"

"I'm here, I'm fine," I shouted. Man, he got riled up easily.

He sat back. "I'll never get used to this. You go all zombie on me and I can't reach your mind. I don't like this. What happened?"

I chewed a nail. "Do vampires have purple eyes when they are using compulsion?"

Kai's eyes went yellow. "Yes, they do. Please tell me you are not having visions of vampires doing compulsion on you!" he roared.

"Wow, so vampires *are* real..." I pondered with a mixture of excitement and fear. I mean they told me that before, but now I was really processing it...

"Aurora, what happened?" Kai pushed again, looking feral.

I quickly explained, but didn't give him details, and

had to talk him out of driving over to Sylvia's right then and there.

"This day is about Sadie," I declared. "She is going to meet her mate. Meeting with Sylvia can wait."

He groaned, but started the engine and careened the car back onto the highway.

---

When we entered the large, grassy park, I could see the Space Needle peeking out in the background, just like my vision. A man and a woman stood near a picnic table, with a large group of people farther back in the grassy area playing soccer. Apparently the Seattle alpha and Kai went way back. He told me they used to be in the same pack together in New Mexico.

"Shamus!" Kai embraced the large man with a red, shaggy beard.

Shamus returned the hug. "Kai! My brother. You didn't say much over the phone, just that this visit involved a possible mate for one of my wolves. All of my guys are in a frenzy with excitement."

"Well, it's a long story, but my newly-changed mate, Aurora, had to see a witch about something. Sadie was there, and the witch did a palm reading for Sadie and said her mate might be in the Seattle pack."

Interesting, I thought. Kai didn't trust him with the truth.

*'I trust Shamus with my life, but not his mate,'* Kai told me.

Double interesting.

Shamus stepped toward me and extended his hand. "You must be Aurora. It's a pleasure to meet you." He smiled genuinely, and I was careful to make only the briefest of eye contact. I took his hand in mine. "A friend of Kai's is a friend of mine."

Shamus' mate then stepped forward and shook my hand. "I'm Petra." She was tall and extremely thin, with dark brown hair and unkind eyes. With her expensive jewelry, too much makeup, and upturned nose, she had an air of snobbery. I had my guard up after what Kai had told me.

'*She's power hungry and money hungry, but she's not a horrible person,*' Kai said in my mind.

Oh, just power and money hungry, the two motivators for every villain in history. Kai tried to cover his chuckle at my thought into a cough.

"Nice to meet you, Petra." I held her gaze a little longer than polite.

She nodded curtly and then she turned to Sadie.

"It's good to see you both again," Sadie greeted them.

Shamus smiled warmly at Sadie. "I would be one proud alpha if one of my boys was your mate, Sadie. This is exciting. Should I have my boys shift and we can see what happens?"

That's how it was in my dream.

"Yes," Kai said, and nodded to Sadie, who began to undress and shift. All of the men on the soccer field suddenly looked our way. They began to undress and I cleared my throat, looking at my shoes.

"You'll get used to it," Petra told me, winking. After a minute of hearing snapping bones and growls, Sadie stood a few feet ahead of us, facing the approaching wolves. She was a beautiful reddish wolf with small black spots and sleek fur. We stood in human form, as did the women and their mated partners on the field. I noticed there were only three mated couples and one child to the twenty or so single males trotting toward Sadie. My eyes were scanning the wolves one by one, but before I could get halfway through the approaching pack, I heard Shamus shout out in joy.

"It's Brett!"

He looked at me and Kai. "He joined my pack two summers ago. Was a lone wolf, broke away from an aggressive pack in Texas. He is such a good guy. They will make a great pair."

I turned to Kai and saw him swallow hard. I had forgotten for a minute that this was his ex-girlfriend. Sadie approached Brett's wolf, he jogged up to her and put his front paws flat with his rear up in the air and yipped. He reminded me of a dog asking to play with his owner. Sadie pounced on him and they rolled a few times before running off into the park. I knew what they felt. Total completeness.

Shamus sighed. "Young love."

Petra spoke next. "Will you want Brett to transfer to your pack or ..."

Kai shook off his thoughts. "No. Sadie and I have

spoken, and in the event she found her mate today, she told me she wishes to transfer to the Seattle pack. She has my blessing."

Shamus put his hand on Kai's shoulder. "Trusting me with Sadie, with a mated female and her future pups, is an honor. I will make sure she is well protected and provided for."

Kai nodded. "I knew you would, friend. That's why I was happy to oblige her request. I just hope you have a spot for a dominant female who thinks she should be your next second-in-command."

We all shared a laugh at that.

A while later, Sadie and Brett changed into human form and got dressed. They kept giving each other side glances and flirty smiles. It was adorable. Was that how Kai and I looked? When Shamus told Brett that Sadie would be joining his pack, he grinned goofily and then approached Kai, extending his hand. "Thank you for allowing Sadie to join my pack. I will take good care of her."

Kai shook his hand briskly and nodded.

Shamus, Petra, and Brett started walking away then, and I moved to go to the car to give him and Sadie privacy to say goodbye, but Kai grabbed my hand to stop me.

"Breaking pack bonds needs a witness from the pack. As my second, it's your job to witness."

"Oh, okay." I stood there frozen. My vision didn't play this part, and as Kai's new mate, witnessing him breaking ties with his ex-girlfriend, I wasn't exactly comfortable with the situation.

Sadie stood strong and lifted her shirt to expose her tan, lean belly. Her eyes ran up and down Kai's body slowly. It was as if she was taking one last look of what she would never have, and I had to suppress a growl.

"I'm sorry, but this will hurt," Kai told her, and she nodded.

Kai turned around and undressed quickly, changing into his wolf form. When he spun back around, he paused for a second and then lunged at Sadie's abdomen, digging his teeth into her side. She whimpered a little but didn't scream. Now I knew why Brett had walked away—he wouldn't have been able to see this. Kai pulled his jaws out of her stomach, and with her blood in his mouth he howled. It was the longest and most haunting howl I had ever heard.

'*Sadie, you are no longer a member of the Mount Hood pack. I cast you out.*' Somehow I knew he had sent this mental message to all of Mount Hood pack. '*I cast you out. I cast you out. I cast you out.*' I felt something tug at my chest and then it was gone. Sadie was gone. She smelled like a foreign wolf to me now. A single tear rolled down her cheek and she nodded. My heart broke a little then; she was a part of Kai's family and leaving in this way, it felt … sad. Kai changed into human form and got dressed, and without another word that's when Sadie began to walk away. When she looked back over her shoulder at Kai, it was the look from my vision. It was goodbye.

It was done. Kai let Sadie go and Sadie found her mate. My second vision had come true. It hit me then. I *was* the Matefinder. In a world where it was hard to find your mates, I found them with ease. The thought put a heavy responsibility on my shoulders, but with it came a newfound pride and sense of purpose. I was meant for this.

"Let's go," Kai said with little emotion, and pulled me gently towards the car.

The drive home was silent and introspective, at least for twenty minutes.

"So tell me more about your vision with the vampire," Kai said with one hand on my thigh and the other on the wheel.

"Tell me how to keep you out of my thoughts," I countered, because it was starting to overwhelm me knowing he could hear nearly everything I was thinking.

He growled. "Aurora..."

"I'm serious! I feel invaded. I get in a horrible accident and you save my life. Then I wake up to find out I'm a mons—a werewolf—and I have a mate. But my mate is also my alpha, so he is inside my head all the time! I'm also a Matefinder, and so I'm hunted and I have visions. Please, Kai, I need a break. It's too much." I whimpered. I hadn't planned on breaking down and exploding on him like that.

Kai pulled the car over and took my face in his hands; I stared into his yellow eyes, his jaw clenched.

"Why is your wolf out?" I asked him, trying to change the subject.

"Because you aren't happy and he is upset about it." Kai closed his eyes and took a deep breath. When he opened them, his warm chocolate eyes stared back at me and he placed a kiss on my forehead. "You're right, you deserve a break. Close your eyes and think of a safe place within nature."

I raised my eyebrows. "What? I don't need calming techniques, I feel fine," I assured him.

He chuckled softly. "I'm teaching you how to close me out of your every thought."

"Oh." I closed my eyes quickly and thought of the creek my twin brother and I used to play at, but that was no good because he drowned there and that was no longer a safe place. Then my mind wandered to the woods that backed on to Kai's house. I thought of my first run as a wolf, the bits of bark that crunched underneath my paws, the smell of cedar and Kai ... that was peace now. That was my home.

"Stay there," Kai whispered. "Now imagine my energy as a bright ball of light sitting next to you."

With my eyes still closed, I was looking around the forest in my mind's eye, and a glowing orb appeared next to my wolf.

"Good. Now bury the glowing ball, bury my essence. Not too deep, just under the surface. We will still be able to communicate through pack bonds, and eventually through our mate bond. But this will make it so I won't get your every thought unless you intend it.

I will just pick up moods and emotions or sense when you are in danger."

I imagined my wolf digging a hole and nudging the orb into the hole with my nose, burying it loosely with dirt. Opening my eyes slowly, I saw Kai staring at me from across the car. God, he was so sexy. That dark, mysterious, rugged, lumberjack kind of guy I always fantasized about.

"Did you get that thought?" I tried.

He shook his head.

*'You are sexy,'* I sent to him, and a huge grin broke out onto his face.

"Whoa, it worked!" I said excitedly. Mind back to myself. Success!

Kai grabbed my face and gave me a passionate kiss that warmed my belly, nipping my bottom lip at the end.

"Now tell me more about that vision."

"Ugh!" I growled playfully. I was hoping for a bit of a break with the heavy news. But his glare said I would be getting no break, so I told him about the vampire who met with Sylvia and how he seemed interested in finding me.

"So a vampire tried to use compulsion on Sylvia to give up your location?" Kai's voice could have cut glass.

I chewed a fingernail. "Yes."

His eyes went yellow and his nails grew to points. I could see patches of fur rippling along his arms as he tried to fight the change.

"Kai?" I was scared; he'd never lost control like this with me before.

"If the bloodsuckers think they can have you, they have another thing coming. You're mine. Mine to protect." He was breathing rapidly and slammed his fist into the steering wheel; the car horn honked and I jumped.

Placing a shaky hand on his arm, my voice shook. "Calm down, you're scaring me."

His mouth popped open in shock and his fingernails immediately went human-short; the fur turned to skin, and his eyes went brown. "Aurora, I'm so sorry. I would never hurt you. I was mad at the bloodsuckers. Not you. Never you." He reached out for my face but I flinched. I don't know why I did; too many years of getting hit when my dad was pissed off. The remote ran out of batteries—smack Aurora. My mother burnt dinner—punch Aurora. Drunk and bored—put a cigarette out on Aurora's neck. My hand instinctively went to the circular scar at the back of my neck.

I shivered thinking of the memories, while Kai shrank back, hurt. I reached out and grabbed his hand. "I have issues, okay?" was all I could offer at the moment. I knew he wouldn't hurt me, but there were some things people never really got over.

He stroked my hand with his thumb. "Okay."

He started the car and we drove the rest of the trip in silence.

## 8
## VAMPIRES

We got a call from the pack about halfway home, telling us that Sylvia was waiting for us at Kai's house.

As we drove up the long, tree-lined driveway to Kai's, I still couldn't fathom how much money this land had cost him. He must own half the mountain. The pack lived in twenty or so separate houses, all within a few miles of each other and Kai owned every single one of them.

"So ... my mother will be coming by tomorrow to meet you. I think I should know a little bit more about how you became so ... financially comfortable." My mom had been texting me, dying to meet him and see where I would live, and I needed to move my stuff up here. So I'd invited her over for a BBQ.

He smiled. "I am a very, very old wolf, Aurora. I have had hundreds of years to amass this wealth. I have a bachelor's degree in engineering, a master's degree in finance, and I even went to medical school.

I've tried my hand at day trading on the stock market, I've dabbled in real estate, and I own some franchises."

Whoa. Wait. Hundreds of years? He was old and mega rich but looked twenty-five. That was super unsettling. My mind was trying to fathom all of this information when suddenly I smelled something weird. Breathing in deeply, I frowned.

"Witches have a distinct smell, as do vampires," Kai said, parking the car. "As you learn more about your wolf, your sense of smell will improve."

"Do you trust Sylvia?" I probed. She seemed nice enough to me, but I wasn't sure if we could trust her.

"I don't trust witches. That being said, I have known Sylvia for a long time and she has never given me cause not to trust her. When it comes to your safety, I trust no one outside this pack." He got out of the car and gestured for me to do the same.

I unlocked my seatbelt and scrambled to catch up with him.

"That smell, that witch smell, do I smell like that? She said I was part witch." I stuck my nose in my armpit and inhaled but came up with nothing but deodorant.

Kai stared into my eyes. "You smell amazing, but yes, you have smelled faintly of witch since I found you at the accident. I knew you weren't full-blooded because your blood didn't taste like witch, but there was something about your blood that had me puzzled. You weren't completely human. It wasn't possible though, so I put it to the back of my mind. Now I'm not so sure."

I recoiled at the thought. My whole life I thought I was human, but then Kai turned me into a werewolf ... but maybe I was destined to be supernatural all along? "What puzzled you about my blood?" I was curious.

We entered the house and stopped outside his home office. "You know when you go to take a sip of water and you realize you have grabbed your friend's glass of Sprite instead? The fizz shocks your tongue and you aren't prepared for it. That is your blood."

With that, he opened his office door, where Sylvia was waiting. My blood tasted like Sprite? Gross. And how the hell did he know what witches' blood tasted like anyway? I didn't want to know.

Sylvia sat across from Kai's desk. Her neck was adorned with blue stones that had gold flecks inlaid in an ornate necklace. She clutched her handbag and stared at Kai as I leaned against the wall.

Finally Kai took a seat before her and motioned with his hands for her to speak.

She quirked a smile. "We are meeting all too often for your liking I'm sure, but there is a matter to discuss."

I stepped forward. "The vampires are after me."

Sylvia's face showed genuine surprise. So she must not have been aware that I'd had a vision of her. That told me two things. One, that her powers weren't limitless. And two, that she could be trusted. She didn't have to come warn me.

"You have the gift of a seer?" she asked me, puzzled.

I shrugged. I didn't know what that was.

Kai cleared his throat. "What do the bloodsuckers want with a werewolf Matefinder?"

Sylvia leaned forward, staring Kai directly in the eyes. "What do the vampires always want?"

"Blood?" I offered.

Kai nodded his head to her. "Money."

She smiled. "Someone is paying big bucks to get the info on your mate, and I'm guessing I'm not the only witch who has been asked."

Kai muttered a curse word. "But I'll bet you are the only one refusing to give her location."

"Hold on," I intervened. "Only Sylvia and the pack know what I am. Who cares if some other witch is asked about me?"

Kai rubbed his palms on his jeans in a nervous gesture I had come to recognize, and nodded to Sylvia.

Sylvia stood and crossed the room, resting a hand on my arm. "Witches can do spells to reveal an object or person's whereabouts. Finder spells are the easiest ones to learn. I did my first finder spell when I was six years old."

My stomach dropped. The room was silent and I began to feel claustrophobic.

I swallowed hard. "So anyone who pays a witch to do a finder spell can get to me?"

"They are probably searching for you right now, dear."

Kai stood up suddenly. "Don't scare her!" he roared at Sylvia, and she backed away from me as my heart began to hammer in my chest.

Sylvia put her hands up and faced down Kai. "Calm down, Alpha. I haven't come all this way to deliver bad news! I have a vested interest in protecting Aurora and I have placed a protection bubble over Mount Hood. Anyone scrying this way won't pinpoint her location. It won't last forever, but it will confuse lower witches. Only a high priest or priestess could break my protection spell, and only after many tries. They won't be looking for a werewolf under the protection of a witch. It won't make sense to them at first."

Kai adjusted his posture. "You have a vested interest in my mate? Why?"

Sylvia sighed. "Because she is a Whiteraven. She's a descendant of my coven. She smelled part witch and I was curious, so I stole a piece of her hair last time I was here and did a descendant spell. She is a witch of my coven, and therefore I offer her my protection."

Kai looked at me. "And that's why I don't like witches!"

Could my life get any more complicated? Before I could comment, Kai walked to the door and opened it.

"Aurora *was* part witch. Now she's a werewolf and she's mine to protect, not yours. Thank you for the protection spell, but we won't need your help any longer. You may leave." There was no denying that was an order, but a piece of me was desperate for more information about this part of my life I knew nothing about.

"Wait." I stood quickly. "I found out a few days ago that my mom isn't my real mom and my real mother is dead. Now I find out I'm related to Sylvia's coven and you want to throw her out?"

Kai's eyes went yellow but I stood my ground. "No, I get a say in what happens to my life. I want to get to know Sylvia, and I want to know more about witches. I want her to come to the barbeque tomorrow to meet my mom."

If I was some witch descendant, I wanted to know how.

Sylvia smiled. "I'd love to." She looked to Kai, asking permission with her eyes.

Kai threw his hands in the air, speaking rapid-fire Hindi to no one in particular. I was kicking myself for not picking the language up during my time in India. "See you tomorrow, then," he finally stated to Sylvia through gritted teeth.

Sylvia smiled and nodded her head. She was in the doorway getting ready to leave when Kai's voice carried across the room.

"Sylvia?"

She turned, looking slightly afraid. "Hmmm?"

"If you ever steal one of Aurora's hairs again, you and I will have a serious problem."

Sylvia pursed her lips, turned away, and left.

Kai then faced me. "Has anyone ever told you that you're not very good at taking orders?"

I backed him into his chair and he sat down, looking up at me with a wild, passionate look in his eyes. Straddling my legs around his waist, I leaned closer. "Yes, every man that has ever tried to order me around has told me that." I leaned in tentatively and kissed him. I really loved kissing him. He never went too far and I felt in control. I was coming to realize I felt completely safe with him.

I pulled at his bottom lip. "Do you want to know the secret to getting me to follow orders?"

He groaned. "Yes."

"Stop giving them." I lifted myself off of him and walked to the door, giving a flirty look over my shoulder.

His eyes were yellow but there was a smile on his face.

*'Woman, you'll be the death of me,'* he stated in my head, and I grinned.

---

I KNOCKED LIGHTLY on Anna's door. It was my door really, but it was her room for the time being. I wasn't exactly complaining about sharing a room with Kai.

"Come in," a bright voice answered on the other side.

Opening the door, I tried to mask my shock. Her face had filled in and she looked like she had gained at least fifteen pounds. She looked healthy. Her cheeks were rosy and her hair was already a couple of inches long. She had a cute red clip pulling some hair away from her face. Wow, she looked beautiful. Jake sat at her bedside and they were both leaning over a photo album and smiling.

Jake looked up when he saw me. "Hi, Aurora. She is taking things pretty well, considering. I'll give you two a moment to talk."

After Jake left the room I sat down and nervously picked at my jeans. I didn't have a formal plan of what I wanted to say to her, I just wanted to make sure she was okay. Let her know that I knew how she felt. She started the conversation for me.

"Jake tells me you were in a car accident. That Kai, who is our alpha, changed you and then you found out you were mates. How romantic." She smiled.

"Romantic is one word for it. Scary, intimidating, horrifying, shocking, *and* romantic is more like it." I smiled and we both shared a laugh.

"Jake tells me that we're mates too. I'm not sure what that really means, but I think he's a good guy—and he is pretty hot, too," she offered with a smile.

I wanted to set her mind at ease. "Well, you haven't done your first shift yet. Once you fully let your wolf out, you will feel what it's like to find your mate. It's pretty incredible, and I'm sure if you ask Jake to take it slow, he will."

She chuckled. "I just escaped death. The last thing I want to do is take things slow. I'm ready to live my life." She reached out, grabbed my hand and squeezed as a tear rolled down her cheek. "Thank you for finding me and for letting Kai change me. I was in so much pain, so defeated. I wanted to fight for my life but the doctors kept telling me to give up. I feel so strong now, and I have so much hope for the future."

My throat swelled up and I was overcome with sudden emotion. I hadn't really felt settled about my mate-finding gift until now. Sitting here, I realized it was a good thing, an incredible gift that could bring joy into people's lives. I thought of Sadie and how happy she must be to have moved on to another pack and settled with her mate. I made up my mind then to be the Matefinder, to fully embrace this gift no matter what. Bringing soul mates together and starting families was something I could do for the rest of my life with no regrets.

I returned the squeeze to her hand. "You're welcome."

---

THAT AFTERNOON, Anna ran with the pack for the first time. You could see the instant bond her wolf had with Jake's. They nuzzled and nipped and ran around like total love-crazy goofballs. Because Anna was a changed wolf, she was told she would have a special power when she shifted. She hadn't discovered her power yet. Kai said it might take a few shifts, or a certain situation to bring it about.

Right before the run, Anna's place in the pack was tested and we learned she was fifth from the top, a very dominant female. Kai was pleased as she was a good replacement for Sadie. He was worried that someone might come to claim her, but no one from her home state of Montana even tried.

I was excited to see that I was becoming more aware of the pack bonds when I was in wolf form. Kai told me that as his second, and eventually when we were mated, I would have access to power through the pack bonds. I began to open myself to each member and the energy they brought to the pack. I sifted through the bonds and felt for Emma. She had such a sweet and naïve energy. She served the pack well with her submissive peaceful nature. Then I felt for Akash. He was such a young and bubbly spirit; I sensed future dominance in him. He might become an alpha of his own one day. Moving on, I silently sifted through the pack members, getting to know each of their energy signatures.

That night we had a huge bonfire in the backyard. Emma, Anna, and I sat together and talked while Kai handed out food. He was an amazing cook. His Indian heritage showed in the meal. He made me a chickpea masala burger that left me drooling for a second helping.

"I have something to discuss," Kai shouted over everyone, and the pack quieted. "Aurora has chosen to stay in contact with her family and friends."

There was a murmur among the wolves and I felt my cheeks redden. "And I support it," he shouted, and everyone quieted again.

"Tomorrow, Aurora's mother will be visiting her under the pretense that Aurora has come to live with me as her boyfriend. To explain the presence of all of you, Aurora has told her mother I run an alcoholic rehabilitation facility."

The collective laughing was hard to ignore. Max stopped chugging his beer mid-swallow.

"Also, Aurora is the owner of a non-profit company called Safe Haven. It's a domestic violence shelter for women and children. They teach self-defense classes as well."

The pack was now looking at me with respect. Some of the more submissive members tipped their heads to me.

"Her main office is in Portland, which will now be staffed by humans so we don't start a territory war. We will purchase a second location in Gresham on the border of our territory. From now on, I ask that all pack members volunteer at the Gresham location on a rotation schedule. This is important to Aurora and to me."

The pack raised their glasses. "Cheers!" called Devon, and the others chimed in with agreement.

I stared across the lawn at Kai. This man just kept on amazing me with his support and kindness. He met my eyes and whatever was left of the walls deep inside of me, the ones I had built to keep me safe, crumbled. In that moment, the look he gave me, I could see my future with him. I could see what it truly meant to find your mate. He would never hurt me—more than that, he would protect me, support me. I had spent so many years learning to protect myself, teaching others to protect themselves, that I didn't realize I had been searching for someone to protect me, to make me feel safe.

We held our gaze with each other as I slowly crossed the yard toward him, his mouth curling into a smile. He licked his lips to wet them and I took stock of his tall, muscular physique, the way his teeth were perfectly straight and bright white; his canines were just a little larger than a human's. His dark brown stubble looked so sexy on his medium-brown skin. I reached him and he lifted me up as I wrapped my legs around his waist, pulling him in for a kiss. We could hear whistling from the pack as we spun around kissing, and I laughed as he sat me down.

"*Meri pyari.*" He pulled my long hair away from my face.

"What does it mean?" I asked.

He gave me a devilish smile. "If I told you, then I would have no secrets."

Anna and Jake approached us from the side. "Aurora, I'm going to move in with Jake now, so you can have your room back." She paused, looking at us wrapped in each other's arms. "If you want." She winked and they left, holding hands.

She wasn't kidding. She was going to live life to the fullest.

After the bonfire, Kai and I were cleaning up dishes in the kitchen. "So, I told my parents about you too," he said, with a hint of nervousness to his voice.

I dropped the plate I was scrubbing in the sink. It landed with a loud thunk but didn't shatter.

"Your parents are alive?!" I asked in shock. "Oh my God, I feel so selfish. I haven't asked you anything about your family. I figured they were long gone. Are they werewolves? What did you tell them about me? Where do they live?"

He laughed. "Slow down. It's okay. My mother, father, sister, and I were all changed in a werewolf attack in Delhi." He paused, thinking about the past. "My sister didn't survive the change, though." A look of sadness crossed his face and then it was gone. "My mother and father turned out to be mates. They have since given birth to my twelve siblings, including Akash. They still live in India. I called and told them that I met my mate."

My mouth dropped open. "You have twelve brothers and sisters?"

He smiled. "Eleven rowdy brothers split between six packs, and one sister. She is the princess of the family and is still a member of my father's pack in Delhi. He's the alpha of the New Delhi pack."

"Whoa." I let that information sink in. "Isn't the population of New Delhi like ten million people?"

Kai took a deep breath. "Yes, and my father's pack is about three hundred strong."

"Three hundred wolves in one pack? It must be hard to be an alpha of a pack that large."

A look crossed Kai's face as if he contemplated telling me something more. "Being such a big pack, fights break out daily. My father spends his time keeping the peace. There are constant battles for territory as my father's pack grows and they fight other packs to open their land. My father is a traditional wolf and a traditional Indian. My sister won't leave the pack until she is mated, and even then my father will fight to have her mate transferred so he can keep an eye on her."

I nodded. "So you left, then? Transferred packs?"

Kai ran a hand through his hair. "You're a dominant wolf, so you know that feeling you get when someone tries to hold you down or order you around and you just want to jump out of your skin?"

"Like earlier in your office when you told me I couldn't see Sylvia anymore?" I reminded him.

He laughed, assaulting me with his charming smile. "Yeah, like that. Well, I battled with more dominant wolves in my father's pack daily. As I grew older, my dominance grew stronger. Brother Wolf didn't like being told what to do. I eventually fought my way to becoming my father's second. But that wasn't high enough for my wolf. We wanted to be alpha. I *knew* I could be alpha."

Oh God. I didn't want to know where this story was going. Did he fight his own father?

"My mother could sense my feelings and asked me to leave before it sparked a challenge fight with my father. I agreed. I transferred to a pack in Australia for a while, and then to a pack with Shamus, and eventually took over Mount Hood. I didn't want a huge pack that couldn't be controlled. I wanted to do things differently." He stared at the bubbles, clearly lost in thought.

"That must have been hard, leaving your family like that." We finished the dishes and then I came to sit on his lap on the barstool.

"I'm more at peace with the decision than my father is. I think he struggles between his human side wanting me to have my own pack, and his wolf wanting to challenge me to prove he could have won a fight. He wants to prove I would always be his second-in-command and never above him. Eventually, Akash transferred here and my mother visits twice a year. So I guess it has worked out."

He rubbed small circles in my lower back and my heart ached for his situation.

"When is the last time you saw your father?" I could see that a part of him was just a boy who wanted his father to approve, but another, stronger part of him was a werewolf that needed to make his own place in the world.

"I see him once a year at the annual alpha conference. Every year most of the alphas and their second-in-commands meet for a conference to discuss pack issues and make laws. My father is on the council. It's pretty intense, and I'm glad every year when it is over."

I jumped up from his lap. "So you're telling me

that every year you put a bunch of dominant alphas in one room and expect them to sit around politely and talk about issues?"

He laughed as he picked me up and walked me down the hallway. "For the most part, only a few fights break out. There are rules to keep things from getting out of control."

He stopped at his bedroom door. "So are you continuing to stay in my room?"

The fact that he asked and gave me the choice brought a smile to my lips. "Of course—as long as you behave," I reminded him playfully, while secretly hoping he wouldn't.

"I make no promises." His eyes roamed up and down my body as he gave me a heated stare. If I were being honest, I kind of liked playing hard to get, proving I could control him, control this relationship. It brought me peace and made my past stay locked down where it belonged.

# 9
# MOTHER

IN THE MORNING, Kai and I ate breakfast hunched over his laptop looking at commercial properties in Gresham for Safe Haven. When he entered a price point of 1.5-2 million dollars my eyes bugged out of my head. "Kai, you can't."

He glared at me playfully. "I'm an alpha. I can do whatever I want."

Holy shit.

We called a realtor on three of our favorite properties, and Kai sent out a few pack members to take videos of them all. Afterwards, Kai and I reclined on the sofa. He was playing with my hair when I started thinking about Sylvia. She was a high priestess witch and I was related to her coven. My biological mother was a Matefinder wolf but I was born a human-witch mix. How did that make sense? I relayed this question to Kai.

His face looked concerned. "I wondered the same

but figured we shouldn't pry into something we might not like the answer to."

I chewed on that. "No, I want the answer. I always want the answers."

He sat up and took a deep breath. "Well then, we can ask Sylvia later today when she comes for the barbeque. I'm sure she has a spell for everything."

I jumped up suddenly and took off my shirt, standing there in my teal lace bra.

Kai grinned. "Now that's my kind of morning surprise."

I laughed and shook my finger at him. "Turn around! I want to go for a run."

Kai let his gaze rest on my bra for a second longer and then lowered his eyes, undressing himself. We shifted incredibly fast and leapt out an open window in the living room, landing on the grass outside.

My paws hit the cold, blades of grass with a satisfying thud. My wolf body was lean but compact with muscle. I still wasn't used to being on all fours but I loved the freeing feeling of this body. Kai yipped next to me and took off running, as I followed. We ran through the forest, all the way to the edge of the mountain and back. My agile wolf body leapt over fallen logs, and pranced in mud puddles, it was wonderful. I loved running with Kai. We were both fast, really fast, and running next to him made me feel free in a way I had never felt before. Later that day, after getting home, I took a shower and then we got the backyard ready for the barbeque. A light sprinkle of rain fell as we set the tables and it created a foggy mist that was the definition of Oregon weather.

I exhaled contentedly. "I love this mountain."

Kai smiled as he put a stack of paper plates down on the table. "Now you see why werewolves can be territorial."

I laughed and nodded. This mountain was ours. I would never let another pack take it from us. I realized in that moment that I was happy, truly happy, something I hadn't felt in a long time. I was excited to see my mom but even more excited for her to bring me all of my stuff. I had called and explained the entire ordeal—or at least the "moving in with the boyfriend" version—to Lexi, my roommate, and apologized profusely for having to move out. Then I told her that I would pay her rent until she could find a new roommate. She had seemed okay with it and I promised her she could visit sometime.

Kai handed me a stack of cups and I placed them at the edge of the table near the water dispenser. The sound of crunching gravel had me spinning around to see Sylvia's car pulling into the driveway. I had also called her and explained the alcoholic treatment center cover up, and she was happy to play along as a therapist or patient.

After greeting Sylvia, I asked her if she wouldn't mind staying later so we could talk, that I had questions for her. She agreed and then went to mingle with the pack. While Sylvia and Emma were chatting, I saw the huge moving truck pull up with my mom at the wheel.

Nervousness flooded through my system, but more so was excitement.

I jumped up eagerly. Kai grabbed my hand and we walked out to greet my mom together. She parked the big truck and hopped down from the high seat. Now that I knew she wasn't my biological mother, I could see that we looked nothing alike. She had dark brown hair to my light blond; she was short, where I was tall. None of that mattered to me. I didn't care, because she *was* my mother. I chose her as my mother now, even knowing she didn't give birth to me. She was the one who held me when I was sick or pushed me to follow my dreams of opening Safe Haven. We had been through so much together—the death of my twin brother, the abuse of my father, and so much more. My mother and I had crawled through a disaster and made it out alive together, because we had each other. She was my chosen mother, always.

Oh my God. My father wasn't my real father. It really sank in now. I had always hoped as a child, when the abuse started, that my mom would one day tell me that he wasn't my real father, that she'd had an affair or something. That was actually the best news I had gotten in a long time.

"Mom!" I ran to her, pulling her into a bone-crushing hug.

She smiled and squeezed me back as I took a deep breath, taking in all of the scents that made her my mom. Apples, cinnamon, dish soap. She'd been baking recently.

Stepping away from her, I motioned to Kai. "Mom, this is Kai."

Kai shook her hand. "It's a pleasure to meet you, ma'am."

My mom looked at me. "Ma'am? Do I look that old?" We shared a laugh and Kai suddenly looked nervous.

"It's a pleasure to meet you too, Kai. You have a beautiful home. You can call me Beth," my mom told him, looking at the large modern house that stood before us.

Kai smiled. "Thank you."

"So you live on the grounds of the rehab center?"

Kai cleared his throat. "Yes, ma'am—umm, Beth. I own over twenty homes on the mountain, which have been converted to sober homes for the patients who come to stay at the facility."

My mom smiled genuinely. "You and Aurora are one and the same, always trying to help others. You're a good boy." She patted his shoulder and shared a look with me.

She liked him. I laughed to myself at the fact that she was treating the alpha of the Mount Hood wolves like a little boy.

We walked toward the backyard and introduced my mother to the pack. We made sure to tell everyone not to bring beer to the event and blow the cover of an alcoholic rehab center. My mom talked with everyone thinking they were struggling alcoholics, and it was pretty comical to watch as she told them all to "stay strong."

When my mom got to where Sylvia was sitting with Emma, I could see Sylvia looking at her with pinched eyebrows. Alarm registered on the witch's face, but she masked the expression and shook my mother's hand. "I'm Dr. Sylvia, the resident psychologist." Sylvia held my mother's hand a little longer than appropriate, and my mom pulled her hand away, looking confused.

"Have we met before?" my mother asked.

Sylvia looked at me as she answered. "Not that I remember."

Okay, something weird was going on, and I would have to ask Sylvia about it later. For now, I needed to let it be.

As we ate, Kai and my mom got to know each other while the pack unloaded the moving truck and I "officially" moved in with Kai. My mom asked Kai a hundred questions about India, and he seemed to enjoy talking to her and teaching her things.

After a few hours, Kai and everyone said goodbye to my mom. I walked her to the truck and pulled out a wad of money I had borrowed from Kai.

"Here ya go, Mom, to cover the cost of gas and the moving truck." She took the money, but after seeing how much it was, her eyes widened.

"Aurora, this would cover ten moving trucks. It's too much." She made a move to give it back to me, but I put my hand up to stop her. I wanted better for her. I tried to help her when I could, but owning a nonprofit didn't exactly make me rich. Now that I was staying with Kai, I could afford to help her. I closed my hand around hers. "I want to help you more, Mom. Let me." I held her gaze and she looked behind me at Kai's large house. It must have cost at least half a million dollars, not to mention his other properties on the mountain.

"Okay," she said, and stuck the money in her pocket.

I hugged her tightly. "Love you."

"You too, sweetie. I'm glad you're happy. I like him. He looks at you as if you're the only woman in the world."

I was shocked at her appraisal. She never liked guys I dated; no one was good enough. I looked nervously at my shoes. "Good, because I think this one will be around for a long time."

She smiled before climbing into the truck and taking off down the long drive. I waited until she got to the end of the driveway and then went in search of Sylvia.

## 10

## MEMORIES

Sylvia, Kai, and I were gathered around the desk in his office.

"What do you mean my mother has a memory blocking spell on her?" I shouted. I felt like shifting. My wolf was close to the surface and I knew my eyes were yellow.

Sylvia patiently continued: "That's not all. I'm the one who put it there. I don't remember it, but when I touched her hand I could smell the spell. It was *my* work. I'm at a loss. I don't understand how I could memory-spell someone and not remember it myself!"

Kai looked pissed. But before he or I could say anything, Sylvia put her hand to her lips. "Oh God."

"What?" I stumbled forward.

Sylvia tucked her hair nervously behind her ear. "I have a very good memory—I'm not *that* old. The only way I wouldn't remember a spell or a client is if I also did a memory-erasing spell on myself. I would only do that if the knowledge I was hiding was life or death."

I felt my breath leave me in a rush. "Is my mom in danger?"

Sylvia shrugged. "I don't think so, but I obviously can't remember."

Okay. I needed answers now or people were going to get hurt. I stepped forward. "Undo it. Make yourself remember. If my mom is in danger, I have to protect her!" I wanted to shift so badly I could feel my inner wolf clawing at my skin with her growing impatience.

"Aurora, calm down. Your wolf is too close to the surface." Kai put a light hand on my shoulder and I took a deep breath.

Sylvia cocked her head to the side as she looked at me, as if seeing something that wasn't there.

"It might not be your mother who is in danger. I could have hidden the memory to keep myself safe, or you. Do you really want to know what was hidden?" she asked me, chewing her lip.

I thought about it. I did want to know. I needed to know.

"Yes," I answered.

Sylvia exhaled loudly and looked at Kai. "I will need powerful blood for the spell."

He turned his gaze on me for a long second, and then held out his wrist to her. Relief poured through me as I realized he was going to do this. For me. Sylvia pulled her bag onto his desk and laid out a white silk cloth. Then she removed a small ornate golden dagger with a matching bowl and placed it on the cloth carefully. Reaching into her bag, she revealed a large clear crystal and another purple crystal, and placed them next to the bowl and dagger.

"Kai, do I have your permission to do the spell here in your home?" she asked the alpha sitting before her.

He looked at me. "I hate magic," he grumbled, and then looked to Sylvia. "Yes, you have my permission."

I cringed. Kai was doing this for me and clearly wouldn't otherwise allow it. I was subtly picking up on cues that werewolves, witches, and vampires kept to themselves.

She nodded, took the dagger to Kai's wrist, and cut him, dropping a few drops of blood into her bowl.

Kai pulled his arm back and staunched the wound as Sylvia splayed her arms out, palms up, and closed her eyes.

"I call on my ancestors and spirit guardians who come in the white light. I provide the powerful blood of an alpha as an offering. Help me to find what was once lost. Open my mind to the memories, no matter the cost."

I could see a white mist coming down from the ceiling and into Sylvia's head. I gasped, and she looked at me with silver-coated irises as her expression became blank. The mist intensified and I stumbled back to avoid it. Kai looked at me oddly, as if he wasn't seeing the mist. A horrified look crossed Sylvia's face, then transformed into a smile as a tear rolled down her cheek. I watched her face play out a dozen expressions as if she were watching a movie. Then the mist retreated and Sylvia's eyes returned to their normal color. She pinned her gaze on me.

"What happened? The mist..." I stuttered.

Sylvia looked shocked. "You saw the mist?" She reached out her hand. "Aurora, I think you have the gift of a seer witch. I might be able to show you everything I just saw. Take my hand."

I reached for her outstretched hand, but Kai stepped in front of me. "I don't trust witch magic."

I looked at Kai and chewed my lip. "I need to see."

I sidestepped Kai and clasped her hand tightly. Then I was pulled into a vision that felt much like the visions I had when I saw a pair of mates.

A younger woman with long blond hair sat on a bed of green grass stroking a large, muscular man's arm. He looked at her and smiled before taking her in for a passionate kiss. "Genevieve..." he whispered.

Then the scene changed, and this time it showed the muscular man who had been with Genevieve turning into a werewolf and running with a pack. It then flashed to Genevieve standing over a spell book, her eyes glazing over white. She was a witch.

Then Genevieve was at home and holding her swollen belly. She was pregnant. The werewolf man stroked her belly. "How can it be? You're a witch and I'm a werewolf. How can you be pregnant with our child?"

Genevieve had been crying; tears streaked her face.

"You don't believe me? I haven't been with anyone else, Vincent!" she screamed.

"I want to believe you! But it's not possible. Werewolves can take witches and humans for lovers, but not as mates. We can only have children with our mates!"

Genevieve stood boldly, her hair standing on end with anger and magic. "Maybe I am your mate! I just happen to be a witch, but I am your soul mate, Vincent Briar! I'm carrying your child, and when the baby is born you will see. If only werewolf mates can produce a child, then how am I pregnant with yours?"

She ran from the house crying.

The next scene showed Genevieve having just given birth, holding a small baby girl and a boy, not just one child but twins. The babies were wrapped in fuzzy blue and pink blankets. Vincent was there. He held them and stroked Genevieve's hair. "I'm sorry I didn't believe you. They are mine, I can see it. They smell like me, too."

She gazed at Vincent and smiled. "I want to name her Ruby, after my grandmother, and I want to name him Cole, after your father."

"I love you. I love them," Vincent said as the scene faded.

I saw Ruby growing up at varying ages—she looked about five, and then twelve, and then she met her mate. She was half witch and half wolf. It seemed that when she shifted with her mate for the first time, her Matefinder abilities manifested. Then the vision showed her wedding day. It showed her changing from wolf to human but also casting spells with Genevieve, her mother. She was some sort of hybrid, the first Matefinder. Then the vision darkened. It showed Genevieve arguing with a vampire and then being killed. Her head torn clean off. Vincent tried to defend her honor and was ripped apart by the vampire coven.

Ruby explored her new abilities, finding mated pairs, but was sad not to have her mother's guidance. Then the vision showed Ruby pregnant and also having twins. She held the babies wrapped in her arms while her mate caressed her face; tears shone on her cheeks. "I want to name her Aurora, and his name will be Drake, after you."

Shock ripped through my body in Kai's office and the vision flickered. I tried to calm my emotions so that I could stay with the vision.

Ruby's husband looked down at her and the children. "Are you sure it has to be this way? I'm an alpha, I can protect them. I *will* keep them safe."

Ruby's eyes glowed yellow. "I've seen her future and mine. We must have them turned human before the first full moon. They will go live with Beth. She is human, so no one will suspect that the twins are supernaturals. We will have a high priestess wipe Beth's memory. She and her husband have been trying to conceive. They will think the babies are their natural children. The priestess will fix her own memory so that no one ever finds out. I've seen it. It's the only way to keep them safe." Ruby cried openly as her husband held her.

The next scene showed a younger-looking Sylvia performing a ceremony on the twin babies. Sylvia looked at Ruby. "You know the price of turning wolf pups into humans?"

Ruby nodded boldly. "The children's mother must take her life before the first full moon after their birth." Ruby's mate wasn't present.

The twins were brought to Beth and her husband's house, and a spell was cast to wipe from their memory that the twins were not theirs.

On the way back from the ceremony, Ruby was captured by a werewolf pack and a dark warlock. They did horrible things to her. Tortured her, starved her, forced her with magic to tell them who their mates were. The wolves started changing innocent children. Ruby's mate and his pack showed up to free her—her mate died protecting her. When her pack freed her of the magic chains binding her, she ran outside and looked at the moon. Not yet full. The pack that had taken her was still fighting. She walked over to the alpha of the pack that had captured her and sealed her death: "I challenge you as alpha of Wide Rim pack."

I knew what was next. I didn't want to see her beheaded. I ripped my hand away from Sylvia, crying, and broke away from the vision. Kai caught me as I fell back; Sylvia ran over to me, and they both held me for a long time as the sobs racked my body. Kai seemed to understand that physically I was okay and that Sylvia and I had shared something intimate. I lay there letting my breathing even out, and it was a long time before I could speak.

"Ruby ... she was my mother," I croaked out.

Sylvia nodded and stroked my hair. "Genevieve was my best friend. I would have done anything for her and Ruby. That explains why I would wipe my memory. Now I remember it all. We were trying to protect you and Drake. Your mother, Ruby, she was a powerful seer. She could see the future. She showed me the future she saw for you and Drake. You wouldn't make it to your fifth birthday without being captured and drained for your blood if she hadn't done what she did."

I breathed out shakily. "She sacrificed herself. My mom, Beth. She was her best friend?"

Sylvia nodded. "Beth and Ruby met in high school and then went off to college together. Became instant friends—they were inseparable." Sylvia was touching her temple and staring off, lost in her thoughts.

I stood up, angry. "So Ruby was a powerful seer, but she couldn't see that if she stuck me with Beth and Tom for parents, I would be beaten. That my mother would be abused and called fat and lazy by my no-good father?"

Sylvia's face softened. "There is a heavy price to pay for changing the future. Maybe she thought that fate was better than being captured, tortured, and killed at five years old before you could ever learn to protect yourself."

"Drake drowned! My childhood was taken from me! I should get to choose my fate. It's my life." I turned to Kai. "I'm going for a run. Don't follow me." I felt magic infuse my words as a command, and Kai looked hurt. In that moment I didn't care. I fled the house, bursting out of the front door crying, and collided right into Emma.

"Oh, Aurora, I'm sorry." She laughed and then saw my face. "What's wrong?"

I stripped down in front of her and changed into my wolf, ignoring her question. I couldn't speak right now. Without asking, she stripped down too and followed me. I could hear her bones slowly cracking as her change took longer. If Kai had followed me I would have been mad, but something about Emma's energy soothed me. I didn't mind. I took off into the thick woods and she stayed a good distance behind me as I ran. I didn't go my fastest, but I was running hard. I could hear Emma panting behind me, trying to keep up. She didn't try to talk to me through the pack's bond and I loved her for it. She seemed to know I needed space, but didn't want me to be alone.

As I ran, I thought of my mother, Beth, and all we had been through. Did she just love me and treat me like a daughter because Sylvia messed with her memories? No, I couldn't believe that. I thought of the sacrifice Ruby made and I got angry. Part of me was grateful Drake and I were placed with my mother, because otherwise I wouldn't know her. Another part of me wondered if Ruby's seer abilities were that good.

What if the future would have naturally changed, and she did all of that but there had been another way? I never bonded with my father, Tom. It was like a piece of me knew he wasn't my real father. When Drake died and my father blamed me, he began drinking. That's when the abuse started.

If Ruby hadn't put Drake and me with my mother, then my father never would have started drinking and abusing us. I could have saved my mother from all of her heartache, saved myself from the darkest parts of my childhood. I stopped at the top of the mountain and howled long and deep, letting the vibrations of the guttural yell cleanse my soul. Then I curled up next to a large pine tree and stared out at nothing, feeling numb and overwhelmed. A moment later Emma trotted over to me. She nuzzled me and curled up beside me.

'*Are you okay?*' Kai sent to me.

'*I'm with Emma,*' I replied, not sure if I was okay or if I would ever be okay. If this Matefinder gene was passed down to future generations, then I didn't want children. I didn't want to curse them to a life of being hunted. And if I didn't want kids, then Kai might not want me...

Emma's soft and submissive presence put me at ease. We lay there a long time, curled up together without talking, and for the first time I understood what it was to be in a pack. It was family. A big extended family that you could have comfortable silences with.

After a while, I stood up and shook off the dried leaves stuck to my fur.

'My whole life has been a lie,' I told Emma, finally able to speak.

She stood and met my gaze. 'Then maybe it's time to start fresh.'

Although her advice was simple, it was sage counsel. I couldn't control my past, and I didn't live there anymore, so I needed to try to move on. This life —being turned into a werewolf—it was a fresh start for me, and I could create from it whatever I wanted.

'Ready to head back?' Emma asked me.

'Yes,' I told her. 'Thank you.' She gave me a nod and we slowly trotted back to Kai's house.

It was late when we got back, and from the looks of the dark houses everyone was asleep. Emma and I shifted quickly in front of Kai's front door and got dressed. She pulled me in a quick hug and I felt the pull of a vision. Again! I was looking at a movie screen in my mind. Emma's belly was swollen with pregnancy and I was walking down an aisle littered with red rose petals. I looked at my feet. They were bare, with henna designs, and adorned with a silver anklet on each foot. A red and gold silk sari was draped over my legs. I looked up, knowing that I would see Kai at the end of an aisle, but then the picture dissolved and Emma was shaking me. My head was on her lap and she was stroking my hair.

"Aurora, come back to me," she whispered. "What is it? Have you found another mate? So soon?"

I opened my eyes and shook my head. "I think I just saw the future—my future, our future." I sat up slowly and turned to Emma.

She made a motion with her hands, urging me to tell her.

"My wedding," I said softly.

"Your wedding!" she screamed, then smiled.

"Shhh. Yeah ... don't tell Kai. I saw you pregnant again, so it must be after Jake's wedding." She motioned to zip her lips, but smiled.

Wow, my wedding. That was intense. I would file that away in my brain and deal with it later. I wasn't sure I was ready for that. Having visions was weird.

Saying goodnight, I gave Emma a big hug and she headed home. I thought I would sneak in the house and just glide into bed without having to talk to Kai about my running off after the drama with Sylvia. But I was halfway through the living room when Kai stood up from the couch and scared me.

Jumping back, I screamed, "Jesus!"

"Nope, just me," he said, putting his hands up.

"Very funny," I muttered, still trying to calm my rapid heartbeat.

He crossed the room quickly and wrapped me in his arms. "I held Sylvia hostage until she told me everything. I'm so sorry, Aurora. For the first time in my life I feel powerless. I wish I could take the pain away for you."

My throat tightened. Kai was a good man. Despite his huge and dominating appearance, he was so soft inside, so lovable. If we were going to have any future together, he deserved the truth.

"If I didn't want children, would you still want to be my mate?"

His eyebrows pinched before he smiled slightly. "First of all, I am your mate whether you want kids, or eat meat, or like the same music as I do. We *are* mates. There is no changing that. Secondly, I have always wanted children. I want to be a father, but if you don't want children … then what can I do? I want you, and I won't force you." He pulled me back and looked into my eyes.

In that moment, I blurted out the stupidest thing. I didn't even think.

"I'm falling in love with you," I admitted, then slapped my hand over my mouth. Wasn't the guy supposed to say that first? I'd had boyfriends, but I never let them get close enough for love. Being in love meant you could get hurt.

A huge grin broke out on his face.

"God, I feel like I've been waiting to hear that from you my whole life." He scooped me up, pressing my body close to his, and started walking me to the bedroom, kissing my neck. I smiled. Okay, maybe saying I love you wasn't that bad.

## 11
## DIWALI

I WAS BEING NUDGED AWAKE. Opening my eyes groggily, I saw Kai, freshly showered and wearing a red silk Indian top, with a smudge of ash on his forehead. I looked at him, confused.

"What's up?" I asked sleepily.

Kai looked nervous. "Well, remember how I told you that I had spoken to my parents about you? My mom and sister have been bugging me to talk to you and today is Diwali. It's a special holiday in India. We always video chat on Diwali so..."

I knew what Diwali was from my six months in India. I sat up so fast I almost smacked his head. "How long do I have to get ready?"

He grinned. "Twenty minutes."

I leapt off the bed and flew into the shower. After blow-drying my long hair and quickly applying light makeup, I went into my room. It was stacked full of the moving boxes my mom had brought. Where was my box of stuff I brought back from India? I tore open the tops of the boxes. Books, no. My boxing gloves, no. Regular clothes, no. A knock at the door.

"Aurora? It's time to call them," Kai told me.

"Be right there!" I screamed as I tore open another box. The sight of my red silk Indian top and bangles made me smile. I threw the top on over skinny jeans and put a stack of red and gold bangles on each wrist. The top was adorned with gold thread, and was a gift from the host family I had stayed with. Throwing open the door, I took in Kai's shocked expression.

"Too much? Trying too hard to impress them? I'll go change." I went to turn around and he caught my elbow.

"Don't you dare! You look amazing." He spun me around and laced his hand behind my lower back, pressing me close to his hips. I stood on my tiptoes as his lips brushed against mine and a moan escaped me. He was a tease and I liked it. Next time his lips came down, they pressed deeper and I opened my mouth, welcoming his tongue. Kissing Kai was my favorite thing. We both pulled away a little breathless and walked hand in hand to his office.

As we sat in front of Kai's computer, I nervously played with my bangles. The video chat icon started ringing and I swallowed hard as the nerves churned in my gut. Kai gave me a smile and squeezed my upper thigh before clicking the green accept button.

The screen came alive with an image of a beautiful woman, Kai's mother, and a younger version of her sitting beside her. They both wore Indian clothing and jeweled bindis on their foreheads.

His mother scanned my outfit and smiled warmly. "Hello, Aurora, I'm Maya. It's so nice to meet you. We have heard so much about you," she said, eyes twinkling.

Kai's sister, who looked to be in her early twenties, waved. "Hi, I'm Diya."

"Hello," I croaked nervously. What had he told them about me?

"*Namaste*, Ma. Happy Diwali." Kai put his hands together in prayer pose and nodded.

"Happy Diwali, *bete*," she replied, beaming at her eldest son.

"So," Diya smiled, "when's the mating ceremony?"

My eyes widened and Kai stiffened beside me. Maya elbowed Diya in the side.

Kai groaned. "We are taking it slow, Diya."

Diya put her hands up. "Okay, okay. I'm just saying my big brother is the first out of thirteen siblings to find his mate. Mom is dying to plan a wedding here."

Maya lightly smacked the back of Diya's head and she frowned.

I turned to Kai, shocked. "You're the first of your siblings to find your mate?" No pressure.

He smiled nervously. "I told you it was rare. Don't mind my sister. She is bored and likes to interfere with everything."

Diya stuck her tongue out in typical little sister fashion.

Maya cleared her throat. "So, Aurora, how do you like Mount Hood?"

I smiled at the graceful change in topic. "I love it. It's so beautiful here. How is the weather in Delhi? If I remember correctly, it's quite pleasant this time of year."

His mother raised her eyebrows. "You've been to Delhi?"

"Yes, ma'am. For six months last year."

His mother and Diya both shared a smile, and we all talked easily for the next hour, Diya taking jabs at Kai and teasing him. I could tell he adored her. She really was the princess in the family. I noticed his father didn't join the call. Eventually, we signed off and I let out a huge sigh of relief.

Kai laughed. "Were they that bad?"

I smiled easily. "No, I'm just nervous. I want them to like me."

He leaned forward. "They will love you, like I do."

My heart beat wildly in my chest at his declaration, and Kai leaned forward and kissed me gently.

"All right, are you ready for your first pack training session? I can't have an out-of-shape second," he teased.

I stood up and glared at him. "Out of shape? Oh, really?"

Kai and I joined the pack in a short walk to another member's house. We went down into a basement that had been converted into a large gym. A boxing ring stood at the far corner; the rest of the floor was covered in padded mats and free weights, similar to Kai's basement. The walls were lined with mirrors, and some weapons hung from the wall. This gym put Safe Haven to shame.

I had changed into tight yoga pants, a sports bra, and pulled my hair up into a high bun. I had been tempted to wear my black belt but thought better of it —better to surprise them. I had been studying mixed martial arts since I was twelve, so this would be fun.

Kai shouted to the group. "Pair up with your partners and start defense techniques. Aurora, you partner with Emma."

Oh my God, he seriously didn't understand what I meant when I said that I ran self-defense classes on the weekends. He thought I was weak. No offense to Emma, but I was stronger than she was.

"No," I told the room loudly, "I want to partner with you."

I pulled myself into southpaw fighting position and saw Kai's eyebrows rise. The pack started whistling and clapping. "Fight, fight, fight!"

Kai shrugged and stepped forward in a relaxed position as the pack made a circle around us. He nodded, accepting the fight, and I nodded back. I moved blindingly fast, delivering a front kick to his chest that had enough force to push him backward, knocking some wind out of him.

He stumbled backward, shocked, and everyone started hollering in excitement as Kai rubbed his chest. "Aurora, I get it. You have some fighting skills, but I don't want to hurt you."

Oh. Hell. No. If we were going to be mates and I was going to be second in this pack, he needed to learn a few things about me. Firstly, you didn't go easy on me because I was a girl ...

I ran at him and launched a flying side kick aimed squarely at his chin. He did a quick shuffle to the left, ducking and avoiding my move. He immediately started to sway to his right and left.

"Okay," he said, and I recognized his moves as capoeira, a Brazilian form of fighting I was less familiar with. In one swift move he did a front flip and delivered a kick inches from my head. I jumped back as fast as I could to get out of the way, but stumbled and landed on my back. Someone in the pack started to chuckle, but immediately quieted when I shot right back up with a perfectly executed kick-up.

Kai was grinning. The pack had abandoned any idea of pairing off. They were cheering us on. Kai charged me again and tried sweeping my feet, but I was quick enough to jump over his leg. We traded several shots for the next couple of minutes, and I managed to dodge a few of his barrage of kicks and check the rest. There was undeniable beauty in the perfection of his technique and fluid motion, but that didn't distract from the pain in my shins and arms that I was trying hard to conceal. Kai was a worthy opponent.

I circled to the left to buy some time, but Kai walked away and approached the cupboard on the wall. Just when I thought he was going to call an end to the sparring session, he grabbed a bo, a traditional ninja staff, from the cabinet, threw it at me and I caught it midair. Then he grabbed one for himself and charged at me.

He ran as fast in human form as he did in wolf form. It caught me off guard. I would have to try running that fast some time. I ran at him to meet him partway, and attacked first with a precise swing at his head that he blocked with his bo.

We faced off and I spun my stick in my left, dominant hand. I had many hours of practice with weapons and the bo was one of them. I charged him again, giving my loudest battle cry, and as I brought my stick up, he blocked it on the way down. We exchanged blows and the room filled with the *clack, clack* of the sticks hitting. He tried a jab at my abdomen that I read early enough, and I was able to rotate away, catching his staff between mine and my body.

Sweat shone on our skin. I hated to admit it, but I got the feeling Kai was going easy on me. This enraged me more, so I feigned right, and Kai took the bait. I quickly changed course and struck my stick out, pulling his stick up high into the air and out of his hands. I smiled and relaxed a little—just as his leg shot out lightning-quick and kicked my legs out from under me. Shit. I fell backward as he pushed his way on top of me and held my stick lightly against my throat.

"I win," he said softly, as some of the pack cheered and some booed. Then he kissed me gently and rolled off me.

"How long have you been training?" I asked him loudly, panting.

A sly grin crept over his face as he stood. "Over a century."

I tried to mask my shock at how long he'd been training. I mean I knew he was old but damn.. "Well," I said with a grin, "I've only been training ten years. Give me more time and I'll beat you blindfolded." Shit-talking was the best part about any sport. Over one hundred years? Exactly how old was he? Note to self: learn more about werewolf aging. Everyone cheered at my comment, seeming to get a kick out of me shit-talking the alpha.

Kai smiled, appraising me, and tipped his head to one of the more dominant wolves. Trent was his name. I remembered him talking to my mother at the barbeque. He was a nice guy, originally from California. "Trent, you spar with Aurora. Don't go easy. Emma, you are with Anna."

I nodded, thinking Trent was a worthy sparring partner. He was packed full of muscle and had a long reach. Max walked over to the far wall, partnered up with Kai, and everyone began sparring with the bo staff. The loud *clack-clack* sound was rhythmic and reminded me of my weekends at Safe Haven. I missed my students. I didn't even get to explain and say goodbye.

After a few minutes of sparring with Trent, I swept my stick out—he tripped backward and slammed onto the padded ground. I stuck my hand out to help him up. "Nice move," he told me as he grabbed my hand. The second our skin touched, I was pulled into a vision.

Kai's sister Diya was crying, crumpled over in a chair as her mother rubbed her back.

"Please, Papa! Let me go. I don't want to stay in Delhi, I love him. I want to join Kai's pack and live with Trent in the States."

An older man with salt and pepper hair, who was the spitting image of Kai, approached Diya with a stern face. "You are my only daughter. I am happy you have found your mate, but I will not permit you to leave. Kai is a strong alpha, but he is not strict enough to do what needs to be done for the good of the pack. His pack is emotional and weak. They cannot protect you like I can. They're not big enough." The veins in his neck were bulging as he tried to contain his rage.

Diya stood, defiantly staring into her father's eyes; her mother looked at the floor in a submissive gesture. "Don't make me go rogue! I want this, Papa. I'm asking for your blessing, but I will go without it." She held her chin high, tears lining her eyes as her father gritted his teeth.

He looked to his mate, Maya. "Why couldn't you bear me a submissive daughter instead of this dominant princess I see before me?" His tone was light; he sounded defeated.

Diya softened, stepping closer to her father. "You will allow it? A pack transfer?"

He sighed. "I will talk to Kai about transferring

your brother Jai along with you. Kai's pack is small. If a war broke out, he wouldn't have enough numbers to fight larger packs. I'll transfer you both. And Trent needs to start video conferencing us. I need to get to know this boy better." He growled.

Diya flew across the room and hugged her father as her mother smiled behind her.

"Kai has never been concerned with being alpha of a big pack, Papa," Diya stated to her father.

"Well, it's time he started," he declared.

Diya went to leave the room and her father stopped her. "The wedding will be in India. That's not up for discussion. You're my only daughter and I want a traditional ceremony."

She nodded and left.

I CAME out of the vision and the pack was standing around me. Kai's eyes were yellow, but he patiently stroked my hair and waited for me to come out of it. I sat up quickly, but then grabbed my head as a wave of dizziness hit me.

*'What happened?'* Kai asked me privately.

I looked into his eyes nervously. *'I found Trent's mate,'* I told him.

He smiled, looking at Trent.

"It's your sister," I said aloud, and Kai's mouth gaped open in shock.

"My little sister! No, there must be a mistake. She's too young!"

I stood up, slowly shaking my head. "She's the same age as me!"

He sighed, and Trent looked at both of us, confused. "Are you okay, Aurora? What's going on?"

I smiled at Trent. "I found your mate."

## 12

## YOUNG LOVE

After two hours of Kai grilling Trent on how he would treat his sister, how many kids they would have, where they would live, when they would have their mating ceremony, and a hundred other things, Kai finally called his sister. I could hear excited screaming on the other end of the phone and it brought a smile to my lips. Kai and I talked before he made the call and agreed to tell his mother, father, and sister about my Matefinder abilities. Although he didn't have the best relationship with his father, he said he could be trusted. His father took mating and werewolf species growth very seriously. Kai said if something ever happened to him, his father would protect me. I didn't even want to think about the prospect of something happening to Kai.

After a few minutes on the phone, Kai's voice changed. "Hello, Papa." His tone took on a serious note and he put the phone on speaker, looking at me and putting a finger to his mouth for me to keep quiet.

"Are you sure this boy is Diya's true mate? We have had prospects before but nothing worked out." His father's voice was that same as it was in my vision. Deep and full of power.

"Yes, I'm sure," Kai replied through clenched teeth.

A heavy sigh. "How can you be sure? Her markings are unique. His wolf may just look similar but not be a match. Is he even good enough for her?"

"He is a good wolf, dominant, loyal, successful, and smart. He will be a good match for Diya." If Kai was offended that his father had just put down one of his pack members, he didn't show it.

"Son, I don't understand how you can be so sure this is Diya's mate. I don't have time for tricks. Mating needs to be taken seriously, especially when my only daughter is involved. How exactly are you sure this boy is your sister's mate?"

Kai chewed at his bottom lip and looked at me.

"To answer that question, I would like to enact *Alpha Secretum*. I have information to share with you that is about one of my wolves. If this information is shared with another pack, it could threaten the growth of our species."

My mouth hung open. We hadn't talked about this part. I guess he didn't fully trust his father. I didn't know what *Alpha Secretum* was, but the hair on my arms was standing up.

"You want to enact *Alpha Secretum*? This must be

serious for you not to trust me in open conversation. Fine," his father declared. "I swear on my pack magic that I will not share the following information outside of my pack."

"Not good enough, Papa. You must not share it outside of telling your mate and Diya."

I could feel his father's rage on the other side of the phone; it was almost a tangible thing.

"You always loved to enact your power, Kai. Just remember that's a trait you got from me. Fine! I swear on my pack magic that I will not share the following information outside of telling my only daughter, Diya, and my mate, Maya." His father's voice could cut glass, it was so full of anger.

Kai nodded, seemingly satisfied. "Aurora, my new mate, is the Matefinder. She has successfully paired two mate couples already. Sadie transferred to the Seattle pack and Jake has found his mate. She had a vision when sparring with Trent. Diya and Trent are mates, she is sure."

I saw a fine mist creep out of the phone and wrap around the words coming out of Kai's mouth. Magic. That must be *Alpha Secretum*, a pack magic that was keeping his words secret. I wondered what would happen if his father broke the oath.

There was silence for a long time. "I've heard stories of ... but ..." He seemed at a loss for words. "This is incredible. Do you know what this could mean for our species, for reproduction?"

Kai gritted his teeth. "Aurora won't be used as a

tool to grow our species. Talk to Diya about what you want to do next and get a hold of me. Goodbye, Papa." And he hung up.

We sat in silence for a moment. "So, your dad seems like an interesting guy," I joked.

Kai chuckled and then changed the subject. "Let's go on a date."

I smiled. "Are you asking or telling me?" I teased.

He pulled me in close and brushed my hair away from my forehead. "Alphas don't ask."

---

I WORE A LITTLE BLACK DRESS, red ballet flats, and bright red lipstick. We decided on a small Indian restaurant that Kai apparently owned. One of the pack members managed it.

Kai was surprised I knew what to order and that I could handle spicy food. He couldn't keep his eyes off me all night, and I liked how it made me feel.

"Tell me about your family," I said, taking a bite of the lentils and rice.

Kai smiled. "Well, my dada, which is my father's father, was a vegetarian like you. He was the nicest man you could ever meet. He loved animals."

"Isn't most of India vegetarian? I thought it was a religious thing?" I had found it so easy to eat vegetarian in India. They had a green dot on food for veg and a red dot for meat on every menu. Easy.

"They are. The humans, at least." Kai winked.

"So tell me a story about your dada," I prodded.

Kai pondered for a moment, looking far off beyond our table, and then started laughing. "Well, when I was a young human boy, I was walking with my grandfather to another village. We were taking a group of cows we owned to sell them as milking cows. A man ahead of us had a small metal cage stuffed full with chickens. There was not one inch of space for the chickens to breathe. Some were bent at such an odd angle that their feet and wings were broken."

"Oh, God." I frowned.

"The second my dada saw the man dragging the cage along the road with the chickens scraping along the ground, he screamed, 'Stop!' My grandfather stormed the man and ripped the string from his hand, taking the cage from him. The guy was furious with my grandfather and asked him what the hell he thought he was doing. My grandfather told him that it was cruel to carry the chickens like this, to cause them pain. The guy actually laughed. He told my grandfather they were going to the slaughterhouse to be sold for meat anyway, so what did it matter? My grandfather told the man that one day he too would die, but he wouldn't want to be tortured beforehand, would he?"

I smiled, liking this story and the type of person his grandfather was. After a moment of silence, I poked him. "So what happened to the chickens?"

Kai seemed to be off in his head, but he focused on me then with a smile. "My dada traded them for all of the money in his pocket, and the watch my grandmother had gotten him. We weren't a wealthy family. It was every luxury we had."

"Whoa." I sat back. Would I have done the same?

"We took them out of the cage and brought them home. We splinted their legs and wings and gave them all names. They squawked around the yard for years." Kai smiled and I smiled, too. I liked stories with happy endings.

After dinner we went home to watch a movie. I changed into yoga pants and a loose, long-sleeved t-shirt. Right before Kai was about to play the movie, he looked at me with the remote in his hand. "I don't want to keep secrets from you."

My heart started beating so fast in my chest I thought it might burst. That wasn't exactly a sentence I liked to hear. "Okay, so don't."

"After you ran off with Emma and I questioned Sylvia, she told me that now that she had her memories back, she remembered something else. Something she didn't show you."

Oh God, what now? I paused, waiting.

"After you were turned human as a baby, Sylvia also put a blanket over your natural witch magic. That blanket is still there, she will remove it and teach you magic if you want." He toyed with the remote, chewing his cheek.

"Oh. More powers, more weird stuff happening to me without my control? Not now. Maybe later, but not now," I assured him. I think we all needed a break from my issues. No way was I adding any more to my plate.

He sighed in relief. I guess Kai wasn't a huge fan of me being part witch.

---

THE NEXT DAY we toured the top two properties we had picked out for Safe Haven. Kai told me price wasn't an issue, so I picked the old high school property. The gymnasium would be perfect for training sessions, the cafeteria could feed a lot of families, and we could stock the classrooms with bunk beds and turn them into apartments for women and children in crisis.

Next, we met with a contractor to plan out what construction needed to be done to the property and how many beds to order. Then Kai had us meet with a marketing firm and had promotional materials printed up for Safe Haven. He also purchased a billboard and hired one of the pack members to oversee the daily tasks of running the facility. I was completely floored by his dedication to my passion project. It made me love him more. We were going to be able to help so many families. Later that day, after calling local businesses for Safe Haven donations, we finally collapsed onto the couch.

Kai stared at me, seemingly in deep thought.

"What?" I prodded.

"You are the ultimate package: beautiful, smart, strong, *and* a good person. How did I get so lucky?"

I gave him a small smile. "Good karma, I guess." I

joked, but what I wanted to say was that I was damaged. That sometimes things happened to children that carried over into adulthood, and although I seemed perfect on the outside, I wasn't. I had invisible scars.

Before he could respond, his cell phone rang. Kai looked at the caller ID. "My father," he groaned.

"Hello, Papa." Kai was very formal with his father. I also noticed that he didn't tone down his dominance with his father like he did with me. He didn't treat his father as an equal. His father pushed and he pushed back.

"I will keep them safe, you know that," he said through gritted teeth.

His father said something else and Kai's nostrils flared. "Fine." He hung up.

I looked at him with raised eyebrows.

"My mother and Diya will be flying out here to meet Trent. My father will be sending my eldest brother, Jai, along for protection, because apparently my pack isn't big enough to protect anyone," he ground out.

My mouth hung open. "So I'm going to meet your family?"

"Yes, they will be here tomorrow," he stated calmly, like it wasn't a big deal.

"Tomorrow!" I sat up. "I need to unpack my room. It's a mess."

Kai laughed. "It's fine. No one will go in there. You

sleep in my room anyway. They can stay in one of the other guest rooms."

I decided not to call him out on the fact that when Anna took my room, I could have easily slept in one of the guest rooms and not his room. I needed to explore the house more. I stood and started walking to my room. "If you think I'm staying in your room with your mother here, you are crazy. Help me unpack."

He groaned getting up. "Aurora, we're mates. They expect some hanky-panky to be going on."

I grinned at "hanky-panky," but let my face grow serious. "No, you only get to make a first impression once. Help me unpack and move all of my stuff out of your room."

He frowned, but followed me into my room.

After unpacking, I spent the night snuggled with Kai in his bed, but swore I wouldn't do so with his family here.

THE NEXT MORNING we were making breakfast when Emma knocked at the door.

"Hey," I answered the door, and saw an ornate gold-lined paper in her hand.

"Special delivery," Emma said, and came inside, handing the paper to Kai.

He glanced at the paper and nodded.

"So?"

"It's from Shamus. Sadie has set a date for her mating ceremony. Our pack is invited, but we don't have to go." He was trying not to show any emotion, but I gathered that wouldn't be the greatest political decision.

"Don't both packs usually go to a mating ceremony when two wolves from separate packs marry?"

"They do," Kai said after a long pause.

"But it's understandable if they don't attend when the old pack's alpha dated the bride for six years and has a new mate," Emma threw out there.

"Six years!" I shouted, louder than I intended.

"Emma," Kai growled. Emma looked down at her feet, mumbling an apology.

"Jesus," I said, "that's a mini marriage."

"Six years to a werewolf isn't a long time," Kai offered.

"Which reminds me..." I pointed my finger at Kai. "How old are you? How does this aging thing work in the werewolf world?" A six-year relationship was a big deal. No wonder Sadie left the pack. Her wolf had found her mate, but did her human side still love Kai? I brushed off the thought.

Kai grinned, seeming to enjoy the change in topic. "I'm quite old in werewolf standards, over two hundred years old. My mother, father, and I are some of the oldest werewolves around today. We have survived because my father quickly became alpha after his change and built a strong pack in Delhi. Then my mother was able to bear children. Having thirteen protective children in a large pack will keep you from getting killed in a fight."

Two hundred years! Two centuries. Whoa. I was dating an old guy who looked like he was in his late twenties. Weird didn't even begin to describe it.

Emma stepped forward. "We don't know much of werewolf aging, but it seems that you age normally until about twenty or twenty-five years old. Then your aging stops until you meet your mate. Once you are mated, you age together, but very, very slowly. It might take fifty years for you to look ten years older.

My mind was reeling. "You stop aging until you are mated?"

Emma nodded. "We think it has something to do with fertility. Some of us never find our mates, but if we are lucky enough, then it can take a very long time. A werewolf can only have so many children before becoming sterile. We go through menopause just like humans."

"But we don't die of old age?"

Kai shared a look with Emma. "The few wolves old enough for us to test that theory on have asked their pack to kill them. It seems that after so many hundreds of years alive they just crave an end."

"That's horrible," I said. I was unsettled by the whole idea.

"My parents were in their forties when they were changed, so they look about fifty today. Since they mated, they have aged only about ten years in the two hundred they have been wolves. Some seem to age faster. We just don't know."

I shook my head. Wow. I looked again at the pretty wedding invite.

"We will go to the wedding and support Sadie." I hadn't meant to say it so final, like a command.

Kai tilted his head to the side and raised his eyebrows. "As you wish."

Maybe being mates really did make us equal.

## 13

## FAMILY

I paced the house, wearing foot marks into the carpet. Kai went to pick up his family from the airport and I had stayed back. Kai didn't think it would be wise for me to be in such a public place, seeing I was being hunted by vampires and witches. I had unpacked my room and cleaned the kitchen. All of the things I hadn't unpacked yet or that I wanted to sell went into the garage. It felt weird to be living with my boyfriend. That was a huge step in a relationship that you usually made after a year or more of dating. I had only known Kai a few weeks!

I face-palmed my forehead. What was I doing? I was so in love. Just thinking of Kai made my stomach flutter. I told him I loved him already? Oh my God, and he'd said it back. It was like I hadn't just gotten the Lycan virus and turned into a werewolf, I had gotten some lovesick mating virus too, and all of my logic and normal tendencies to push guys away had gone right out the window!

I heard a car door shut and I froze. *They're here!* Oh God, I felt sick with nerves. Trent was probably as nervous as I was. He had Skyped with Diya the night before, but they still didn't know each other very well. We told Trent we would let Diya settle in and then we would call him over.

I could hear voices at the door, then Kai's key was in the lock. Oh God, I was seriously going to be sick. Why was I so nervous? I was only meeting my two-hundred-year-old mate's mother and only sister. Didn't he say something about a brother coming too? The door began to open and I panicked.

I ran down the hall and into the bathroom, shut the bathroom door and ran the water, looking into the mirror and smoothing my hair. I was wearing light makeup and had my pearl earrings on. I'd decided on dark blue skinny jeans and a bright teal long-sleeve sweater. I had met my other boyfriends' parents before, so why was this different?

*Because he is your mate. You love him*, my inner wolf whispered to me.

She was right. I did love him. I was nervous because I cared. This was a serious relationship and I wanted his family to like me, to love me. I didn't have a big family, but I wanted to be a part of this one.

I let my inner wolf take over and she sent a calm feeling through my system. Her instinct was to be dominant, to show his family that I was worthy of their approval but that I did not need it. I looked in the mirror and saw my golden-yellow wolf eyes looking back at me. I deserved Kai—we deserved each other. I hoped his family liked me but if not, oh well. I took a deep breath and my wolf faded. I turned off the water and left the bathroom.

Kai was in the kitchen making tea, the boiling water sending steam up into his face. His mother wore a deep-red sari and had gold bangles on, and his sister wore jeans and an Indian top. They both had a jeweled bindi on and were sitting in two chairs just beyond the kitchen, in the dining nook. A twenty-year-old-looking young man stood behind Kai, just as mountainous in size, peering over his shoulder. He must be his brother Jai.

Jai frowned. "You're putting too much ginger in."

Kai groaned. "You haven't changed a bit. Still trying to boss me around in the kitchen."

"Well, if you knew how to make proper Indian tea, then I wouldn't have to," Jai retorted.

I cleared my throat and everyone turned. "Hello, I'm Aurora."

Kai's mother, Maya, stood and clasped her hands together. "You are even more beautiful in person," she exclaimed, barely meeting my eyes. She was submissive, I realized in surprise.

Diya jumped up and ran over to me, giving me a brief hug, bringing the scent of sandalwood with her. "Hello, sister."

I stood there silently for a moment, unsure of what to say. I wasn't expecting such a warm welcome.

"Let her breathe, Diya," Jai told her with a mild Indian accent.

Kai smiled at me. "Would you like some chai?" After six months spent in India, I knew better than to turn down an offer of chai.

"Sure." I nodded as Diya pulled me over to the table.

"This is so cool, Kai and I finding our mates at the same time," Diya exclaimed, her almond-shaped eyes wide with excitement.

I took a deep breath in through my nostrils. They smelled of foreign wolves, but they also smelled familiar, friendly. I was still getting used to how my wolf interpreted things.

"How are you adjusting, dear? It's a lot to take in," his mother asked me. The way she looked at me, with such a caring gaze, made me drop my guard a little.

"Oh, well, I'm just doing my best," I offered. His mother's brow pinched together.

"Being changed, and then finding out you are second in the pack, and then meeting your mate—it's a lot ..." his mother said.

I felt my throat tighten. What the hell? I hadn't planned on this. Don't cry.

"Ma ..." Kai growled lightly and brought over a tray with steaming cups of chai.

His mother lowered her gaze and shrugged. "Sorry, dear. I can't help what I feel. It overwhelms me."

I looked at her, confused.

Jai stepped forward then. "My mother is a changed wolf, so her gift is that she can feel emotions. She was also a psychologist for a couple of decades in the sixties. It makes for an intrusive combo. You can't keep anything from her. She will shrink you until every last emotion has been turned to peace."

Maya swatted Jai. "Oh, stop it! I can't help it. I was just trying to get to know her. I'm sorry if I intruded, Aurora."

I smiled lightly. "That's okay. I know what it's like to not be able to turn your gift off." I sipped my chai slowly.

The entire table was silent for a moment and then Kai cleared his throat. Only Jai looked confused. I had forgotten they hadn't told him.

"Well, Diya, I'm sure you are dying to meet Trent. Let's all take a run." Kai motioned us outside.

*'My family is here. Let's go for a run,'* Kai sent to the pack.

---

THE ENTIRE PACK assembled in front of and behind Kai's house. Trent and Diya shared a nervous hug and a little small talk before joining us in the open area in front of the house. It was sweet to see Akash run to his mother and give her a big hug; she cupped his face in her hands and kissed his forehead, which he promptly wiped off. Kai then asked us all to shift. Everyone kept their eyes at the ground as we undressed and changed forms. I had shifted less than a handful of times, so I was still nervous that something could go wrong and I would get stuck in some halfway form. But after some mild pain and nausea, I shifted without incident. As usual, Kai and I were the first to be finished with our change. I shook my fur and rolled in the soft grass as Kai trotted over and nuzzled me. A few moments later, I turned my attention to the pack and saw Trent and Diya rolling on the ground playing. They were mates. Exact opposite markings. The third couple I had brought together.

Wow, I had a purpose in life, a good purpose. I brought families together; I helped people find love. A huge weight I had been carrying lifted off my chest. This gift was a blessing more than it was a curse, and I was truly feeling settled in my own skin.

I turned to find Kai's mother staring at me as if she sensed my release of emotion. She trotted over and nudged me lightly with her snout. After a small yip, she took off into the forest and I gave her retreating body a wolfish grin. There was nothing my wolf liked more than a good chase. Kai and I took off after her, feeling the thrill of the chase. The wind streaked through my fur as my paws pounded the damp forest floor. The pack fanned out around us and we all ran down our usual path, howling and yipping. I felt so free when I ran, like nothing in the world could bother me.

We were making our way down the back side of

the mountain when I smelled something ... off. It was like how a foreign wolf smelled, but not. More coppery. Before I could ask Kai about it, he ran to my side. His mother, who had been leading the pack stopped dead, and howled deep and long.

*'Vampires. Pack formation. Protect Aurora and my family,'* Kai sent out to the pack. With that command, the pack shifted their formation and made a circle around me, his mother, Jai, and Diya. Akash didn't come into the circle but joined in, protecting us. I looked around for the source of the smell but saw nothing. Then three vampires dropped from the trees above and landed ten feet from us. I bared my teeth and growled. They didn't smell friendly, and I had a bad feeling about this.

My wolf eyes roamed over them, two men and one woman, cataloging their features. They were impossibly pale and cruel looking, with sunken cheeks, yet their features were beautiful, like they had stepped out of a macabre painting.

"Hello, Alpha." The male vampire moved fifty feet to his right in a matter of seconds as the female moved behind the circle just as quickly. Holy shit, they were fast! They had surrounded us.

"We are here on an investigative mission into your newly-changed female," the tallest of the males instructed in a deep, smooth voice. "The Portland alpha says she smells quite unique. Let us meet with her and no one gets hurt."

I thought I had seen Kai at his fastest before, but

the speed at which he moved now was akin to the vampires. He lunged forward and clamped his jaws down on the vampire's neck, tearing out his throat. Before I had time to express my shock, the second vampire glided up into the air and landed inside the circle, right in front of Jai, Diya, Maya, and me.

The third vampire, I could see, had begun fighting Devon and a few other wolves. He was striking the wolves in the rib cage with iron-fisted blows. The vampire Kai had injured was miraculously still alive and had his arms around Kai, squeezing so hard I could hear bones breaking. *No!* I was about to move when I saw Anna dart towards the vampire. She got up on her hind legs and clamped her teeth around the vampire's wrist, yanking it back with a sick crunch. Kai's wolf dropped to the ground and Anna jumped up on her hind legs and pushed the vampire back with her front paws, sending him flying backward fifty feet. His body slammed into a large tree and cracked it in half.

Holy mother. I guess we knew what Anna's new power was: extreme strength. Kai observed Anna with surprise, and with one nod they went after the vampire together.

I was so busy watching Kai's fight that I didn't see the female vampire in the middle of the circle lunge for Kai's mom until it had already happened. She was a submissive, and Diya and Jai were both less dominant than me. I could feel it—I had an overwhelming urge to protect them all. Being dominant didn't mean you were physically the strongest—I knew that—but it did mean I had to try to protect them.

This must be what Kai felt like all the time for the entire pack. I threw myself on the vampire's back and knocked her to the ground. Kai's mom, now free, crawled to the safety of the far corner of the circle. The ghoulish female stood facing me with an ugly sneer, and pulled out a thin silver chain from her pocket. Before I could even track her movements, she had my paws bound beneath me.

I gave her a wolfish grin. I was immune to silver, and when it didn't burn me or begin to make me weak, I saw fear flash in her eyes. That's when Jai lunged for her. He captured one of her wrists in his mouth, and Diya went for her other hand, pinning her down. I yanked my paws apart and tore the silver chain in two with ease.

'*Decapitation or a stake through the heart,*' I heard Emma say into my mind. She must have been watching this all go down from somewhere. I realized Jai and Diya were pinning her down for me to finish her off. The vampire tried to fling them off, but two full-grown werewolves were too much for her. Could I kill a vampire? Could I decapitate someone? The answer came from deep within me—the new me.

If it meant I was protecting my pack, my family, then yes.

I crouched on my hind legs, but just before I was about to pounce, the vampire jumped high up in the air, Jai and Diya still hanging from her hands, and came down hard, slamming them both to the ground. A resounding thump rang out as their bodies hit the hard forest floor. Both Jai and Diya let go and whimpered in pain. Then, lightning-quick, the vampire strode across the inner circle, took a handful of Kai's mother's fur in her hand, and started pulling. Kai's mom whined and growled, trying to bite the vampire to no avail.

That was all I needed to see to know what I was capable of. I was a vegetarian, I was a do-gooder, but I was also a werewolf, and in that moment I knew I was capable of murder. Something within me snapped. I sprang back and leapt at the vampire, baring my teeth, and came down on her chest, knocking her back. Before she could push me off, I dove for her neck and bit down hard, locking my jaws in a death clench while thrusting my body into a roll and using the momentum to pull her head clean off. It all happened in an instant, but it felt like an eternity.

Her body turned to ash; the head in my mouth disintegrated, leaving behind a black, chalky powder that tasted of death. My heart was hammering in my chest. It all happened so fast, I wasn't sure it was over.

I ran to check on Kai's mother and she was staring at me with wide eyes. Then she lowered her head in thanks and nuzzled me. Suddenly, I felt like I was being watched. Sure enough, turning, I saw Kai and the pack staring at me. All the vampires were dead. Three distinct piles of ash lay on the ground. Kai was the first one to tilt his head back and howl, and we all followed.

Someone had tried to take one of ours, to harm us. This was our land, our family, our pack, and we would protect what was ours.

We ran back to the house slowly, reflecting on the attack. Twice, Kai asked me if I was okay and both times I assured him I was. I didn't really have a choice, I had to be okay. This was my life now; I was hunted and I was a hunter. I just didn't want those I loved to get hurt. I was starting to see the rationale in my birth mother's choices for my life.

When we got back, I shifted quickly and ran inside before the rest of the pack was done changing. Kai tried to follow me but I shook my head. I needed a break and I needed a shower. I could still taste the ash on my tongue. As I let the water beat on my back, my mind wandered back to what had just happened. So the Portland alpha was behind this attack? He smelled something different about me ... that I was part witch? That I was the Matefinder? How would he even know that? Unless legend said the Matefinder was part witch. Was this the last time vampires or anyone would come for me? Not likely. Maybe I should run away? The second the thought was out, my heart protested. I couldn't leave Kai—I loved him. But I also wanted to protect those I loved.

'Don't worry,' Kai told me. *'I can feel your struggle raging inside my head. Anyone who comes for you will meet the same fate as those vampires. You are safe.'*

*'I don't care about my safety, I care about yours,'* I replied to him.

*'As long as you are with me, I will be fine. The only way I can get hurt is if something happens to you.'*

I sighed and turned off the tap. Drying off, I brushed my teeth and changed my clothes. When I came out into the kitchen I expected some big awkward talk about the vampire fight. Instead, some Indian dance music was playing and Diya was dancing with her mother. They were laughing as if we hadn't just killed three vampires. Trent and Jai were talking quietly, watching them, and Kai was cooking. I stood there, unsure of what to do.

Kai's mom spotted me. "Aurora! Come dance with us."

I smiled, and shouted over the music, "You will have to teach me. I'm not much of a dancer."

Maya pulled me into the living room and motioned her hands in a pattern while shaking her hips and dropping her shoulder. I tried to follow what she did and Diya busted up laughing. "Oh my God, you're horrible!" she teased playfully.

Her comment brought a smile to my lips, as Jai smacked his forehead. "Watch out, gori girl trying to Bollywood dance."

"Hey!" I shouted at him, chucking a couch pillow his way and then joining him and Trent on the sofa, abandoning all ideas of becoming a great Bollywood dancer.

"What's a gori girl?" I asked Jai.

He nudged me with his elbow. "White girl."

I stuck my tongue out at him but I had another question. "What does *meri pyari* mean?"

Jai grinned and looked toward Kai in the kitchen. "Did he call you that?"

I nodded.

"It means, 'my beloved.'"

My heart rate picked up and I glanced at Kai. As if he sensed me watching, he looked up from chopping veggies and held my gaze. I blew him an air kiss and he smiled, then motioned his head to my room. I rolled my eyes and shook my head, no. Such a guy!

---

Dinner was amazing; the food had so much flavor. I think I impressed his family by eating the Indian food with my hands and talking about my time in Delhi.

"I miss India, mostly for its shopping," I told them.

Diya smiled, nodding with approval. "Ahhh ... so you like to shop? My kind of girl."

Jai put his hand out, stopping Diya from talking further. "Can we please just take one second to talk about how amazing it was when Aurora ripped that vamp's head off to save Mom?" Jai said.

I froze, and Kai's mom kicked Jai under the table.

Jai looked at me. "What? Was that her first kill?"

I sat there frozen. Flashes of my father lying on the kitchen floor, blood dripping out of his stomach, filled my mind.

"My first kill as a werewolf, yes."

Kai met my eyes and seemed sad.

"Oh," Jai said.

Kai spoke gruffly. "She has been a werewolf for under a month. You think she's racked up a bunch of kills?"

"Sorry, bro." Jai looked at his plate and I suddenly felt bad for him. He was just trying to be nice.

"I was kind of a badass, wasn't I?" I asked the table.

Jai smiled and Diya nodded.

"You were!" Jai exclaimed.

"What are you going to do about the Portland alpha sending three vampires to capture your mate?" his mother asked casually. There was no hint of submissiveness in her voice. This woman could be deadly if she wanted to be.

Kai lightly dabbed his mouth with a cloth. "I'm going to kill him," Kai said, staring right at me, and I spat water out onto the table.

## 14
## KILL OR BE KILLED

"What!" I shouted and stood.

Kai stood as well and his nostrils flared as we locked eyes. *Challenge.*

"No! You almost died when you fought him last." I held his gaze.

"No?" he shouted, staring back. I could feel the hair rising on my arms as sweat broke out on my upper lip.

"How long do you think she can hold his gaze?" Jai asked, and his mother swatted his head and shushed him.

"Aurora, you are *mine*. If someone thinks they can take you from me, there is only one response they deserve. Death."

My breath was ragged now, and even Kai looked strained. What was I doing challenging him like this?

I broke the connection and stared at my feet. "I

don't want you hurt like that. Not ever again." I sounded defeated, like a little girl.

Everyone at the table was deadly silent as I collapsed back into my chair, dreading the thought of ever seeing him hurt like that again. Kai walked over and picked me up, carrying me to my room. He struggled to open the door as I laid my head on his chest, and tears fell down my cheek. When we got inside, he dropped me on the bed and curled up next me, kissing my forehead.

"Believe it or not, I am a good fighter. I have been around so long because I have survived many, many fights. Fights of dominance, fights for territory, fights for alpha status, and whatever else. I can and will fight for my mate. If he sent vampires once, he will do it again. He is known for running a dirty pack. I have heard recent rumors that his unmated women are treated like sex toys and his men fight to the death over dominance. They all live in poverty and steal from humans, so I would be doing the world a favor."

I sighed. He was right.

"So you're just going to barge in there and kill him? Won't they smell you coming?" I asked.

"They will smell me coming. If I were to barge in there in a rage, I would be torn apart by his pack. I'm going to request a meeting and then I'm going to challenge him for alpha status of his pack. It's the only way to ensure a clean fight. It's a fight to the death and no one can intervene."

"So, if you are tearing their alpha apart, no one can jump in?"

"Correct. Pack law will make sure. My pack would report it and a werewolf from the council would come dispose of the person who intervened."

Dispose of? Jeez.

"What if he is about to kill you? You expect me to stand there and watch you die?"

I twirled my hair around my finger in a nervous gesture. He grabbed my hand and brought it to his lips. "I'm not going to die. I have too much to live for now."

I lay with my head on his chest for a few more moments, and then Kai and I left the room together. I said goodnight to his family, and they were kind enough to act like we hadn't just gotten in a big dominance fight. Maybe it was common in werewolf culture. I went to the bathroom to get ready for bed, and as I was coming out of the bathroom, I noticed Kai in my bedroom.

"What are you doing in here?" I whispered.

He pouted. "Come on, we're mates. My mother doesn't care."

I put my hand out. "We are mates, but we are not yet mated. So no. You need to leave. I don't want them thinking bad of me."

Kai looked hurt but brushed it off. "I forgot, I'm just your boyfriend," he said, before shutting the door behind him.

Great, the last thing I needed was Kai mad at me. I lay down and tried to sleep, but I kept tossing and turning, thinking of the vampires, of being hunted, of my argument with Kai. I thought of Sylvia saying I had witch powers that she could activate. I thought of everything you shouldn't think of if you are trying to sleep.

Finally, I turned to look at the clock. One a.m. God, I really needed sleep. I chewed on my bottom lip, making a decision. Opening my door slowly, I peeked out. All clear. I crept down the hall to Kai's room. The second I turned the handle, he sat up quickly and stared at the door. His hair was ruffled and he looked adorably sexy.

He smiled. "What took you so long?"

I grinned, shut the door, and climbed into bed with him. The second his arms closed around me, my mind shut off and I slept easily.

The next morning was a mandatory weekly pack barbeque. Even the wolves who lived on the edge of our territory drove in for the event. I took time to get to know each wolf. Sammy was fifteen and our youngest wolf; he was best friends with Akash. Besides Emma, Anna, and me, there was only one other female and she was unmated. Her name was Oksana and she was Ukrainian. She lived on the edge of our territory with her boyfriend Dominic, who was also in our pack, but they weren't mates.

Diya and Trent were really getting along well. You could see the romance budding between them, and she looked genuinely happy. Trent looked head over heels in love with her already. He looked at her a certain way that said he adored her. It reminded me of the way Kai looked at me.

After we had eaten, Kai cleared his throat. "As you all know, we had some vampires trespass on our territory and try to take one of our pack members. This deed cannot go unpunished!" He roared the last sentence, letting some of his alpha power leak through. The pack rumbled their approval as the hair on my arms stood on end.

"We know the Portland pack is behind this, so I have decided to challenge Dane for alpha status of his pack and take over his territory."

You could hear a pin drop. No one said anything; the more submissive wolves looked scared and the dominant wolves looked proud.

"I know merging our pack with new members will be hard at first. If you are currently fourth in the pack, you might be eighth after we merge. I have never been a wolf seeking out a big pack or a large territory. Dane runs a dirty pack, as you all have heard. When I kill him and take over, some of his pack mates won't want to stay under my command. Others will be relieved. I will run this new pack the same way I always have. Minimal fights, respect, and you will all still be family to me."

I could see the pack's expressions change. They trusted Kai. They would do anything for him.

"Aurora is special," Kai said. "A bigger pack and more territory also means we can better protect her against future enemies. The three vampires who came for her will not be the last. She has a beautiful gift that has already seen three of our pack members mated. Soon, we will have small pups running around this mountain. There will be weddings. This pack will grow, but not because we are after numbers—because we want to grow as a family."

Everyone clapped, and I felt tears line my eyes. It had been weird not to see any children around. It would be nice to see families grow.

THE NEXT MORNING Kai and I were silent over breakfast with his family. He had called Dane and requested a pack-to-pack meeting about the territory violation with the vampires, and Dane had accepted.

"Do you think he knows what you are planning?" I finally asked out loud.

"Yes, he will be ready to fight," Kai answered.

I swallowed hard. Kai's mother put a hand over mine. "Do you know why my son didn't stay in Delhi under my husband's authority?"

"A little bit," I confessed.

Kai cut her a look but she dismissed it. "Kai is more dominant than my husband. He could have fought him and taken charge of the entire New Delhi pack. He would have won. His father knows that. He will win this fight tomorrow, and any other after that."

I admired her confidence in Kai. I was tempted to ask her if she knew about Dane's silver teeth, but thought better of it. If support was what he needed, I could do that.

"I know," I told her, and looked at Kai with a forced smile. I just hoped she was right.

It took six cars, but we all drove out to the Portland pack's meeting place. Emma and Devon stayed back to keep a presence in our territory.

As we pulled up to meet the Portland pack in the large open park area, I started feeling nervous. What if Kai was gravely injured like the last time? What if someone in our pack tried to fight him injured, for alpha status? I would protect him again if I had to. Kai parked the car and leaned across the seat to gently grasp my face. His mother, sister, and two brothers were in the back of the SUV, watching.

"I love you and I will be fine." He gave me a passionate but chaste kiss and then exited the car. Taking a deep breath, I got out of the car as well, and we all walked in human form toward the group of people standing in the meadow.

I caught a whiff of cigar and aftershave. *Foreign wolf.* Dane's pack was quite large. Twice the size of ours by my quick count. The women were skinny and looked broken. They clung to the men in fear and it made me sick.

Dane stepped forward. "To what do we owe the pleasure of being able to gaze upon your delicious new female werewolf?" He licked his silver teeth and gave me a stare that made my blood run cold. I glared back, tilting my chin up. If Kai didn't kill this guy, maybe I would.

Kai clenched his jaw but otherwise didn't show that the comment bothered him. "I challenge you, Dane Hurst, for alpha status to your pack and all of your territory. You sent three vampires after my mate, and you run a dirty pack. If I don't get rid of you, the council eventually will."

Dane began unbuttoning his shirt as if he'd expected this. "Challenge accepted."

His second-in-command handed him a blue glass bottle and he began to chug the contents. "Silver water," Dane told us all with a grin.

My stomach dropped. Bastard. I took a deep breath, put on my game face, and walked over to Kai, who was undressing as the two packs made a wide circle around us.

"Kick his ass," I told Kai. "He looked at me like I was a piece of meat, and his females look half-starved and scared."

Kai grinned. "Gladly." He shifted lightning-fast and took off, throwing himself onto Dane's half-shifted back. Dane was curled in a ball, protecting his jugular with his hands until he could fully shift, but Kai wasted no time chewing the back of his neck, ripping chunks of flesh away.

Oh God, this was hard to watch, but I couldn't look away. I backed out of the circle and found myself between Diya and Kai's mother. Dane had fully shifted, and now threw Kai off of his back with brutal force. My mate landed hard and I heard the cracking of bones as the breath left his lungs in a whoosh. I put my hand over my mouth in fear, but Kai's mom pulled my hand down from my face and held it tightly.

She leaned in and whispered, "I've seen my husband through many fights. They are only as strong as we let them be. If you cry out or he risks a glance at you and you are anything but strong and fierce, he may make a mistake that could cost him his life."

I held my head high and masked my fear. Sure enough, Kai got up and risked a half-second glance my way before charging Dane. He kept going for the throat and tearing chunks away. Each time Dane tried to bite him, Kai would quickly dash the other way. He was freaky fast, but I could tell the silver was getting to him. I was pretty sure that when Kai bit Dane and got his blood into his mouth, the liquid silver was getting into Kai's system. You could see that Kai's pace was slowing and his movements were less coordinated.

Then, Kai made a mistake. He didn't get away quickly enough and Dane clamped his jaws around his left shoulder and closed down. Kai tried to shake him off, but couldn't.

Next to Diya I heard Max swear. "He is going to try to weaken him with silver poisoning. If only he had your immunity, Aurora."

Kai's mother whipped her head towards me. "You have silver immunity?"

I nodded. "Yes, but I don't know why."

"Who cares why? Quickly, open your mate bond," she instructed me.

"My what?" I couldn't take my eyes off Kai, but I made up my mind then. If he looked like he was going to die, I was going to intervene. Damn the council, let them come after me. I didn't want to live in a world where he didn't exist.

Kai's mother grabbed the side of my face and stared at me with glowing yellow eyes. "Open your mind to Kai *now*! Mates can share powers for a short time! It would be stronger if you had gone through the mating ceremony, but even without that your bond will give him enough to strengthen him. He can win this fight!"

My heart leapt at her words. I was immediately reminded of the glowing ball in the woods that I'd buried. Closing my eyes, I ran to the spot in my mind where I had buried the orb and saw a faint glow under the dirt. I dug it up and quickly threw the ball into the air, where it burst into a million twinkling stars that covered my body like a fine mist—like magic. My eyes stayed closed, and Kai's mother whispered in my ear.

"Give him your silver immunity. Imagine it as a liquid leaving your body and joining his."

I did as she asked. I had always been good at visualization, so now I thought of a shimmery stream leaving my heart, envisioned it as a magic liquid that held the power to give the user immunity to silver. Then I opened my eyes, and to my shock I saw a fine mist floating from me to Kai just as I had envisioned, drenching Kai with the imaginary liquid. The moment

I did this, Kai's eyes snapped open and he threw Dane off of him with a burst of strength. It was incredible. He spared no time in lunging for Dane's half-torn throat, and clamping his jaws over his neck.

Dane struggled, but was in no position to fight back. Kai pulled his wolf body into a standing position, with Dane still dangling from his mouth, used his claws to grasp Dane's shoulders, dug his claws in, and in one tug ripped Dane's head from his body.

Our pack began to cheer, and I sighed in relief. Kai had done it; he'd beaten him. Dane's second-in-command shifted into wolf form then and ran away with a few other wolves. They weren't going to stick around, I guess. Everyone else stood still and stared at Kai as he shifted and changed into clothes.

Most of Dane's pack lowered their heads in respect. The ones who didn't were dominant males, or submissive females who looked too terrified to do anything. Kai was still catching his breath, and his wounds would need time to fully heal, so I stepped forward.

"Kai has rightfully won this pack and these lands. But he won't make you his wolves by force. We're more than pack. We're family. If anyone else wants to leave, then go—find another pack to run with, because we run a clean pack. No dominance fights. We treasure and protect our females, we help them find their mates. We have homes and enough food for everyone. If you want to be a part of our family, then step forward."

I glanced at Kai, who had pride in his eyes.

"A worthy mate and second-in-command," I heard Kai's mother whisper to Diya.

Kai's shoulder wound wasn't healing well, and I could see the bluish iridescent fluid still leaking from it. Silver. He looked exhausted.

Dane's entire pack stepped forward and got on one knee, all but two people. One was a hard-looking man with dominance in his eyes and scars on his face. The other was a woman who looked like a survivor, like she had been through hell and back and didn't want to take any more shit from abusive males—looked like me the night I killed my father to save my mother's life.

The scar-faced man stepped forward. "How can I assure a high position in the pack without a fight? I'm third in this pack."

Kai acknowledged him with a nod. "If fighting for dominance is the only way to calm Brother Wolf, then you will have to find another pack. If you are okay with letting Brother Wolf out and staring into my most dominant wolves' eyes, then we can establish your place in the pack without hurting my family members. If that doesn't settle Brother Wolf, then I will grant you leave to find another pack."

The guy raised his eyebrows. "That works for me." Something else crossed his face, but it was too quick for me to read.

Lastly, the woman stepped forward. "My name is Isabelle. Dane attacked me on my way home from work. He took my money, ripped my flesh apart, and left me for dead. I survived the change, much to his delight, and I have wished every day since then that I hadn't. I don't know where my family is now. I have a husband and two small children. It's been two years. Every time I tried to run away, Dane beat me, and eventually held me captive in his basement. Rarely let me out. I know I can't go back to being human, but I won't go back to being a slave. I want to see my family again."

She held her chin high, and her jaw was set, but I saw her lip quiver. Her wrists, I could see now, were bound with thin silver chains, and I felt sick looking at how mistreated she was.

Kai began to speak when I stepped forward, but I turned and quieted him with my eyes. I walked slowly and lowered my gaze so I wouldn't spook her. I could feel her dominance, yet she was fragile. She reminded me of the women at my shelter. I knew how to deal with them.

"Kai is a good alpha and a kind man. I got into a car accident and almost died, but he saved me. I survived the change too, and when I told him I didn't want to fake my death, that I wanted to continue to see my family, he allowed it. My mom just came to a pack barbeque last weekend…"

Tears were streaming down the woman's face, but I knew she needed more—she didn't trust anyone at this point. She needed proof. "If you join our pack tonight, first thing tomorrow morning we'll take you to find your family … or you can leave. Be a lone wolf."

Tentatively, I reached for her hands and began to

gently remove the silver chains that constrained her. She stiffened, but allowed me to help. A mix of surprise and pain shone in her eyes as she stared at me silently.

'*She wouldn't last a day as a lone wolf,*' Kai told me.

'*Don't underestimate a victim of abuse,*' I fired back into his mind.

With new tears on her face which seemed to exude from relief, she let her hands fall to the sides and stepped forward. I could see the fresh burn marks on her skin as Isabelle bent on one knee, accepting my promise.

Kai nodded to me and raised his hands high. "I call on my ancestors and invite in the pack magic that bonds us all, makes us a family. Let me lead you, let me protect you."

All of the new pack members were lining up.

"Do you promise to obey me and share all that you are with this pack?" I could see sweat had broken out on Kai's forehead. The fight had taken a lot out of him.

"I do, Alpha," the first person said, and rolled up his sleeve. Kai transformed his fingers to claws, and swiped at the flesh of the young man's forearm. The man winced and clawed at Kai's forearm, then they touched their forearms together.

"Blood of my blood," they recited in unison.

"Welcome to my pack, son," Kai told the young man. The pack roared and cheered behind Kai, welcoming the new member. I was faintly aware of a new string of consciousness added to the pack's energy.

*'You okay?'* I asked Kai.

*'Yes, just pushing out this liquid silver. Will be fine with a good night's sleep and a couple of rare steaks.'* He smiled, knowing that would gross me out.

Kai walked to the next person and repeated the ceremony. When he had finished inviting the last member, Kai's arm was dripping bright crimson blood and he looked absolutely exhausted. His shoulder was healing, but there were still deep gashes in him. He needed sleep and food, but he was alive. That's all I cared about.

Just as I was approaching him to suggest we get him home, the unthinkable happened.

The scar-faced male that had been third in the Portland pack advanced toward Kai with yellow eyes. "I challenge you for alpha status of this pack."

The collective intake of breath from the pack gave me chills. That statement was a death sentence for my mate. I saw a flash of fear flicker across Kai's vision before it was gone. Cold, hard anger replaced it.

Suddenly Kai's mother was by my side. "A pack's second-in-command can fight in place of an injured alpha." She whispered.

I didn't hesitate. "As second-in-command, I accept your challenge on behalf of my injured alpha." Fear and anger washed through me in equal measure. Oh, shit. Did I just do that?

Kai's nostrils flared as he glared at his mother, sending ripples of fur down his body. "I forbid it!" he roared.

The man who had challenged him pinned me with a hard gaze. "Too late. She accepted. If I win, I take this pack and you become my second," he told Kai. "If I let you ..."

"Then when I am healed I will challenge you and kill you!" Kai roared at the man. "Withdraw your request!"

"No. Challenge accepted." The scar-faced man started to shift.

Okay, this was just another guy who preyed on weak people. I had prepared my whole life for this moment. All of Safe Haven, my martial arts training, it was all to keep bastards like this from taking advantage of the weak. I wasn't weak, though, and I was going to prove it.

I took a hint from Kai's style of fighting and shifted instantly, running at the man full speed. I slammed into him, knocking him back in his half-shifted form. Glancing at Kai, I saw that he had shifted into his werewolf form. His mother had a chunk of his fur in her hand, holding him back. I knew then that if it looked like I was losing, Kai would intervene and the council would later kill him.

I tore at the werewolf's jugular as his half-clawed hands raked down my back, causing me to let out a high-pitched yelp.

*'Don't drag this out*, Kai told me. *'You want a fast kill. He is wolf-born, I can feel it. No powers.'*

I backed out of his hold and came from a different angle. He was fully in wolf form now and I lunged at him, but he rolled to the side, avoiding me. I caught his tail in my mouth and dragged him toward me. He howled in pain, and when he was close enough I used my front paws to dig into his hind legs and pull him underneath me. Being underneath your attacker was the worst and most vulnerable position possible. He was squirming and strong, but I was fast. I saw an opening and lunged, taking his neck in my mouth. He was swiping at my belly with his hind paws, but I ignored the pain as I chewed into his neck. Sister Wolf had taken over and nothing about this grossed me out. Vegetarian Aurora was nowhere to be found. I wanted him dead. I wanted his head separated from his body. I wanted to taste his blood—to protect my mate and my pack. This was a means to an end.

Once I had a good hold, I shook his neck in my jaws and his body flopped like a ragdoll. I think he had lost consciousness. With one last burst of effort, I gave a hard pull to the right and ripped his head clean off. His body crumpled beneath me and I turned to see Kai's wolf two feet away, ready to intervene at any moment. Luckily he hadn't. I gave a loud howl then and the pack began shifting. It was unspoken, but we needed a run, together, for the first time as a new pack in our new territory. My stomach was already healing, which amazed me beyond belief.

'Don't ever do that again,' Kai told me with a venomous tone, and ran off beside Jai. I sat there in silence for a moment, and then followed with my tail between my legs.

## 15

## REUNITED

The next morning, Kai, Isabelle, and I sat together in Kai's office. The phone jumped in her hands as she trembled, so she set it back down. "I don't even know if he has the same number ... if he has remarried. I don't know what to say." She looked at her hands and picked at her nails.

Kai had agreed she could reunite with her family and, depending on her wishes, we would figure out a living situation. Kai had barely talked to me last night for fighting in his place. He'd slept in his room, and I'd barely slept in mine.

"Let me call him," I offered. "I can start the call off and you can jump in when you are ready. Okay?"

Isabelle began to weep. "Is this really happening? You guys will let me see my family? I can see my kids? Every day?"

She had limp brown hair that framed a face full of scars. This woman had taken many beatings, with silver I didn't doubt. Only silver would scar a werewolf this bad. She was emaciated and broken, and I didn't think she believed us, that this was really happening. Poor thing. My throat tightened with emotion.

Kai walked over to her slowly. "Dane wasn't an alpha, he was a power-hungry monster. An alpha takes care of his pack like family. I will treat you like you are my own sister. I would *never* separate a mother from her children. I can clear it with the council. In rare cases, humans are permitted knowledge of our kind. Your children can come live here on the mountain with you, and we will protect them as pack. Your husband can too, if you like. Children are a treasured gift in werewolf society. It doesn't matter if they are human or not."

Isabelle gave a weak smile. "I can feel that your words are true. Make the call, Aurora. I'll dial the number." She pressed the buttons slowly, and handed me the phone.

I cleared my throat, as I heard it, thinking of a story to say when he answered—if he answered.

"Hello, this is Tristan." I had the phone on speaker and Isabelle squeezed my arm hard when she heard his voice. Tears spilled over her cheeks.

I kept my voice light and airy: "Hi, my name is Aurora, and I live up in Mount Hood ..."

"What can I do for you?" I could hear children in

the background laughing. Isabelle's face was frozen in shock at the sound.

"I have a woman here who says her name is Isabelle," I told him bluntly. "She looks pretty shaken up, and underfed. She says she escaped capture and is your wife."

There was silence. "You people don't stop, do you? You're sick. Prank-calling bastards."

"Tristan!" Isabelle shouted, choking on a half sob.

"Oh my God!" He choked at the sound of her voice. A second later he started weeping uncontrollably into the phone. I felt my throat swell with emotion. "Izzy! Oh my God! Is that you?"

"It's me." She wept.

"Are you okay?" he shouted frantically. "I've never stopped looking for you. Have you called the police? Where are you? I'm coming. KIDS! Mommy is on the phone!"

"It's been a long time, and it hasn't been easy but I'm okay now. I thought you might have moved on..." She let that sentiment linger. I suddenly felt like I shouldn't be in here, witnessing this very private conversation.

"Are you crazy?" he said tenderly. "No, no, no—where are you? Give me an address right now. The kids are so big. Violet is four and Connor is six. I show them your picture every night."

Isabelle was sobbing as I rattled off the address, telling Tristan not to involve the police, that we would explain why later.

After a few moments of shocked silence, we called Diya over to help put makeup on Isabelle's bruises and scars to make her more presentable for her family. I lent her some clean, colorful clothes, then Kai and I waited outside with her. I prepped Isabelle to tell her husband that she didn't want a media circus—that the man who did this to her was dead and she was safe now.

Meanwhile, Kai put in an urgent call to the council to ask for permission to bring three humans into the pack. The fact that there were children involved would get it approved quickly. Children in packs were rare, even if they were human. Also, Dane did a bad thing and brought a person into the pack after mugging and attacking her—and then had kept her hostage. She could go to the media and expose our kind. This all made a good case for telling her husband of our race. The kids could learn later, when they were older. When I questioned how pack bonds worked on humans, he said pack magic worked to bring any species into the pack, if an alpha allowed it.

A maroon Ford Explorer made its way up the hill on to Kai's property and Isabelle shrieked. "Tristan! Connor, Violet!" She ran toward the car. Her husband braked hard, the tires kicking up bits of gravel, and jumped out. Running toward her at full speed, he picked her up, spinning her around as they embraced. They were both crying freely as the children got out of the car and ran to their mother, clinging to her legs.

Kai reached over and held my hand. All was forgiven.

---

Since the vampire attack, Kai had increased pack training sessions to once a day. A week after Isabelle reunited with her family, Kai was given approval from the council to expose our kind to Isabelle's husband, Tristan, and to make her family part of the pack. They only made one condition—a witch needed to put a spell on him so that if he tried to tell other humans our secret, he wouldn't be able to.

Tristan seemed shocked at first, but was turning out to be a great guy and was taking the news fairly well. He was a firefighter and strongly built so he didn't seem too intimidated by the dominant males in the pack. Kai had a special ceremony to introduce him and the children. This gave them our scent so that other werewolves would know they were claimed, and not to mess with them. Kai also gave them a house on the mountain, because an unmated female werewolf living in Portland was a disaster waiting to happen.

It bothered me that Isabelle was considered unmated even though she was married. Kai explained that eventually Tristan would grow old and die, and Izzy would live over a hundred years. She could search for her werewolf mate after Tristan was gone. That thought unsettled me. What if Tristan was her mate but if he never changed into a werewolf, we wouldn't know? My mind chewed on this for hours.

When Sylvia put the spell on Tristan, she also told me she could open up my magic so that I could better protect myself from vampires and any other threat. I was tempted, but Kai seemed against the idea so I declined. After the spell was put on Tristan, I confronted Kai about something that was bothering me.

"So no one knows of our kind? We have been around hundreds of years and it's still a secret?"

Kai looked at me for a long time, weighing something in his mind.

"None of the general human population know about our kind," he answered.

That was vague. I pressed him. "Okay, but some humans know about our kind?"

Kai exhaled loudly and leaned in to whisper in my ear. We were outside and a few wolves were lingering about.

"Every intelligence agency in almost every country knows about the three supernatural races. We scare them, and they keep tabs on us, but they don't approach us. Many younger wolves don't know that the government knows about us. It's better that way."

My mouth dropped open. "So the CIA could be watching us right now?" I whispered back.

Kai shrugged. "Possibly. I know a few wolves who work for the CIA that we could ask." He winked.

So we had people on the inside? Interesting. I

wondered, if the government ever felt our kind were a threat, if they would take us out. I shivered at the thought.

THE NEXT DAY I awoke slowly. Sadie's wedding was today, and Diya and the rest of Kai's family were going home tomorrow. It had been a thought-provoking week. Kai had woken early to go meet with pack members living in Portland and establish a bond. Everyone had found their place in the pack. I was still second and Emma was no longer the most submissive member. I was lying in bed stretching my back when my door suddenly flew open. I jumped up quickly and got into a fighting stance as Diya flew across the room with her hand out and shoved it in my face.

"Trent proposed! Oh my God! Isn't it beautiful?" she gushed.

Now that I was convinced it wasn't an intruder, I relaxed, and looked down at her hand. There was a modest princess-cut ring on her left ring finger. Taking her hand, I brought it closer to my face.

"It's beautiful," I agreed. Wow, they moved fast. Anna and Jake were talking of a mating ceremony too. Was I jealous? I had asked Kai to go slowly. Was I even ready for marriage? She dropped her hand and hugged me.

"Don't worry, you will get one too and yours will be bigger, if I know my brother." She gestured to my hand and I blushed, unsure of what to say.

"So, when's the big day?" I asked, to change the subject.

"I have to talk to Papa, but the sooner the better! I love Trent." She swooned and dropped on my bed just as Emma burst into the room clutching a small, white, plastic pregnancy test.

My mouth dropped open. This was quite the exciting morning.

"I'm pregnant!" Emma screeched.

Diya and I started screaming like teenagers, then laughed a little at our ridiculousness. If my vision was correct, Kai and I would be married in the next four to five months. Emma had been heavily pregnant in my wedding vision. Holy shit.

## 16
## UNITED

I LOOKED down at the deep blue silk dress that clung to my petite figure. My hair was a spill of curls that were expertly pinned all over my head and cascaded over my left shoulder. My lips were stained red and I was wearing heavy eye makeup. Diya had made me over and I liked what she had done.

Most of the old Mount Hood pack was en route to Sadie's wedding, while the new Portland members stayed back to defend our territory. Kai was driving his family and me to Seattle and kept giving me sexy side glances in the car. I smiled. He cleaned up well; his wild hair was slicked back and he wore a gray linen suit with a bright blue shirt.

*'You look amazing,'* I told him through our mental bond.

He gave a soft growl. *'Amazing doesn't begin to cover how you look, my dear. That red lipstick is driving me crazy.'*

I smiled and puckered my lips.

---

Sadie's wedding was in a rose garden at the house of a Seattle pack member. It was a full moon and the sun had just set. As Kai and I tried to find our seats, I saw that the aisle was lined with white flower petals and tea lights. It felt magical. A man standing at the altar wearing a large Native American headdress was holding a dagger encrusted with rubies.

I took a deep breath and inhaled his scent. He wasn't a werewolf or a witch, but he didn't smell human. Kai chuckled beside me.

"Trying to figure out what he is?"

I nodded.

"Shamans are their own species. They are closest to Spirit, and some of them are shapeshifters, so they know of our kind. They have been performing our mating ceremonies ever since I can remember."

I looked closer at the man. He could have been forty or seventy, it was hard to tell. He had a tattoo of a jaguar on his arm, and a sharpened bone hung from a thread on his neck, while his wrists were wrapped in leather cuffs and adorned with turquoise.

Kai leaned in and whispered. "Legend says that the shamans hold the power of our fertility. Long ago, any female werewolf could give birth to pups. It didn't matter if she was mated or not. But then the werewolves did something to anger the natives and the natives made all of the female werewolves infertile. Unless they were mated and blessed by the Great Spirit in a ceremony, they couldn't reproduce."

Chills ran up and down my arms. Just then, the shaman looked at me and I locked eyes with him. Everything around me froze. *Literally*. Kai was stuck leaning into my ear, and all of the seated wolves were frozen in midair. It was like time had stopped but I could still move. What the hell was going on?

I felt my heart rate pick up; fear flooded my system as I wondered if I was in danger. The shaman came walking toward me and I put myself in a fighting stance, unsure of what was happening. I didn't like that my pack was helpless if someone were to attack, and I was about to change into my wolf when the shaman spoke.

"I come in peace, little sister," the shaman said to me with his hand raised.

"Did you do this?" I gestured around at the frozen crowd in awe.

He nodded. "I have a message for you, sister. My name is Nahuel, and Spirit has blessed you with a great purpose. My ancestors have cursed the werewolves for a long time. Werewolves were greedy hunters and didn't share their meat. They became territorial and didn't share their land. They reproduced quickly and were wasteful like the humans. But we did not foresee that our curse would reduce the population of the werewolves so quickly. We only wanted to teach them a lesson, to respect Mother Earth and all of her inhabitants. Now, the werewolves are on the brink of extinction and the balance is being threatened."

My mouth hung open at his admission to cursing our kind and reducing our population. He simply went on, ignoring my shock.

"Vampires are a threat to humans, and werewolves protect the humans. Witches are neutral to all species, so if everyone serves their purpose, then there is balance. But there is now an alarming amount of vampires in relation to the werewolves. If the vampires choose to attack, they could wipe out the werewolves, and eventually the human race. This *cannot* happen. I perform mating ceremonies to pay a debt to the werewolves because the curse my people laid on them cannot be undone. But I perform them all too little. Your presence here will change that. As the Matefinder, you will bring together many mated pairings, with Spirit's help."

He knew what I was? I was breathing deeply, trying not to freak out. *I think I'm having a panic attack*, I thought. I don't know what made me think of Isabelle and Tristan, but I blurted out, "Our pack member Isabelle is married to a human and they are in love. They have human children and are happy. How can she have a mate waiting out there for her? It doesn't seem right. I don't understand how mated pairs are brought together…"

The shaman nodded kindly, seeming unperturbed by my random thoughts. "Nothing seems right on this side of the veil. In the spirit world, it makes more sense.

You have many loves in your lifetime whether you are human, vampire, witch, or werewolf—people you have chosen to share your energy with, people who lift your spirit. But then there are soul mates. Soul mates choose to spend the most time together in a lifetime. They challenge each other, support one another, and grow together. It's the hardest and most rewarding pairing." He glanced at Kai and smiled. "Your pack mate Isabelle will share a good life with Tristan, but if Spirit allows she will also share her life with her mate. As a werewolf, you are divided, your human half and your wolf half. Isabelle's human half loves Tristan and her wolf half respects him, but when you meet your mate, both halves love that person. You become one."

That made sense to me. I felt settled thinking of it that way and so I nodded.

"So that's the message you have for me? My race is dying and vampires could take over, so I was sent here to find mates? Well, I have only found three mates in about two weeks, so it might take a couple of decades to find enough to grow my race." It felt a little ridiculous saying it like that. I hadn't meant for it to sound so sarcastic, but it did.

He stepped even closer to me, fully entering my personal space, bringing the smell of freshly burnt sage with him.

"No, little sister. My message for you is that, in the near future, Spirit is going to download you with hundreds of mate couplings at once. It will be scary and somewhat debilitating. After this information gets out, everyone will know who you are. All of the packs will benefit from your gift, so they will vow to protect you. You are to come out to your kind. It's the only way to ensure you are safe. Your mother hid from her people and died a young woman. If you expose yourself at the right time, to as many of your kind as you can, you will ensure your safety, and unite your people with one common goal. As pups start being born and children's laughter is heard among the packs, they will know it is so because of you. So when the vampires come for you, let every wolf fight in your honor." His face took on a menacing look and the hairs on my arms were standing.

I swallowed hard. "Why would the vampires come for me?" Hundreds of mate pairings at once? Download? Like I was a computer? My head was spinning.

He looked down at his dagger and then up at the moon. "Because of the balance. You have the gift of finding mates for your kind. But you also have the gift of giving fertility to female vampires. It's in your blood. Literally. If a female vampire drinks your blood, she could mate with a male vampire and have a vampire child." He sighed, resigned.

I stumbled over Kai's frozen body, falling on all fours, panting on the grass. What the hell did he just say? Vampire *children*!

"And they know this? The vampires?" I shuddered, looking up at Nahuel from my place on the grass. The thought of small children acting like those deadly vampires in the woods made me sick. The shaman reached down and helped me stand.

"Their queen knows this, and she will stop at nothing to make you her blood slave. Good luck, Aurora. Spirit has equipped you with all that you need to fight for the light, but there is also darkness inside of you. You must embrace all of your powers to become who you truly are."

I stared into his seemingly endless eyes and saw something flicker, and an image take shape. I saw a flash of Sylvia putting her hands on my head and mist pouring out of my body. I also saw the image of my father putting a cigarette out on the palm of my hand when I was nine. I shuddered. Maybe there was darkness inside of me. Thinking of the abuse I endured as a child ignited a ball of rage inside of me.

"I can't hold time much longer," he told me as he pulled a black Apache tear from his satchel. "If you need my counsel, just bury this in the earth. I am here as your guide, and I owe a debt to your people." Then he nodded and walked up to the front, just like that.

I sat down in shock just as the people started moving and talking again. They all looked around, confused, and next to me Kai took in a deep inhale through his nose. He grabbed my arm. "You smell like magic."

I sighed. "I will tell you later. This is Sadie's day." There was no way in hell I could explain any of what had just happened. I wasn't even sure I believed it. I wanted to rock in a corner in denial and cry.

Kai and some of the more dominant wolves looked at the shaman with suspicion, but didn't confront him. Something told me they knew that wouldn't be a good idea. If he could stop time, who knew what else he was capable of?

*'Are you hurt?'* Kai pressed the issue.

Physically no. Mentally was another answer. *'No.'* I told him.

Kai settled as the music played and the wedding party began walking the aisle. *The balance.* Werewolves were here to protect humans? It seemed right. The thought of the human race or the werewolf race going extinct sent chills down my spine. A world run by vampires taking human blood slaves was a horrible thought. Vampire children were an even more horrible thought. I was sent here to restore the balance between the different species? That was a heavy responsibility. Life had just gotten way more complicated.

The music changed and I turned my head. Sadie had begun her walk down the aisle and she looked breathtaking. Her hair was pulled back to show her strong face. She had light makeup on to showcase her natural beauty, and a thin white silk dress clung to her muscular body. As she passed us, she held Kai's gaze for a few seconds and my heart spiked with jealousy. Kai pulled my hand on top of his and stroked my palm with his thumb. I took a deep breath. *'You're mine,'* Kai told me, *'and I am yours.'*

I relaxed into the chair as Sadie met Brett at the

altar. Nahuel's hands raised, in a high arc above the couple. He was holding a smoking sage bundle and began fanning smoke around the pair, while they held hands, facing each other. Then Nahuel tied a blue silk ribbon to Sadie's left wrist. "This represents your human half." He did the same on Brett's wrist. And then tied a white silk ribbon to both of their right wrists. "This represents your wolf."

Both of their eyes showed yellow.

Nahuel projected his voice to the crowd: "Werewolves are courageous, strong, loyal, and successful at hunting. Werewolves are in fact so loyal that they mate for life. If lucky enough to find their mate, it will be the only one they ever have."

Kai laced his fingers tighter through mine.

"You come to me as two parts in one body, human and wolf. You come as two souls with one purpose—to be mated for life, to start a family if you choose."

Nahuel's face took on a relaxed expression as his eyes clouded over, turning white. "This pairing is blessed by Spirit." As Sadie and Brett held hands, Nahuel began to braid the four strings together. "I join your souls as one. May you have no secrets from one another. I join your souls as one. May you protect one another until death. I join your souls as one. May you respect each other as equals, regardless of pack rank. I join your souls as one. May fertility be bestowed upon your family. I join your souls as one. May you love each other for the rest of your long, long lives." The braid was complete and the entire altar was coated in a fine white magical mist. "It is done, so be it." Sadie and Brett stared into each other's eyes and silent tears began to fall on their cheeks.

It was a beautiful moment to witness.

Kai leaned in to whisper in my ear: "They say during the mating ceremony that Spirit shows you everything about your mate, so there are no secrets. Your past, your faults, your strengths. It is said to bring the couple even closer together, and is what bonds them for life. It's ten times what you felt when you first looked at me as a wolf."

A tear sprang up in my eye as emotion overwhelmed me. It was beautiful. I remembered what I was shown when I first realized Kai was my mate. To see more … I couldn't imagine. What Nahuel had said, and the tears falling down Sadie's cheeks—it was all so breathtaking. I turned in my seat and looked into Kai's eyes.

'*I love you*,' I told him, and something else passed between us in that look, something unspoken, causing him to smile so big that all of his teeth showed.

THE ENTIRE RIDE home consisted of Kai and me arguing in my head. I think his mother knew what was going on because I could see her in the rearview mirror just staring at us.

Kai was pestering me to tell him more about why he smelled magic on me. I kept telling him we would talk about it when we got home. I didn't want to give him details in front of his family. It was too much to explain in our heads. Surely waiting a few hours wouldn't kill him.

*'Did he put magic on me? Did he threaten you? If so, then I don't want to drive home, I want to go back and have a little chat with him,'* Kai roared.

I sighed.

"Fine!" I screamed in the car, making Diya and Maya both jump. "He stopped time and told me that Spirit had crazy plans for me because a war with the vampires is coming! He was warning me, okay? Happy?"

Kai's knuckles went white while his mother leaned forward. "Tell us what he said about the vampires, dear," she tried to coax me.

Kai shook his head. "No. I'm sorry, Mother, but you are not pack. I need to protect my pack and my mate. I will learn of what was said and decide if I want to share it with other packs." There was finality in his voice. The alpha had spoken. His mother sat back and lowered her head in a submissive gesture while I chewed on my lip, feeling bad.

*'See? I told you!'* I shouted into Kai's mind. *'Why did you push me?'*

*'When we get home, I want you to replay every single word that the shaman spoke to you.'*

I sighed. It was already past midnight. This was going to be a long night.

---

I WOKE up groggy and unrested the next day. Kai and I had been up until dawn arguing about what the shaman had told me. He wanted to take the Apache tear from me, thinking it was spelled; he didn't want me having it, but I kept it anyway. He was unsettled with what had been said and he didn't want me coming out to the werewolves. He also didn't like the idea of me being downloaded with hundreds of mate pairings. It broke my heart when he said that for the first time in his life he felt helpless to protect someone.

I rolled over to see his half of my bed empty. After showering and getting dressed, I made my way into the kitchen. A bunch of the pack members had come over to say goodbye to Diya, Jai, and Maya.

"Why didn't you wake me?" I asked Kai.

He kissed the top of my head. "I was just about to. I figured you needed the rest. Pack barbeque before my family leaves. It will be the first barbeque with the entire pack. Everyone is coming in from Portland."

I smiled, but turned around quickly when I felt a small tug on my finger. It was Violet. We had all become enamored with Isabelle's children.

"Is it true you are a veterinarian? I want to be a veterinarian, too!" she shouted. I smiled, picking her up and placing her on my hip.

"I'm a veg-e-tarian, but I'm sure you will make a wonderful vet-er-i-narian." I said the two different words slowly.

The girl giggled and touched my nose. "You're pretty," she told me, and I could feel Kai's eyes on me.

"You're prettier," I told her back, nudging her nose with mine.

"You will make a wonderful mother," Kai's mother said as she stood next to me and Violet. I met Kai's eyes and blushed. I wanted children, I always had, but not if they would be born into an unsafe world. I wouldn't have children selfishly, and I didn't want my daughter to be hunted by vampires as I was. Truthfully, I didn't know what I wanted. But the thought of having a child with my nose and Kai's eyes, with both of our strong spirits, made my belly flutter.

Isabelle, who we now affectionately called Izzy, came and grabbed Violet from me. "Is she bothering you? She has been asking me all morning to come and see you."

I smiled. "It would be impossible for her or Connor to bother me."

She laughed. "Okay, then I'll send them both your way the next time they have a tantrum about eating their vegetables."

We all laughed. Izzy seemed to have come out of her shell. I knew all too well what that kind of trauma did to dampen your spirit, but with her family by her side she had bounced back. Tristan was working a twenty-four-hour shift at the local fire station, so when he was gone the pack pitched in to help out. I was relieved to see her whole family had settled well after the move from Portland.

We made our way outside as the rest of the pack

arrived. One hundred and seven members in all, including Tristan and the children.

Kai jumped up onto a picnic table and addressed the crowd. "Weekly pack barbecues are mandatory, as well as daily training sessions from now on. We can train apart in smaller groups, but once a week we train together as a family." Kai's words settled into us and there was no doubt it was the vampire attack that had him increase training sessions.

"I have some exciting news to share with you all." Kai nodded to Emma, who tipped her head back at him.

"Emma is pregnant," Kai announced.

The pack roared with excitement, clapping and cheering as Emma blushed and held her stomach.

"We have been blessed with more members. Soon Violet and Connor won't be the only children running around the mountain. Our family is growing, and I am honored to welcome two new family members. My blood sister and brother, Diya and Jai, will be joining our pack after Trent and Diya wed." More clapping as Trent gave Diya a kiss.

"This coming weekend, Aurora and I will have to travel to the annual alpha council meeting. I will be leaving the rest of you to protect Emma and the young. When we get back, there will be much to discuss."

His eyes bore into me.

*'Council meeting?'* I asked him. *'When were you going to tell me?'*

*'I don't want to bring you, it's not safe. But every*

*alpha and their second must be in attendance. I think this is where Spirit will give you the pairings. You'll probably expose yourself at this conference, but I am helpless to stop it.'*

My blood ran cold. Hundreds of alphas and their seconds all in one place? That's why Kai was so mad last night when I told him what the shaman said. If that's when I had this massive downloading vision, I would have no other choice but to expose myself. It was scary, but it also might be brilliant. It might be the only way to keep the werewolves from turning against me. I could tell from the look on Kai's face that he would do everything in his power to keep me from going to this conference.

## 17

## PROTECT

The entire week was spent training hard. I pressured Kai and he told me more about this council meeting. Once a year, alphas and their seconds got together to talk about werewolf law and territory, hand down judgments, and most importantly, talk about mating and the issues with our dwindling race. This year it was being held in Canada. Hundreds of our kind would converge on a four-star, werewolf-owned hotel, and carry out the weekend like a business conference.

An alpha and their second were mandated to attend. Kai had pleaded with the council to allow him to bring Max instead of me since I wasn't exactly caught up on werewolf politics, but it was forbidden. I had to attend. I wasn't sure whether to be scared or excited.

Something had been bugging me all week. I hadn't talked to Sylvia since she had offered to open me up to my powers as a witch. I'd given it a lot of thought and now I wondered if it wouldn't help me to have all of my witch powers opened up. After that vampire attack and the chilling warning from Nahuel, it made sense. I slowly padded down the stairs, and approached Kai in our small training room in the basement. He was lifting weights. Sweat gleamed on his muscles and I was glad to see he was alone.

"I want to see Sylvia about opening myself up to my witch powers," I blurted out. I was never good with keeping secrets.

Kai finished his rep and placed the weights slowly on the ground. I had to tell myself to focus on the task at hand and not trail my eyes all over his half-naked, glistening body. He wiped his face clean and looked at me.

"Why?" he asked in a voice devoid of emotion.

"I know you want me to be one hundred percent werewolf, but I'm not. I want to explore this part of myself. It might help me one day if I get into trouble. I could protect myself better." I chewed my lip nervously. I also had a super curious personality and the thought of doing a spell excited the crap out of me.

"Okay." He sighed, sounding defeated. "I agree, it might help you if you were to have more tools in your arsenal."

Really, no big fight? "Thanks for understanding." I gave him a kiss and left to call Sylvia.

Sylvia requested privacy, much to Kai's dissatisfaction. We hiked to a dense part of the woods a few miles from the house. Sylvia had a large blanket spread out with a bunch of crystals, herbs, and a large, worn book.

I sat there nervously while she set up. "So, I heard you had a run-in with the vampires?" she asked coyly.

"We did. There were three … and I killed one." I tried not to react to the look of shock that quickly passed over her face. She didn't think I was capable of killing a vampire? Or she thought it was dangerous for me?

Her face quickly masked the shock and she nodded. "And are you okay with that? I mean, it must have been scary."

I shrugged. "It was, but it was them or me, so I'm fine with defending my life and protecting my family."

Sylvia smiled, so that seemed to be the right thing to say. She had taken a motherly role in my life and I was grateful to have someone to freely speak with. "Good. Now, when I remove this spell that has been encasing your energy, you will have full use of your witch powers. You will need to train with me in order to learn how to use them. Your lineage is strong, and with proper practice you could become a high priestess like me. I have spoken to the rest of my coven. Even though this is unusual—when you are ready, and if you want to—we would like you to inherit your place as a witch in our coven. We understand you are a part of Kai's pack and consider yourself a werewolf, but I wanted to make you the offer, in case this is something you would consider.

I wanted to, badly, but I knew Kai wasn't exactly comfortable with my witch blood. I had always been an avid fantasy reader. One book series I liked was about a witch clan. They had different colored candles for different spells, and I ached to know if this was true now that I knew witches were real.

"I will talk to Kai and think about it," I told her honestly.

She nodded. "Today you will receive your full given name."

"Given name?"

Sylvia nodded. "You know me simply as Sylvia, so you can do me little harm without knowing my full *given* name. When I release your powers, I will name you. Your full magical given name must be kept between the two of us. It's a name given by Spirit through me, and will enhance your powers. If someone were to know this full name, they could also hold great power over you."

I swallowed hard. I guess I had to trust that Sylvia wouldn't try to hold great power over me. As if she knew what I was thinking, she smiled.

"The person who names you can never use your full name for bad intentions. Are you ready?"

I nodded. Now or never.

Sylvia threw her hands up to the sky, standing before me as I sat on the blanket. "I call on my great ancestors, my coven, the Great Spirit, gods and goddesses, and all those who come in the white light. I claim Aurora Maiden Whitefeather as a magic wielder. With intent to protect her, Aurora's witch powers were hidden." A wind picked up and tossed Sylvia's hair in the breeze; her eyes turned white. "I release her powers now! Break down all barriers, Great Spirit, and let her fully walk in her life path. I claim her powers for the light!" She placed her hands on my head.

I was knocked forward on the blanket. It felt like a lightning bolt had struck me. My eyes watered; electricity ran down my spine, and it felt like my nerves were on fire. White mist flowed out from my pores. It climbed across the grass, up the trees, and beyond. Sylvia just stood there and watched in fascination, her jaw slack.

"My stars! I haven't seen this much magic come from any one person in my entire magical life," she exclaimed.

I was panting, my palms out flat on the grass, that electrical feeling finally starting to recede.

*'What's wrong? I'm coming,'* Kai sent.

I couldn't let him see me like this. He would kill Sylvia for hurting me. Even unintentionally.

*'No. I'm fine. Stay where you are,'* I told him. I could feel his hurt through the pack bond. He didn't reply.

Sylvia bent down to my level. "Just breathe. I'm so sorry, I didn't know it would be like this. You have been storing so much magic, it all just ... exploded when I released it."

I breathed deeply, slowly feeling less dizzy, and sat up. "Why do I have so much magic?" I asked between ragged breaths. "I'm a half-breed. Shouldn't I be half as powerful?"

Sylvia chewed on her nail, deep in thought. "I don't think you were born this powerful. I don't remember this much magic in you when you were a baby. Now that my memories have been given back to me, I have spent a lot of time thinking."

"So what is this?" I gestured to the mist surrounding us.

"We have never seen a witch who was turned into a werewolf. We are immune to werewolf and vampire bites. We don't change. We just die. Because your mother had you turned human before the first full moon of your life, and because she had your witch powers hidden, you were simply a human. Then Kai changed you. Changed wolves, as you know, have a very different power structure than wolf-born. Maybe when Kai changed you, it ignited and enhanced your witch powers, only we couldn't see it because they were still hidden but never truly went away. I don't know ... it's just a theory."

I put my head in my hands. "I'm such a freak."

"You're not a freak. You're special." Sylvia smiled, her long auburn hair catching the sun's rays and resembling fire.

*Same thing,* I thought, but she was trying to be nice so I returned her smile.

"The fact that you can see the mist, which is what

magic looks like, tells me you are already a very strong witch. That day in Kai's study when you saw the mist, I was a bit in shock, really. Only very trained witches can *see* magic. Most witches just smell or sense it half the time. That will give you an advantage in defending yourself against other magic users."

"Great," I said sarcastically. I already had vampires after me. I didn't need witches as well. I had wanted to ask Sylvia something since my conversation with the shaman. I figured now was as good a time as any. "Sylvia, why do witches do business with vampires if they are so bad?"

She smoothed her long auburn hair over one shoulder. "There are white witches, like me, and dark witches. White witches do spells to help people, and this sometimes requires vampire blood. In return, we help the vampires with simple spells, to increase their strength, to heal their human blood slaves, or to find a lost object. Dark witches do very bad things in return for blood payment. But witches are neutral, so we serve all. We do business with humans, vampires, and werewolves. That's our place."

"If there came a time to choose between being on the side of the vampires or the side of the werewolves, do you think the witches would choose?" I asked her, trying not to let the fear show in my voice.

Her eyebrows pinched in concern. "Is there something I should know, Aurora?"

I shook my head. "Not yet." I was trying to be

truthful, and I really had no proof yet that what the shaman said was true.

"Humans have persecuted witches for hundreds of years. They fear what they do not know. They have always been the weak race, and yet there is something beautiful about their short and passionate life spans. They are so helpless. I guess if something ever happened where witches had to choose, my coven would side with the humans and whoever protected them." She placed her hand over mine and I nodded. That's what I needed to hear.

"Call me if you have questions about your new abilities, and think about what I said, about joining my clan. We do a weekly spell casting and meditation that I would love for you to be a part of. But I understand this is all overwhelming, so just take some time."

I wasn't sure time would help, but I nodded and helped her gather her things, then we made our way back to the house.

I saw Sylvia off and then I walked inside, prepared for a possible showdown with Kai. He was against me opening myself up to my witch powers, and he would have felt my distress during the spell. When I walked in, I saw Kai was sitting in a reading chair with an old book in his lap. Breathing in deeply, he looked at me, his head quirked to the side. "You smell different," he said.

I smelled my arm. "Should I shower?"

Kai smirked. "No, your natural scent. You smell

like a witch now." The way he said, it didn't sound like a good thing.

"Oh, yeah, about that..." I sat on his lap, needing to be close to him as he played with the texture on my jeans. I told him what had happened with Sylvia, and that she'd invited me to join her clan. There was a long pause.

"You want to be a witch *and* a werewolf?" His voice was deadpan but I knew he wasn't happy about this.

"I want to be who I am," I answered truthfully.

His resolve broke. "I love who you are, and if that means you are a witch, then so be it. Just don't do any weird magic on me."

I laughed and leaned closer, brushing my lips against his, causing him to moan lightly as I ran my fingers through his thick hair.

"And don't steal my hair," he added.

We both laughed at that, but then Kai gave me a hooded stare as he eyed my cleavage. I licked my lips, purposely trying to entice him. As he leaned in to kiss me, there was a knock at the door.

Kai groaned. "Come in, Max," he muttered, and I just smiled as I inhaled through my nose. Yep, it was Max. I was still amazed at my new werewolf abilities.

Max peeked his head in. "Ready?"

Kai looked at me. "Yes." He stood. "I'm running an errand with Max. I'll be back in a few hours." He winked at me.

"Okay, I'll go check on Emma." I followed them

out and headed over to Emma's. Even though she wasn't that far along yet, the entire pack had been going over to help her cook or clean so that she didn't strain herself. She didn't argue, but I could tell she didn't want to be babied too much. We couldn't help it though; our first pup would be born to one of our most cherished and submissive wolves. The instinct to protect her was overwhelming.

# 18
## YES

Now that we had the Portland territory, it didn't seem necessary to open a new Gresham location of Safe Haven, but Kai assured me he still wanted to invest the money in the cause, and today was its grand opening, just one day before Kai and I left for the alpha council meeting.

I had hired my mother to manage the Portland location, and offered her a nice salary. This would eventually get her out of that crappy trailer she lived in.

Kai was a genius when it came to running a business. He paid for billboards to attract donations, and now we had blankets, clothing, and water bottles flooding our two sites. We also had large businesses donating money, and volunteers in exchange for good press and their logo on our signs. The center was practically running itself on donations, something I had barely managed before.

As Kai exited the freeway to the new Safe Haven location, I could see a line had formed around the block. Women and children clutched pillowcases and teddy bears, all waiting to get into the center.

"My God," Kai breathed.

My heart hammered in my chest as I leaned forward in my seat. There must have been thirty families on the street, waiting for us to open. A few were peering in the glass doors. A large sign above the converted high school read, "Grand opening, Safe Haven: A new place to call home, for families of domestic violence." There were news vans and reporters outside as well. Seeing the little girl with her teddy bear brought back too many haunting memories of my own. I had to shake them off and focus. These women and children needed us.

A few cars full of pack members followed us into the parking lot. I hadn't expected such a big turnout the first day. Before Kai had even put the car in park, I jumped out and headed toward the door with keys in hand. Kai was right behind me, and some of the women backed away and looked down, fearful of his large stature.

"Welcome to Safe Haven, everyone!" I shouted to the crowd as a news camera was shoved in my face.

Kai pulled the keys from my hand and spoke to the crowd. "You are safe now. You may stay here as long as you need to, and there is no charge. Please come in."

Kai unlocked the doors. The cameraman moved to capture a shot of the crowd entering, and Kai plucked it out of the man's hand and pointed it toward the floor.

"Some of these women have left abusive situations, and those abusers will be looking for them. You are not to film the women and children's faces, only the volunteers and the facility. Do you understand me?" Kai's voice was growly and pissed off.

The reporter stood next to the cameraman; they both nodded their understanding nervously to Kai.

The pack helped the women and children get settled into their rooms, and began handing out water bottles, hygiene kits, and welcome packets. I spent most of the morning just watching in stunned silence and welcoming each family. This was so much bigger than I had ever imagined. I was overwhelmed with joy. This was good work, work I was proud of.

Kai had warned me that the upcoming alpha conference would be hard. There would be a lot of dominant males and very few women. Also, I was technically unmated, so that would play a part. But today I didn't care. As I saw the little children jumping on the bunk beds in their new rooms, the mothers trying to cover their bruises with their hair, I knew I was doing good. If I died now, I would have left my positive mark on the world.

The logistics were set. The pack would take shifts guarding Safe Haven from any abusive persons looking for their families. We would all rotate teaching self-defense classes, to whoever wanted them, in the multipurpose gym. Kai had also set up a once-a-month job fair for the jobless women to try to get back on their feet. It was more than my mother and I had when we tried to leave my dad dozens of times. In the end, it was death that parted us from my father—luckily, not mine or my mother's. I shivered, thinking of that night.

"You okay?" Kai asked me. We had been driving home in silence and I was reflecting on the day. Smiling, I reached over to grab his hand.

"I'm more than okay. I'm happy," I assured him.

He grinned. "Good." And cleared his throat. "I knew opening Safe Haven would bring in women and children that came from abuse, but ... I don't think I was prepared for what I saw today. I wanted to make them all a part of our pack so that I could take care of them and protect them. That one little girl had a bruise in the shape of a hand on her arm. Did you see that? I could kill whoever did that to her!"

I nodded. "That's why I opened Safe Haven in the first place. So many women are dreaming of the day they can walk out of their abusive situations, but they don't have the money or the guts. At least we can give them a place to stay and some food in their bellies." I shrugged.

"We will give them more than that." Kai turned to look at me and I held his gaze. "We will give them futures."

That's when I knew, without a doubt, this man was made for me and I for him.

By the time we pulled up to the house, it was dark

out. I jumped out of the car and was halfway to the door when Kai spoke behind me.

"Wanna go for a run?" he asked.

I spun around, grinning. "Yes." Running in my wolf form was my new favorite thing.

Kai looked nervous as he fumbled with the buttons on his shirt.

"You okay?" I asked.

"Yeah." He brushed me off and shifted quickly, dashing into the forest. Okay, weirdo.

I quickly stripped down and shifted, taking off after him. He had confided to me earlier that he was nervous to take me to the alpha council meeting. Hell, I was nervous myself. If the shaman could be believed, I was going to have a pretty crazy time there having visions of hundreds of mates and revealing my gift to the werewolf community. But Kai had become my rock, not just my alpha but my mate. I needed him not to be weird. I needed him normal. To think of it, he had been weird all day. Maybe seeing all those women at the shelter had reminded Kai of my dark past and freaked him out.

I couldn't see him anywhere, so I stuck my nose close to the ground and picked up his scent near a cluster of pine trees. Darting between them, I went around the back side of our property, near Emma and Devon's house. None of the pack members had backyard fences. We all roamed each others' property freely. I was about to call out for Kai when I came out into a clearing and saw hundreds of tea lights. A soft blue blanket covered the ground and a picnic dinner had been set up. Kai had shifted to human form and changed into clothes. I gave him a wolfish grin. I loved surprises and this one was epic. Moonlight dinner right after opening a second Safe Haven location ... perfect. Music played softly from a CD player as Kai looked at me with a grin.

"Shift and then change. I brought you some clothes." He turned his back to give me privacy. This was super romantic. Here I thought he had been acting weird, and he was just trying to surprise me with a picnic date.

Shifting quickly, I slipped into the short red dress he had picked out from my closet, then I walked barefoot over to him and wrapped my arms around him from behind. When he spun around, I saw a small, navy-blue, velvet ring box in his hands. My heart started pulsing wildly as my breath hitched.

"Aurora, that night that you got into the car accident was the worst and best night of my life. When I saw you lying there on the road bleeding out, you looked so innocent and beautiful. I couldn't imagine you dying. Then, when I changed you, I feared you wouldn't survive. When you survived, I feared you would be someone else's mate. I have felt pulled to you since I first saw you and now I know why. You are my soul mate. I know you haven't had the best view of men, but I will never hurt you, I will always protect you. Your passions will become mine and I will support you in whatever you do. I respect that you want to take things slowly, but I will go crazy if you don't say you will marry me. Marry me now, marry me in ten years, but please tell me you will marry me."

Tears were streaming down my face as I looked down at his hands, which held a large circle-cut diamond ring.

"Yes! I will marry you," I croaked out, and then laughed as he picked me up and spun me around. I laughed louder as joy bubbled up through me.

There's this thing we do as victims of abuse. We tell ourselves we'll never be happy, we'll never trust, but in that moment I shattered all that negative self-talk. My past was gone. I shed it right then and there. Kai was my future and I had never been happier. He kissed me sweetly and I relished the feeling of his soft, pillowy lips, my fingers raking down the side of the stubble dotting his jawline. He was mine. Forever. He gently set me down and pulled back, meeting my gaze.

"Not in ten years, right?" he prodded.

I smiled. "How about three months?"

## 19

## ALPHA

I woke up the day of the council meeting and immediately my eyes flew to my left hand. There it was. Oh my God, I was getting married. A light snore next to me drew my attention to the muscular mountain of a man that was my fiancé. Kai looked so calm when he was asleep, almost submissive.

His eyes popped opened. "Morning, fiancée." He smiled.

"How did you sleep?"

"Better than I have in decades." He rolled on top of me, holding his weight up with his muscular arms, and bent his head down to kiss me. As his hips pressed into mine, I gave a soft moan that had him nipping my bottom lip.

Then the alarm went off on the nightstand, and he groaned. "We have a plane to catch."

"And don't look the council members in the eyes," Kai drilled into me.

"Okay," I muttered for the fiftieth time.

"And don't take your ring off. You're mine," he lightly chastised.

I rolled my eyes. "Okay, okay, okay." Kai had been drilling me with rules for the council meeting. We were ten thousand feet in the air and I was nervous enough. I hadn't had any visions since Diya and Trent's mate vision. Still, the shaman's words echoed in my mind. Kai said the council members were made up of the oldest, strongest, most dominant werewolves in the world. Their word was law and their packs were made up of enforcers that could wipe you out of existence. I shuddered. They'd better not come for me or my pack. My inner wolf agreed. Most nerve-racking of all, his father was one of the council members. I had yet to meet him properly; this would be the first time.

We stood in front of a sign that read, "NAWAC." We were at the entrance of a fancy four-star hotel. Hundreds of werewolves were pushing past us into the revolving doors, bringing their foreign wolf scents with them.

*'North American Werewolf Alpha Council,'* Kai sent to me.

"Ready?" he asked.

I could only nod, grabbing his hand I following him into the entrance of the building. Nerves didn't even begin to describe how I felt. Right away, something felt off. I noticed people turned to slowly stare at me. As we passed they breathed in deeply, as if smelling me.

"Shit, I forgot," Kai swore, and put a protective hand on my lower back.

"What?" I asked, as more and more people began to look my way.

*'You smell like a witch. Werewolves don't like witches.'*

We were already at the doors of the large conference room and Kai seemed unsure if he wanted to go in or turn around. Two large men flanked each side of the door. My heart stopped when one inhaled deeply.

"We don't allow her kind in here, brother, you know that," the man told Kai, eyeing me like I was some side piece.

Kai's face took on a menacing look. "She's my mate," Kai said with alpha-infused magic lacing his words. I could feel the power Kai had put out, like a wet blanket on my skin.

I shifted part of my face to a werewolf and made a low growl, showing the guard that I was in fact one of them.

The man looked at me, confused, but shook it off, opening the door with his head bowed to Kai.

We entered the huge room and my gaze carried the length of the space, taking in the hundreds of chairs that had been set up, all facing a stage where the twelve council members sat. Eleven were male; only one was female. They all wore hardened expressions and sat a few feet apart. I could feel how they radiated power; it pressed on my skin and made me want to bow my head. There was mist hovering just above their skin like an aura. These were the most dominant wolves in the world.

As if they saw me looking, they glanced my way and I picked out Kai's father immediately. Large stature, medium-dark skin, and the same wild, unruly hair. Was that pride in his eyes? I quickly looked to the ground as I remembered Kai's advice not to make eye contact, but I could still feel their eyes on me.

"Hey, strangers," a familiar voice snapped me out of my trance.

Shamus and his second approached Kai and me, but when Shamus reached me, he stopped abruptly.

"Kai, with all due respect, why does Aurora smell like a full-blown witch?" Shamus looked around the room and I saw that almost every eye was on us.

Kai started breathing heavily, veins popping in his neck. "This was a bad idea. We're leaving." He grabbed my arm to leave when a voice boomed from the stage.

"Kai, you dare bring a witch into one of our sacred council meetings? You know better!"

Kai spun around and faced the council member. I stared at the man's leather-clad feet. "She is my mate!" Kai roared.

"She smells like a witch. She has you fooled. This is some kind of magic she's done on you! Guards!" the councilman yelled. Kai and I must have been thinking the same thing, because we both shifted into our wolf form at the same time. I shook my fur quickly to crawl out of my clothes, and took stock of the situation. This was bad. Why had I talked to Sylvia about unleashing my witch powers? Stupid. Now I looked like some imposter, and if these people wanted it done, we would be torn apart right here.

I heard gasps as people saw my wolf form.

On the stage, the female council member stood.

"She's a werewolf? Why does she smell of witch? She must have done a spell to take on a wolf's form." Her gaze went from Kai to me, no doubt wondering how we had the same markings.

*'Why isn't your dad saying anything?'* I asked Kai.

*'Because I made him take the oath!'* he replied. *'He can't talk about you without putting his whole pack at risk. We are on our own.'*

Shit. Shamus approached the council and bowed his head lightly. "She is a werewolf. One of Kai's wolves, Sadie, recently joined my pack and I have seen her thoughts. Sadie was there when Aurora survived the change. Aurora has the protection of me and my pack, so look for another explanation of why she smells of witch." There was a subtle threat laced into his voice, and his second took up a stance in front of me. Shamus backed up slowly until he flanked Kai's right side. Off to the side, I noticed the guards had shifted now and were surrounding us.

"You think if we wanted her dead that you four could stop it?" roared the female councilwoman.

She burst from the stage and began to walk toward

me, the crowd parting letting her pass. Kai bent low and growled, positioning himself in front of me.

*'If anyone makes a move against us, I want you to run,'* he told me. *'You are fast, you can get out. They won't expect it.'*

*'If anyone makes a move against us, I'm going to rip their head off,'* I sent back to him. *'I'm not leaving you.'*

The council member now stood a few feet from Kai, her towering presence commanding attention.

"Kai, I thought better of you. You are such a wise and powerful wolf. We have asked you thrice to join the council and thrice you have denied us. It would be a shame to dispose of you..."

I growled deeply and prepared to pounce on her. *No one* was disposing of my mate.

Kai's father stepped finally forward. "She's a werewolf!" he roared. I could feel power radiating off of him. It slapped out at us, brushing our fur. Would he fight for us? I wasn't sure.

The councilwoman looked back over her shoulder at him. "Don't protect your son. Has she bewitched you, too? I know what I smell! My nose does not lie."

I looked the councilwoman in the eyes. I didn't care if it was against the rules, this bitch needed to know she wasn't hurting my family—no one was. The second I locked eyes with her, her face fell. She stumbled back in shock, and that's when the vision hit me.

*'Oh shit, bad timing,'* I muttered before collapsing in weakness.

This vision wasn't like the others. This was a simultaneous explosion of knowledge in my head, but part of my consciousness remained with my body. It was terrifying. I knew without a doubt that the councilwoman's name was Jane and she was lonely. A lifetime of loneliness had made her bitter. When she rose to a position of councilwoman, it had satisfied her to a certain degree, but she yearned for more. She yearned for a mate and children. She had many lovers, but nothing compared to the bond you had with a mate. She knew something was missing, and I knew where her mate was. It was painful. My visions had never hurt before, but this one crippled me. My head threatened to explode, and I heard Kai whine beside me.

I was vaguely aware of Jane approaching me, and Kai growled.

"At ease, wolf. She is one of us. I see that now. What is happening to her?" she asked Kai. Was that concern in her voice?

Kai took a deep breath. "She is the Matefinder," he replied; he must have changed form. There was a collective gasp of the surrounding wolves. "And with all due respect, if you touch her, I will kill you."

In my vision I could see the councilwoman's mate playing cards with his fellow pack members in a small pack in Utah. He was a mid-level pack member with a nice smile. Then I saw her wedding, and later, her laughing children running through the snow. I became aware of energy signatures. Each wolf in this building had different energy, and I was out of my body now. I could see my wolf lying on the floor shaking as Kai whined next to me. My soul was out, walking around to each wolf, touching their faces, looking into their eyes. With each contact, I was given the exact location of their mate. If they were already mated, I moved on. Sometimes, I was given multiple people in their pack mate's location. An hour must have gone by before I reached the last person in the room, so I made my way back to my body. Kai was half-dressed, looking utterly gutted. My wolf lay in his lap; he stroked my fur. There was a crowd now. Jane sat patiently in human form a few feet from my body. Just as I was going to fall back into my body, I heard a wind chime behind me and turned toward the noise.

The Shaman Nahuel was standing a few feet from me. He looked spectral and unreal.

"Trust your people with the truth. It's all you have to protect you. The war has begun. The future you see in your visions can change. The future is always changing. Emma may not survive long enough to see her pup born. You may not survive long enough to wed Kai. Now more than ever, the wolves are on the brink of extinction. The vampires have waged war." He raised his hand, bowed his head, and then he was gone.

I stood over my body, mouth agape at the shaman's words. What the hell?!

"Aurora! You come back to me this instant!" Kai was screaming now, and I felt the pull; I fell into my body all at once and woke up. I immediately began to shift into human form and Jane threw a tablecloth over my naked body. I needed to be human in order to talk my way out of this.

Meeting Jane's eyes, I told her, "I know who your mate is."

Her hand flew to her mouth. "Is this a sick joke? The Matefinder is dead, a legend."

"She's a witch," a male council member screamed from the stage.

Jane extended her hand and looked at Kai. "Let me use my power on her. To make them see."

I looked at Kai, confused.

"She's a projector," he told me. "She can project your vision to anyone's mind. She will be able to see inside your head. You won't be able to keep anything from her. Makes for a useful gift when interrogating people." Kai grumbled the last part.

She would know I was part witch. She would know there was a war starting with the vampires. She would know everything about my past. I looked in her eyes and was surprised to see kindness there. She wanted to believe me, wanted to find her mate. I had to trust her. Like Nahuel said, I had to trust my people.

I reached for her hand. The second my skin touched hers, I felt her presence in my mind and it all became too much. My body became heavy and blackness hit me. I crumpled into Kai's waiting arms.

## 20

## EMMA

I CAME to and was aware of whispering. I felt a smooth, comfortable bed beneath my body, and opened my eyes to see that I was in a hotel room. The council members surrounded me; Kai was inches from my face, as usual. Groaning, I tried to sit up but winced. I had a splitting headache.

"Ten hours," Kai breathed, and his eyes turned yellow as he gave me space to sit up.

I grabbed my head. "Huh?"

"You were unconscious for ten hours. Don't ever do that again."

"I don't plan on it. Talk softly. My head is killing me."

Jane stepped forward then. "Aurora, I saw everything. I projected your vision of the mates to the wolves in attendance here today—but I withheld any knowledge of the shaman's prophecy about the vampire war. That, I have only shared with the council." She pulled at the hem of her shirt anxiously.

Kai's face looked strained; his father wore an angry expression. There was something they weren't telling me. I tuned into our pack bond and felt ... rage.

I sat up straighter; all worries of my headache fled. "What else aren't you telling me?"

Kai held my hand softly and spoke through gritted teeth. "While we were away here at the conference, the vampires kidnapped a female from our pack. It happened right after you collapsed."

"No!" I screamed, and my blood ran cold. "Who is it? Who did they take?"

I knew before the answer left his mouth. I could feel her energy through the pack bond—*fear*.

"Emma," he whispered.

A sob escaped me. How dare they? She was pregnant and she was ours! The lamp on the side table near the bed suddenly exploded. Everyone flinched except for me. My chest was rising and falling as I tried to contain my rage; a fine mist leaked out from my pores. The vampires were sending us a message. They were sending *me* a message. How dare they take a pregnant female from *my* pack. In this moment, I felt murderous. A painting flew off of the wall and crashed to the floor.

"Aurora!" Kai barked, and I looked up. Two of the council members had shifted into their wolf forms and the rest were regarding me fearfully. Kai's father was the only one who looked intrigued. Oh crap. My witch magic was out of control. I closed my eyes and took a deep breath.

"Take me home, Kai. We need to get Emma back."

---

THE SECOND WE landed at the airport in Portland, Kai was on his phone. The pack had been frantically following vampire scents all day, but it hadn't led to much. They found a few well-known vampire bars and covens, but none that had Emma. She had been taken from her home, and Max and Devon nearly died trying to protect her. They were still recovering from their injuries.

We pulled our car up to the house to see that the entire pack had assembled. They spilled out into the lawn covering Kai's entire property. We had pulled in all of our peripheral wolves, and every wolf from Portland. Kai also received a call from Shamus that he would send some of his wolves to help us get Emma back. My mate stood on a picnic table in the backyard and addressed the entire pack.

"Emma was taken from us and we will not rest until she is back home. A pregnant female member of the pack is the most cherished, the most loved. The vampires have sent a message—they intend to wipe out our race!" Kai dropped the big bomb and the wolves shouted in rage. A few shifted and howled.

"That isn't going to happen. I protect what is *mine* and Emma is MINE! She is *yours*!" Kai roared and his alpha magic rippled through the pack bond, bringing a murderous rage with it. I had to fight the urge to shift. My wolf wanted out. I had to find Emma. I could vaguely feel her through the bond and what I felt wasn't good. If they hurt her, if she lost her baby ... I couldn't even think about it.

An idea crossed my mind then. I broke into a run as Kai shouted my name. Running from the backyard and toward Emma's house, I burst through the door. Four long strides and I was in the bathroom she shared with Devon. I scanned the counter and landed on what I was looking for, her hairbrush. The tiny red hairs gave me hope.

---

Sylvia came the second I called and she didn't come alone. She brought two other witches with her. Shamus had driven from Seattle with his wolves as well, and we all gathered around our living room.

I approached Sylvia with the hairbrush. "The vampires have taken a pregnant female member from our pack. We have to find her. I have Emma's hairbrush and I was hoping you could do a spell to find her location."

Sylvia looked calm, but the other two witches seemed nervous.

Sylvia addressed the room. "This morning we were sent a message from the vampires as well. They told us they were waging war with the wolves ... and if we interfered they would burn our coven to the ground. Similar messages were given to other covens across the country."

I was shocked at the news, but no one else in the room seemed to be. I guess that was how the vampires did things. Kai nodded. "We understand if you need to protect your coven."

Sylvia smiled. "Threatening to burn us doesn't exactly make us like you. Vampires have always acted above us. They think they are the strongest race. Our coven will help you and any other wolf packs in need."

I stared at the two witches she'd brought with her. "Do you agree?" I asked them, because they seemed hesitant.

The older of the two nodded. "I won't lie, I sense trouble for our coven if we help you. Witches are supposed to be neutral. But what's neutral about watching an entire supernatural race get wiped out? Who will protect the humans if the wolves are gone? We must take a side, even if we don't live to see the results."

Sylvia's eyes flared white. "We will live. Everyone always underestimates a witch." The hairs on my arms stood on end. Kai looked at me thoughtfully.

Sylvia grabbed the brush from me. She spread out a map of the United States, and pulled a pendulum from a black velvet sack. One of the witches walked around the room pouring a circle of white salt, enclosing both wolves and witches inside. Sylvia pulled a few hairs from the brush and wound them around the pendulum, then she turned to Kai. "I need powerful blood for this spell."

He extended his arm without hesitation and she sliced him, taking a few small drops onto the point of a sharp, clear crystal. The three witches stood in a semi-circle then, holding hands around the map.

"This casting is blessed. Protect us from harm or prying eyes. With the power of three, I invoke thee!" Mist poured out of the three witches' hands and I inched forward. There was a circle of mist hovering above the map, and it fascinated me. I hadn't yet been able to take Sylvia up on her offer to attend a weekly spell-casting meeting. This was as close as I was going to get for now.

Sylvia took a deep breath and chanted: "A wrong has been done. Help us make it right. Find this girl on this night. The vampires stole her from her bed. We offer these hairs from her head. Point out her location, show us now. Help us find her, show us how!"

She held the pendulum over the map and it spun wildly. The other witches were holding hands in a circle above the map, the last witch's hand resting on Sylvia's shoulder to complete the circle. Mist was starting to move in a funnel above the witches' heads. My jaw hung open in wonder at the sight.

"We're being blocked," Sylvia grumbled.

"Dark witches aid these vampires," one of the other witches said. "Black magic keeps their location secret."

"No!" I shouted, and mist started seeping out of my skin. This wasn't happening! Emma would be the first werewolf in our pack to have a child. She brought so much hope and happiness to this pack. She was such a sweet person and she had become my best friend. We weren't giving up that easily.

Sylvia's eyes met mine and something unspoken passed between us. I walked toward the circle, placed my hand inside Sylvia's, and held the pendulum with my other. I felt another hand clasp over my shoulder, and the new circle was complete.

"Emma is ours. We're not giving up on her. She's a good person and no amount of dark magic can conceal her from me!" I shouted. A blast of mist shot out of my hand and the spinning pendulum stilled. I heard the wolves suck in a breath and I glanced over to Kai.

He looked disappointed.

*'I'm still a werewolf. I'm just a witch, too,'* I told him. He pursed his lips and nodded.

I looked down to see that the pendulum was pointing to Los Angeles. "Gotcha," I said. If she was hurt, heads would roll.

Who was I kidding? Heads would roll either way.

Pain exploded behind my forehead and I shrieked. I saw the face of a dark-haired witch in my mind's eye. Sylvia ripped the pendulum from my hand, breaking the circle to toss the pendulum into a pile of white salt. "Be gone!" she shouted, and the pressure in my head eased. The dark-haired witch was gone from my mind, but the fear of her presence stayed in my gut.

---

Kai and Shamus stood side by side, addressing their packs together. Everyone had come together in an effort to go after Emma, though Kai had ordered forty-five wolves to stay back and protect the territory. If this was a trap, we didn't want any more wolves getting taken while we were gone. Sadie was out of town on her honeymoon and had no idea Emma had been taken. Kai tried to get me to stay, but I insisted on going to help bring Emma home. Devon was healing nicely, and Kai had okayed him to go along as well. If Kai were kidnapped, it would be impossible to keep me from my mate, and I expected no different from Devon, injured or not.

Kai disappeared for a few minutes and returned with two large duffle bags. Crouching down, he unzipped them and pulled out a crossbow, silver stakes, and various other weapons.

"Whoa!" I exclaimed. "You've had these this entire time?"

Kai nodded. "We have never needed them before. Vampires and werewolves generally leave each other alone. Guess we will be carrying them more often."

He began tossing them out to select wolves in the pack, then he gave a bag to Shamus. "I want half the rescue party to be human with weapons, and half on all fours. These bloodsuckers will pay for taking Emma."

Every menacing face that looked back and nodded, only served to increase my hope that we would get Emma out of there alive.

## 21

## DUFF

On the way to the airport, seventy-six wolves in all, Kai had his hand protectively on my thigh as I played with my engagement ring, which I had strung on a silver chain around my neck. When I had shifted at the council meeting, it had fallen to the ground, later retrieved by Kai. I didn't want that to happen again. Most of the mated wolves had rings around their necks, or tattooed rings on their fingers. Since I was immune to silver, I thought it might make a nice secondary weapon.

"If I could lock you up in the closet and leave you behind, I would," Kai told me, with one hand on the wheel of our SUV. "But then you wouldn't trust me and I couldn't live with that."

I glanced at him, and nodded. If he locked me up I would kick his alpha butt for sure.

"We're getting Emma back *together*," was all I said, staring out the window at the trees as they flew past.

Truth was, I had a horrible feeling. There was a pit in my stomach; something told me we should turn back.

"With all of the flying we have been doing, I might invest in a private plane," Kai mused. "Luke has his pilot's license."

We pulled around to a small side entrance of the airport, where the private planes were kept. One of Shamus' pack members was going to sneak all of our weapons aboard our private chartered jet. We dropped the bags off with him, and then pulled the SUV around to the main entrance. It was late and this part of the airport was all but deserted. A man in a nice suit approached us, asked for our names and the name of our private pilot. There were about fifteen SUVs in our party, and I glanced in the rearview mirror at the line of cars behind me. As Kai rolled the window down, I got a whiff of something. *Vampire.* Kai must have smelled it too, because instead of talking to the man, he hit the gas and charged the gate. The metal doors scraped against the car as they popped open. I was thrust forward slightly with the force of the hit, and at the same time I heard a thump on our roof. Glancing behind us, out the back window, I saw dozens of vampires raining down on the cars from the roof of the airport's small side building.

"What the hell! Can they fly?" I asked Kai. He swerved hard to the right and the vampire holding onto the roof of our car tumbled off the side, hitting the pavement. Kai, Devon, Max, Isabelle, and I were all in the same car. Max and Devon were already pulling weapons, while Izzy watched the spectacle with a cool façade. It took a lot to rile her up; she was tough as nails and had volunteered to help get Emma back.

"They can jump really high—kinda the same thing." Kai got on his phone as he was speeding toward a large white plane on the tarmac. The cars behind us made a barricade by parking themselves sideways to block the vampires from coming near.

I looked at Kai and he nodded as if confirming my thoughts. We were going to have to save Emma alone. Just the five of us.

"Go! Start down the runway!" he screamed to the pilot over his phone.

Luckily the pilot for hire was a wolf or this might have been hard to explain. The plane started rolling and Kai slammed on the brakes. We all opened our doors, jumped out of the car, and started running. My feet hit the pavement and I took off. Izzy was ahead of me, running next to the rolling plane just as the door to the plane opened and a stewardess put her arm out and lifted Izzy up. Next was Max, and then Devon. Once inside, Max reached out for me, and I was about to take it when I heard Kai scream behind me.

Turning around, I saw a vampire on Kai's back, biting my mate's neck. I turned, shifting instantly, shredding my clothes, and barreled in Kai's direction on all fours, forgetting the plane entirely. Max was screaming my name as I lunged through the air and sank my teeth into the vampire's right arm, using the momentum to pull him off of Kai. The vamp and I hit the pavement and rolled as Kai shifted into his wolf form. The vampire took one look at me and smiled. Then he popped up into the air and glided away from us and back into the bigger fight at the gate. What the hell? Since when do they run away?

I could hear Max screaming again, and looked to see the plane's wheels just barely leaving the tarmac about a hundred feet away from us. The door was still open. Kai and I shared a look and then we took off running. I had never run so fast in my life. I almost tripped over my own paws, I was running with such blinding speed. I was the one to reach the plane first. With one giant leap, I lunged in through the small opening, scraping my back on the top of the door, and tumbled, smacking my shoulder against a seat.

I quickly moved out of the way as Kai landed hard right next to me. The plane shook a little with his weight and he whimpered, but otherwise seemed okay. The vampire bite on his shoulder was bleeding, oozing a blackish fluid. I had started shifting back into my human form when I noticed that the female stewardess smelled like a human. She pulled a first-aid kit from an upper cabinet and laid it in front of Kai.

Once we had both shifted, the stewardess threw Kai and I one of those small scratchy airplane blankets. I wrapped mine under my arms like a dress and looked at Max. "Can you get us some clothes? Did the weapons make it on the plane?" I wasn't sure what provisions we had, and I was still mourning the brand new fifty-dollar bra I'd just ripped in half.

Max nodded. "Weapons are here," he told me, and threw us some clothes. They weren't mine, nor were they female, but that didn't matter.

I looked at Kai. "You got bit by a vampire. What does that mean?" I was hoping it didn't mean what I thought it did, but I was trying to stay calm.

He smiled. "Very painful. Will take a few days to heal. But I'll be fine."

I let out a relieved sigh.

I looked again at the stewardess. She didn't seem fazed; she was making cups of ice for drinks and humming to herself.

Noticing my stare, she said, "It's okay, I'm a duff."

"A duff?" I began to clean Kai's wound with the kit she'd laid out.

"My parents are witches but I was born without magic—a lower-class citizen in the witch world. I make my living by serving the supernatural community, but I have no power."

Oh. Well, that sucked.

Kai spoke to my mind: *'Some dark witches put curses on other witches' unborn children. These children are born without magic but are given the knowledge of the supernatural community.'*

'That's horrible.'

He nodded.

Izzy spoke up. "So what the hell was that? Why didn't we see them coming? Do you think the pack we left back at home are okay?"

Kai considered this. "I can sense the feelings of the

wolves we left behind on the mountain. They are worried for Emma but they're not under attack. We left enough members back that they should be okay if the vampires do attack. We know that territory better than anyone. Everyone will protect Tristan and the kids. Don't worry."

Izzy seemed assured, but before she could speak again we all felt it, like a knife to the heart, as one of our peripheral wolves, Joey, who had come to the airport with us, was killed. It was like a string being pulled through my body and out of my heart. His pack essence was there one moment and then gone the next. Kai screamed in pain and the stewardess dropped a glass, which shattered everywhere.

The vampires were picking off our already small numbers one by one, and it only served to increase my rage. We flew the rest of the way to Los Angeles in silent mourning.

---

THE STEWARDESS HANDED Kai a satellite phone. "It's the Los Angeles alpha," she told him.

Kai groaned. He hadn't had time to stop and ask our permission for coming into the Los Angeles alpha's territory. Someone from the pack we left back must have called him. If he was calling us, it wasn't good. Maybe he was denying us permission. Anger flared up inside me and I growled lightly, but Kai silenced me with one look.

"Hello, Kristoff," Kai grumbled into the phone. By his tone of voice it didn't seem he thought this would be a good call either. After a few seconds Kai sat up straighter. "Excuse me?"

I leaned in trying to listen, but the noise from the plane was too loud, even for my sensitive werewolf hearing.

"Well, we would appreciate that. Thank you. We should be landing shortly." With that, Kai hung up.

We all stared at him, waiting.

"The Los Angeles alpha will be sending a few cars and ten of his strongest men," Kai said, dumbfounded. "They have sniffed out the vampire hideout and want to help us get Emma." I was guessing alphas didn't usually reach out and help other alphas like this on a regular basis.

Max made a low whistle.

Kai looked at me. "Werewolves usually keep to themselves and fight to the death over protecting their territory. It seems now that they will do anything if it helps you, Aurora. Kristoff sends his thanks for finding his mate at the conference."

Yes! Kristoff. He'd been in the room when I'd gotten the vision. I remembered his mate clearly. Black straight hair with blunt-cut bangs.

I shifted nervously in my seat. "Whatever helps Emma." Searching the pack bonds, I could feel she was still there, but the connection was weak. If they drugged her or hurt her … I couldn't even think about it!

*'I've tried to contact Emma multiple times, but I'm being blocked,'* Kai told me. *'So is Devon.'*

It was that witch! The one who saw me looking for them when I did the pendulum spell with Sylvia. If I had trained with Sylvia maybe I could break through and reach Emma, give her hope. I tried to send her a message but felt nothing. I glanced over at Devon; he looked so lost.

"We are beginning our descent," the pilot said over the speaker.

No witch, no vampire, no supernatural could hide Emma from us now. I could feel a bloodthirsty craze starting to hum just under my skin. Emma was an innocent and she would be saved.

---

SIXTEEN WAS A GOOD NUMBER. It was how old I was when I got freedom from my drunken father in the form of my license and an old beat-up car. It was the amount of money I had in my bank account before I started Safe Haven. It was also the number of wolves we were about to barge into the vampire den with to save Emma.

We surrounded the old house on Melrose Avenue and I could smell Emma inside. I also smelled witches and vampires, a lot of them. It was dusk, and I had been told on the ride over that dark witches did spells on powerful vampires to give them sunlight immunity, so attacking in the daytime wouldn't increase our chances.

Kai turned to me and placed a silver stake in my hand. It had a rubber grip to protect werewolf skin—not that it mattered much to me. "You're a good fighter. You will be a bigger help to Emma in human form. You go in last." It was a command, but his eyes held vulnerability. He was trying to protect me. As long as I helped get Emma out, I didn't care. I wouldn't push him on this. I nodded and gripped the cold stake in my hand, ready for blood.

Kai lightly kissed my cheek and then began to shift. I took in a deep breath to calm myself. I had never been religious—what kind of God lets kids get abused? But I sent up a silent prayer now. Please let Emma be okay. Let her baby live through this.

The most haunting howl cut through the night. I saw Devon smashing through a side window in his wolf form, with Kai following in right behind him. The fight had begun. I crept around the side of the house, where one of the Los Angeles pack wolves had smashed in the front door. Hissing and screaming rang out into the night as two vampires, doused in flames, fled through the front door. Before I could take a step toward the house, a cold hand clamped around my neck.

"Aurora, dear," a female voice said behind me. "Thank you for coming. I am Layla, queen of the North American vampire clan. You should be honored to be in my presence." Chills ran up my spine, but I wasted no time. Grabbing her palm, I threw myself forward and flipped her over my back. She slammed to the pavement and I turned to run, just as two heavying hands grabbed my shoulders and shoved my face into the dirt. Groaning, I tried to kick out, but it was no use. The female I had thrown was crouched now and peering at me with her head tilted to the side. Totally creepy. Her hair was strawberry-blond and fell to her waist in waves. She was pale; her eyes were black and her fangs stuck out, pressing on her bottom lip. She inhaled deeply and smiled. "You know, people that fight back always taste better."

My heart was hammering inside my chest. I wanted to call for help, but I didn't want to take any help away from Emma.

"This was always a trap, wasn't it?" I asked her. She knew my name and she seemed ready for me.

Her lips twisted into a sadistic smile as I was jerked to my feet and made to stand.

"You were always the prize, yes. Haven't you heard? Your blood can give all of the vampire women in my command the power of fertility." She cooed and dragged a finger across my collarbone.

My stomach dropped. It was just as Nahuel warned me. No. *'Kai!'*

The dark witch that I had seen in my mind's eye walked around from behind me. She smelled like witch and smoke, like clove cigarettes and evil. She ran a bony hand through her long black hair and grinned. "I have blocked you from communicating with your pack. It's just us." A fine mist covered the both of us and I knew she was right. Layla, the vampire queen, smiled at the dark witch. They were working together. I was screwed.

A black van turned the corner then, and came to a screeching halt beside us. I froze. Men dressed in all-black military gear suspended from nearby trees rappelled down to street level. The vampires hissed and I looked around, confused, and took in a deep breath. Humans? They must have been in the trees the entire time. What the hell?

The humans advanced with silver-pointed crossbows and I swallowed hard. They all wore a white symbol embroidered on their black chests. They looked like hunters—seasoned supernatural hunters, if there were such a thing.

*'Kai, run! Human hunters!'* I pushed the thought out with a little bit of what I hoped was magic. I saw mist leaving my body and hoped the message went through.

A few of the humans raised their crossbows just as the witch threw her hands in the air and black smoke exploded everywhere. I couldn't see two feet in front of me. I took in a huge breath and started coughing, stumbling backward; it was burning my eyes and lungs. Someone grabbed me from behind and started pulling me backward. I rammed my heel into what I thought might be a groin and was rewarded with a moan. Then I was hit with a hard object at the base of my skull and blackness took me.

## 22

## RAIDOS

I came to with a raging headache. Groaning, I licked my lips. My mouth was so dry my tongue felt swollen. Gingerly, I peeled open my eyes and squinted at the bright lights, taking in my surroundings. I was tied with silver chains to a chair, in a large room with rows and rows of bench-type seating. About ten people were sitting on benches before me, but they stood now that I was awake and aimed their crossbows at my chest. I was in the center of the room on a dais and it took me a second to realize I was in a church. A crazy thought struck me then. Would I burn alive? I looked down at my body. I guess not.

A man stepped forward. "Aurora?"

I swallowed, trying to figure out how I wanted to play this. They looked scared, but they also looked like they wouldn't hesitate to kill me.

"Yes, my name is Aurora. Who are you?"

He looked to a woman on his right and she nodded, seemingly giving him permission.

"We are from a special branch of the international intelligence community. Those who know of us call us RAIDOS. Research And Intelligence Division On Supernaturals. Our mission has always been to gather intelligence on your kind. How much information you give us will determine if we let you live."

Oh, shit. I nodded and tried to keep my wolf from coming out. I could tell by the fact that they stepped back a few feet that I hadn't succeeded. I knew my eyes were yellow, and I took a few deep breaths to calm myself.

"Well, I have only been a supernatural for a few weeks. I was human for the first twenty-two years of my life."

I was going to downplay this—act dumb. The woman placed a tape recorder in front of me. "If you answer all of our questions, and we determine you are not a threat to the human race, we will let you go."

I looked at her and I could tell from the way she was communicating with the other man that they were in a romantic relationship.

I nodded. "I feel it fair to warn you that the longer you keep me here, the more chance you have of encountering my mate. He will bring our entire wolf pack and they will rip your fragile human bodies apart."

She raised her crossbow and pointed it at me. "Don't make threats."

I leaned forward. "It was a warning. I cannot communicate with my mate because the witch did something to my pack bonds. But he *will* find me and he won't ask questions. This church won't keep them out."

A few of the RAIDOS agents exchanged looks, then a petite woman with short blond hair stepped forward. "So you will answer our questions?"

My mother was human. Hell, I was human a month ago. Of course I wanted the human race to survive. But I also needed to protect my pack, so I needed to give them information—but not too much.

"Yes, unless I feel you shouldn't be given certain information for the safety of my kind."

The blond woman nodded, seeming to be okay with that answer. "My name is Dr. Tavern, and I am the communications psychologist for RAIDOS. We have been tracking the three supernatural communities for about twenty-five years now. We have intercepted your phones, email, and anything we could, without getting too close to your homes for fear you could smell us. We know you are a werewolf, and after listening in on the vampires' conversations, that you may be able to help them have children. They wish to kill off your kind and take humanity under their ownership as blood slaves with their newly-created spawn. So I guess the biggest question we have is ... whose side are you on? The vampires or the humans?"

Jesus. She knew everything. More than even I knew.

I decided a little humor was in order here. "Couldn't you tell how much we werewolves love vampires by the way we stormed that house and started killing them?"

Her lips curled into the slightest smile.

"Werewolves protect humans," I told her honestly. "It's always been this way. They kidnapped one of our pregnant females, and we're here to get her back."

She nodded as if she knew this.

"Why aren't the silver chains hurting you? We have heard other wolves talk about silver incapacitating them."

"Most wolves can't handle silver. I'm immune to its effects."

The psychologist nodded. "She is cooperating. Untie her. Give her water."

The man who had approached me earlier seemed unsure but did as he was told. The second he unlocked my chains I could have shifted and jumped out of the nearby stained-glass window, but I didn't. If a vampire war was coming, we needed allies. I only hoped it was possible to become allies with these people.

I rubbed my wrists and grabbed the water bottle.

"Thank you," I muttered and took a long swig.

Dr. Tavern nodded. "You said you were human a few weeks ago. What happened? Do werewolves turn humans just to increase their numbers?"

"No, that is against werewolf law. I was in a bad car accident on Mount Hood. I was dying and my mate found me. He is an alpha and he changed me, hoping I would survive."

"Kai?" the psychologist asked.

Shit, they knew a lot. I suddenly felt very protective. I opened my pack bond but I couldn't sense Kai. Did it not work if we were too far away, or had the witch done something?

The psychologist seemed to register my apprehension. "We have a drone that flies above Mount Hood. We have been watching Kai and his pack for a while. He does things differently. There are no fights in his pack, they don't do anything illegal—he even pays his taxes."

I breathed a little easier. "Yes, once Kai changed me I found out he was my mate."

The psychologist seemed to mull something over. "I like you, Aurora. You seem very caring, protective, and intelligent. Many of the same qualities we find in humans. But I want you to answer this next question very, very honestly. Your life depends on it."

I sat up straighter and eyed the doorway, calculating how fast I could run to it.

"Are you the Matefinder, and what does that mean?"

Well, shit. So much for not revealing too much. My wolf came to the surface then and I felt the need to run. Surely, if they knew I could help grow the werewolf race exponentially, they would kill me. I decided to downplay it.

"Yes, I am the Matefinder. There is always one

Matefinder in existence to help wolves from faraway packs find their mates. It's not a big deal."

Dr. Tavern chewed her lip, assessing me. "And is it true that without finding your mate you cannot conceive children?"

There was no way around this question. I knew where she was going and I stood up, suddenly angry. "Yes! I find mates so we can marry and have a family just like you! YES! If you kill me right now, then the werewolf population will significantly decrease over time. But if you kill me, there will also be fewer wolves to help you fight the vampires in the future."

All ten RAIDOS agents had their crossbows pointed at me. All except the psychologist. She was completely still and regarding me thoughtfully.

"I guess we have a decision to make. Either we as humans work alone to ensure the human race survives, or we form an alliance," Dr. Tavern suggested.

We stared at each other. *Challenge*, my wolf said. If they made a move to kill me, I would fight. I would probably die, but I would fight.

*'Aurora? We're coming! I can smell you. We're close. Hold on!'* Kai voice finally broke through our bond and relief poured through me.

Dr. Tavern's phone beeped and she broke eye contact to look at it. Relief seemed to flood through her and she extended her hand to me.

"We can start small. I would like to start an alliance from the West Coast branch of RAIDOS to the Mount

Hood pack." She held her hand out, waiting for my response.

Would Kai be okay with this? Did someone just text her telling her to offer an alliance? Kai wouldn't like that they were watching us, but what could we do? We both had a common enemy and a common goal.

I shook her hand firmly. "Deal. My mate and our pack are close now. You should all leave. This isn't the best way for you to meet him."

She nodded and handed me a thin phone. "We will be in touch."

*'I'm safe,'* I sent to Kai. *'We have a lot to talk about. Is Emma with you?'*

I held my breath.

*'We have her. She's fine.'*

My throat tightened with emotion. Emma was okay. Thank God.

The RAIDOS group had their gear packed and were out the back door in record time. They functioned like a well-oiled machine, and if I was being honest, they scared me. I began to walk outside just as their black van pulled away, the tires peeling out. Turning, I saw Kai running down the street in wolf form, a pack of wolves running behind him. Breaking into a sprint, I ran toward him, slowing when I noticed he was hurt. A thick trail of blood trickled behind him.

He nearly knocked me over when he saw me and I dug my fingers into his fur, letting him smell me.

"You're hurt," I said out loud.

*'I nearly tore the head off of every vampire when I realized you had been taken.'*

Izzy was limping and Max had a huge gash in his shoulder. Oh God, where was Devon?

"Devon?" I asked.

*'He's with Emma. They are waiting for us.'*

I sagged with relief as the Los Angeles alpha approached me in human form. "I have a hotel you can stay at until you are healed for travel."

I nodded. "Thank you."

Kai nipped my hand. *'What the hell happened, Aurora? You said human hunters had come. Then I couldn't find you.'*

*'We have a lot to talk about. Not here.'* I rubbed the sore spot on my head where I had been knocked out, and followed the Los Angeles alpha, hoping my mate wouldn't kill me when he found out I had made an alliance with the human government.

## 23

## LIFE

As soon as we reached the hotel lobby, I smelled Emma and broke into a run, following my nose. I ran down the long hallway and stopped at door 137.

"Emma!" I pounded on the door. Devon opened it and I saw that his arm was in a sling and he had a black eye. He stepped aside to let me in and I ran to the bed, where Emma sat eating room service. I could sense Kai behind me. He had shifted to human form before we entered the hotel.

"Did they hurt you?" I hugged her hard and she squeezed me back.

"Not really." She had a few bruises but nothing bad. "Once I stopped fighting back, they were okay."

Kai approached her. "Emma, I will never let this happen again. I promise, you and your baby will be safe with me from now on. But I understand if you want to switch to a bigger pack."

My mouth opened in shock. Of course Kai would

feel guilty; he was supposed to keep her safe. A pregnant female needed the most protection, but to switch packs over this? Would she? Maybe Emma would be safer in a bigger pack.

Emma held out her hands and Kai took them. "I will never leave this pack. You are my family. You were out of town and no one thought the bloodsuckers were a threat to us. If I left the pack based on the grounds that you couldn't protect me, I would have to leave my husband too. He was there and almost died trying to fight them. No one is switching packs."

They shared a look and there was so much love there it gave me goose bumps. Kai would protect any one of his pack members, but Emma was special to him. Like a true sister.

A man entered the room with the Los Angeles alpha then. "Kai, this is the pack doctor you requested."

Kai shook the doctor's hand, a short but kind-looking submissive. I would imagine a werewolf doctor would have to be a submissive. You wouldn't want a dominant male tending to you when you were injured.

"Emma is pregnant. Can you check on the baby? Make sure it's okay?" Kai asked him. Devon placed a protective hand on her belly, stroking his thumb across her skin.

The doctor nodded and left. He returned a few minutes later with a handheld ultrasound machine. My heart was in my throat. This baby had better be healthy.

Kai, Devon, and I all hovered around the bed as the doctor placed some gel on Emma's belly.

"How far along are you?" he asked her in a hushed voice.

"I don't know. I just took a home pregnancy test and found out. We had arranged for a doctor's visit, but then I was taken."

He nodded. He placed a wand against her belly and a black blob appeared. When he moved it a little, you could see a flicker inside the blob.

"The baby's heartbeat ... perfectly healthy. You are about nine weeks along," the doctor said, and smiled.

I looked up then and saw we all had tears in our eyes. Even Kai. Creating life was an amazing thing, and Emma and the baby were safe. All was well.

The second we got inside our own hotel room, Kai collapsed onto the bed out of exhaustion and closed his eyes. I approached him slowly.

"The government has been watching the supernatural community for over twenty years. They kidnapped me tonight, tied me with silver chains, and threatened to kill me if I didn't answer their questions. In the end, we created an alliance. Our common goal is to kill vampires and keep humanity safe."

Kai's eyes flew open and flared yellow. He sat bolt upright. "What the hell did you just say?"

Forty-five minutes later, Kai and I were eating room service, and he was still probing me about my encounter with RAIDOS.

"They have a drone flying over Mount Hood?" he screamed as he chewed his rare steak and I tried not to gag over the smell of the meat.

"Kai, they are the government! What they lack in magical abilities, they make up for in intelligence and money."

Kai seemed to consider my reasoning. "They knew my name? They knew to tie you up with silver? I don't like it."

"Think about it from their angle. They know you exist but they have sat back quietly and watched. Then they overhear the vampires say, 'Hmmm, let's wipe out the werewolves and make a huge vampire nation with tons of human blood slaves.'" I shook my hands for emphasis. "'Oh, and while we are at it, let's have vampire bloodsucking babies because this Matefinder girl can help us!'"

Kai groaned. "I see your point."

I pulled out the phone that had been sitting in my pocket. "They gave me this, said they would be in touch."

Kai snatched it from me. "We need to tell the council right away. And I want to meet them. And I want that damn drone off my mountain!"

I stroked my finger across his chest. "First we need a shower."

He raised his eyebrows, all traces of his former anger gone. "We? As in together?"

I laughed and stood, stripping off my shirt and walked into the bathroom, leaving the door open.

After our shower, where Kai was barely able to retain his label as a gentleman, Kai called his father and told him how some government agents had detained me. That's all he said over the phone—we didn't know who was listening. His father said the council would be visiting us soon. No time or place was given, but maybe that was better. I was sure RAIDOS could be trusted not to kill us as long as they didn't have reason. But there were a lot of reasons. As soon as we weren't useful for them, or if they felt threatened, they could annihilate our kind, and the thought made me shiver.

---

IN THE FEW weeks since we had gotten Emma back, Diya had been busy planning her wedding back in Delhi, and we video-chatted often. I wasn't even sure where to begin with wedding planning of my own, so Diya and Emma said they would take care of everything for me. Every few days they would ask me simple things like what my favorite flower was or my favorite color. Kai's mother had asked me if I wanted to wear a sari on our wedding day and I told her yes. I loved Indian culture, and the thought of wearing a red sari just like in my vision made me happy.

I called my mother to share the news of our engagement and she was actually happy—a little apprehensive that it was all happening so fast, but happy.

Kai stepped up security on the mountain and at all of the pack houses in Portland. Each home had state-of-the-art security and was equipped with a large arsenal of vampire-killing weapons. Our daily training sessions now included staking a vampire and how best to fight them. We all knew we were preparing for something, we just weren't sure what exactly.

I had just reached home after teaching a self-defense class with Izzy at Safe Haven, and we were exiting the car, when I smelled something—foreign wolves. I looked around and noticed a few black cars that weren't pack. Izzy looked at me oddly, but I sent her home and told her I would call her if I needed her.

*'Who's here?'* I asked Kai.

*'My father and the rest of the council. Come in quietly and don't speak.'*

What the hell? Don't speak? Did this guy know me at all?

I tried to smooth my hair down. I was sweaty and wearing a tank-top with yoga pants. Not exactly how I wanted to greet the council. I hadn't even been properly introduced to Kai's father last time, so this was bound to be a little awkward. Using my key, I opened the door and stepped inside.

The twelve council members were seated on the couches in the living room; some had pulled chairs up in a circle. Kai was standing in the middle of the room with a dry-erase board perched above the fireplace mantel. He looked at me and put a finger to his lips.

On the board, Kai had written a message to the council that the surrounding area was being watched by supernatural human hunters, and we weren't safe to speak freely. I heard a car door slam just as I was about to shut the door. I inhaled and smelled a witch—Sylvia. What was she doing here? I creased my eyebrows in confusion.

'What's going on?' I asked Kai through our bond.

'We need to talk about RAIDOS, but they are listening. Just now we found out that one of the trees out back is bugged. Sylvia is going to magically keep our conversation safe.'

Holy shit. They were bugging our trees! Sylvia gave a light knock and I let her in. She locked eyes with me first and nodded. Then she glanced around briefly at the council, and seemed to know what was going on, because she didn't speak. Reaching her hand into her bag, she pulled some white salt from it and began sprinkling it around. Part of me thrummed with excitement watching her do the spell. I wanted to learn to do magic too, I decided. After spreading the salt, she placed a purple crystal in the center of the room and began walking around to each council member, holding out her hand.

"I need a piece of your hair," she whispered. They reluctantly gave it to her, and when she came to me I happily gave her a piece. I watched, fascinated, as she wound each person's hair around the purple crystal in the center of the room. Then she whispered, "Let their words make no sound. Let none hear it all around." A fine mist crept out of the crystal and created a dome above our heads. Badass.

She spoke loudly now. "You may speak freely. I will wait outside. Come get me when you are finished."

"Thank you, Sylvia," Kai told her. I noticed he was trusting her more and more. That was good, because I really wanted to learn more about witches and spell craft.

Kai's father stepped toward me. "First let me properly introduce myself. I am Raj, Kai's father. I'm sorry we have to keep meeting under these dire circumstances." I shook his outstretched hand and didn't make eye contact for fear of seeming rude.

"It's nice to meet you, sir," I told him, as Kai walked over and placed a hand on my shoulder.

Jane stood and smiled at me. "Aurora, I never got to thank you for helping me find my mate."

I nodded and gave her a polite smile.

A large Native American councilman placed both of his palms up. "Enough pleasantries, tell us everything you know about this government group that's tracking supernaturals. We haven't been told anything!"

He was rightfully distressed, so I took a deep breath and told them everything.

"You offered an alliance!" Raj shouted, and I tried not to let my wolf out.

"Yes, I offered an alliance between RAIDOS and *my* pack. I am second-in-command, I did what I felt was best for our pack ... especially when they held a crossbow to my heart." I met Kai's father's eyes briefly, and then glanced at Kai. He looked proud to see someone standing up to his father.

"You are not a council member. You cannot offer an alliance with humans. That's the council's decision," Raj challenged.

Okay, now I was getting pissed off. "I was knocked unconscious, tied up with silver chains, and my life was threatened! I can do whatever the hell I want!" I shouted, and immediately recoiled. Raj and I weren't getting off to the best start; I didn't want things to go down this road. He looked like he wanted to take my head off, but Kai stepped forward and placed himself between his father and me.

"What would you have her do, Papa? Reject an alliance so they have reason to kill her? There is a war coming and we need allies. The witches have agreed to side with us. Now we have allied with humans. Together we may be able to save our race. Together we can stay alive long enough to live out the new relationships and pregnancies that my mate has helped start!"

His father looked to the other council members and nodded. They seemed to be having a conversation in their heads. How could they do that?

"Then there are two more things left to discuss," Jane told us. "Should we publicly reveal our species to the humans? And would you both like seats on the council?"

What did she just say? I did *not* see that one coming.

"NO and NO," Kai answered. "Aurora and I aren't interested in politics, and the humans aren't ready for knowledge of our kind."

Okay, I would have liked to answer for myself, but I agreed. I didn't want to be on some stuffy council. But I wasn't sure I agreed with Kai about the humans not being ready for knowledge of our kind. If a vampire war was coming and the humans were going to be enslaved, then maybe they deserved to know who was fighting for them.

"Do we all agree that if there comes a time to fight for the humans, we protect them?" I asked. Somehow this had become my task—to make sure we would be there to protect the humans. Protect our pack, yes, but protect them as well.

The Native American councilman stepped forward again. "I know you are new to this life, Aurora. Kai may not have had time to tell you all of the stories. It has, and always will be, a werewolf's duty to protect the humans from vampires. Without that, the balance would tilt and we would be thrust into a future none of us want to see." He held my gaze and in his eyes I was reminded of Nahuel. As I continued to stare, I suddenly became very sleepy. Then I was falling backward, but was caught by Nahuel inside of another vision.

We were standing in a deserted field with a huge water treatment plant in front of us. I'd never been sucked into a vision this way before. It was disorienting. I looked at Nahuel expectantly and he looked unhappy.

"It's beginning," he told me. I peered at the doors of the treatment plant to see three vampires walk out.

"What's beginning? What are they doing?" I asked him, motioning to the vampires ahead.

Nahuel rubbed his hands together. "I'm not supposed to show you this. But the balance has been tipped toward the dark. I might as well try to tip it back to the light. If it's going to go one way, I want it to go our way."

His words were cryptic and terrifying.

"I don't understand! Explain it. Help me." I felt desperate and I could feel his anxiety about the situation as well.

"The vampires have poured silver water into every major water supply plant in all of the big cities. They want to weaken the wolves and then attack."

My hand flew to cover my mouth in shock; pure horror flooded my body. "No!" I ran toward the three men coming out of the building. They had huge oil drums full of silver water; they were rolling them in. This would slowly weaken the wolves so that over time their injuries wouldn't heal and they would die.

Nahuel caught my arm. "They can't see us. We are in the future."

"So we can stop it? What day does it happen?" I suddenly felt hope burst in my chest.

He looked sad again, hopeless. "I can only see a few hours into the future. It will happen today."

I grabbed his face and turned it toward me. "Wipe that look off of your face. This hasn't happened yet! You don't know me very well yet, but I don't give up! I've been through a lot of shit in my life, and I didn't make it out by giving up."

His lips curled into a smile then and he placed his forehead against mine. "Little sister, I have not given up. I wear this face because I've seen too much."

"Why do you keep calling me 'little sister?'" I asked, completely at ease with how close he was to my face. Something about him disarmed me.

He pulled his face back and wore a blank expression. "That is not my story to tell."

All of a sudden I was spinning and came back to my body in a series of jerks.

Kai was in wolf form in front of me; his eyes looked menacing. His muzzle hung open as he panted in anxiety. The council was backed up against the wall of our living room and my head lay in Sylvia's lap.

"I feel sick." I grabbed my stomach. That vision was unlike the others. Had he truly taken me to the future?

Kai shifted into his human form, covering himself with a blanket from the couch. His yellow eyes were halfway threaded with chocolate brown as he approached me. The council leaned forward, peering at me, waiting for me to speak.

"Maybe everyone should wait outside until Kai calms down," Raj told the council.

"No!" I stood quickly, sending a wave of dizziness through me.

"Get on the phone, email, use your pack bond, do whatever you have to, to warn as many wolves as you can..." I was breathless—I wouldn't have been shown the future if I couldn't change it. I had to believe that.

The council stood eerily still. "Warn them of what?" Kai asked me.

"The vampires are trying to wipe us out. They're spilling liquid silver into the waterways. It's going to happen any minute!" I waived my hands frantically.

Raj's eyes widened in shock. "Do you mean to tell us you have seen the future?"

"Yes! Hurry." Why did they look so unsure? God, I was sick of being questioned. I advanced on Jane quickly and the muscles in her arms flexed as if she expected me to attack. I held out my hand.

"Make them see," I told her. "We have no time."

She relaxed and nodded, taking my outstretched hand, I could feel her sifting through my mind. I wanted to push her out, but held still. I heard Sylvia gasp behind me, and Jane broke away with her mouth open. Then she closed her eyes and tipped her head down. All of the council members wore shocked expressions. Kai stumbled backward with wide eyes. She had sent my vision to them.

*'The vampires are trying to kill off our kind. We need to protect the water supply. Portland wolves, split up. Half of you go to the wholesale market and buy as many water bottles as they have. The other half, bring your weapons and protect the Portland water supply. Mount Hood wolves, same thing. I don't care who does what. Figure it out and move NOW!'*

My head was still ringing with Kai's mental command. He whipped out his cell phone and called Shamus, telling him to spread the word.

"We won't reach everyone in time!" I screamed desperately.

Sylvia approached Kai's father. All of the council members were mentally warning their packs, and all wearing the same expression, lost in deep thought.

"I've seen your bond with the other people here. You're all connected." Sylvia put her hand out, waving it in the air. Raj's eyes glowed yellow.

"Calm down, Alpha. I think I can help you." Sylvia nodded me over and I stumbled forward.

"What is it? What can we do?" I asked her.

"It's a very powerful spell. It's a communication spell between an entire species. It's been done once before, to warn the witches of the burnings in the Salem witch trials. It would take all of these alphas' blood and your power as a witch to help me."

"Let's do it," I told her.

"Hang on a second," Raj told us, looking down his nose at Sylvia. "I'm not giving this witch my blood."

My eyes flashed yellow. "Then you will be

responsible for the death of our kind!" I shouted boldly. I felt heat at my back and turned to see Kai walking forward to face off with his father.

"You will do this. We don't have time to argue. I don't trust witches but I trust Sylvia." Kai was barely holding on to his wolf form, I could see it.

Kai's father let loose a growl. "You don't tell me what to do, son!" They locked eyes. Oh God. I could see where this was going. This was going to end in a challenge.

I looked at Sylvia. "Help," I mouthed.

She chewed her lip nervously and reached into her purse, withdrawing a fistful of powder. She threw it in Kai's and Raj's faces simultaneously and whispered, "Sleep."

They both crumpled to the ground. The council seemed in shock at what she had just done. They stood there motionless, just staring. Kai lay at an awkward angle near his father, so I straightened his body and looked at Sylvia for direction.

She pursed her lips. "Hopefully they won't kill me," she said.

"They won't, I'll protect you." I looked at the council members. "Extend your arms and we may be able to save our kind."

Something seemed to pass between them. This was our best shot and they knew it. If embracing a little witch magic was what needed to be done for the good of whole, then so be it. They extended their arms one by one, and Sylvia gave me the task of collecting the blood. Just a prick from each person was needed, including myself. I pricked Kai and Raj carefully, aware that any moment they could wake up.

Once I had the droplets of blood inside an ornate glass vessel, I approached Sylvia.

"We must do this outside, in nature," Sylvia declared. We all followed her outside, where she looked to the council. "This spell is powered very differently from any other. It is is fueled by love—love for each other, love for your kind, love for your mate, your children. Any love you can conjure in your mind, you must do it now!"

Everyone stood together apprehensively and closed their eyes to concentrate. I was glad to see they were taking this seriously. I thought of my mother then, of Drake, of Kai. My first kiss with Kai flashed through my mind and my belly warmed. I'd been through some dark times, but I had a lot of love too.

I felt Sylvia's hand slip into mine. "Give me all the mist you got," she whispered, referring to the magic I carried.

Taking a deep breath, I opened my eyes. I imagined the mist inside of me, magic, and let it leak out of my pores. It tingled across my skin and warmed at the same time. It was never-ending, I could feel that. It was everywhere, in the trees, the stars, the rain. The Earth was magic! A huge cloud of mist leapt out of my body and slammed into the council members. They rocked on their heels but stayed standing.

Sylvia raised our hands to the sky. "Let every

member of the four-legged race hear my call! Your survival is threatened. The vampires will attack your water supply with silver. Protect it now!"

Thunder rumbled overhead as rain began to fall. It felt miraculous and terrifying all at once. The message had been received, I just knew it. Then the RAIDOS cell phone rang in my pocket. We had given it a *Batman* ringtone, unmistakable. Shit.

Sylvia let go of my hand. "So be it," she said, and looked at me.

"So be it," I repeated, not sure why.

I answered the phone. "Hello?"

"This is Dr. Tavern. Our ETA to the Sandy water treatment facility is thirty minutes."

"Uh." I didn't know what to say. I looked up at the sky, searching for a drone.

"Well, we are allies now, aren't we? We're coming to help," she told me.

I smiled. Maybe this ally thing was going to turn out okay. "Meet you there."

The council received word that the message had been heard. People were calling and asking what to do. Some were panicked, but most were prepared. I crossed the yard quickly with Sylvia to help her awaken Kai and Raj with more spell powder. I needed my mate alert and awake for what was to come. The second she was done, I told her to leave and avoid their rage.

Kai sat up quickly and grabbed his head. Raj

looked at his son murderously. "I'm going to kill that witch!"

I stepped forward. "No you're not. She has my protection, and since I found your daughter's mate, I figure you owe me." I smiled a little for good measure. I was sure deep down, past the alpha bullshit, he was a nice guy. Or at least I was hoping so.

His father looked pissed for a second and then appraised me with pride, lips quirking into a smile. "She is your perfect match, son." Then he met my eyes. "Welcome to the family, Aurora."

I chuckled as he stood and brushed past me, leaving with the rest of the council. Not exactly how I'd envisioned meeting my future father-in-law, but hey, no family was perfect. The urgency of the situation pressed down on me. I helped Kai stand and we ran to the door together. A few pack members were driving up the driveway with a truck full of water bottles. Kai followed after me.

"What happened?" he asked, confused.

I shifted. *'I'll tell you on the way.'*

## 24

## ALLIANCE

Kai didn't question me, he just tore off his shirt and shifted instantly, following my fast pace down the mountain toward the small town of Sandy, which supplied Mount Hood's water. After explaining to Kai that we had sent a message to all wolves about the water, I also explained about the call from RAIDOS.

*'So we're meeting the humans at the Sandy water plant to fight vampires together?'* he mocked.

'Yep.'

*'Well, they better not get in my way.'* He sped past me, dashing through the trees. We would get there faster in our wolf form; people would hopefully mistake us for a blur of an animal. Sandy was a twenty-mile run as the crow flies. If we had taken a car it would have been a fifty-mile winding road.

After about twenty minutes of relentless running, we made it down the mountain and out into the heavily populated area. We slowed near a gas station and saw a black helicopter landing in the distance, in the general area of the water facility. Weaving in and out of a few parked cars, we made it back onto a side street devoid of people.

From there, we sprinted to the water facility gates. It was dark, but my werewolf eyes could see a commotion just inside. The black helicopter had landed near a side entrance and the RAIDOS team had trickled in the gate that was blasted open. A few RAIDOS agents were perched on the roof, using crossbows to shoot at the vampires down in the courtyard.

There must have been fifty of the bloodsuckers, protecting six large drums of liquid silver. A few of our other pack members who'd been closer when they received the warning had already arrived and were fighting alongside the RAIDOS team. It was chaos. Just as we neared the main gate, a female vampire rose high into the air and landed on top of my back. Rolling quickly, I heard the satisfying crunch of her bones beneath my big wolf body. I twisted out of her grasp and turned to face her. It was the vampire queen from that night in LA—Layla. I bared my teeth, and saw Kai preparing to pounce on her. She looked right at him and whispered, "Freeze." Her eyes flickered with a purple haze. He didn't move—he barely breathed. It was like he was made of cement.

'*Compulsion,*' he said into my mind.

I allowed a low rumble to rock my chest. She'd frozen my mate. She was as good as dead. Then she turned her gaze on me. "You will change into your human form and offer me your blood." I could hear strange sounds in her voice. Were those hummingbird wings? Her eyes were glowing purple; however, I felt no desire to do as she asked. Her compulsion didn't work on me.

I lunged for her throat, my teeth bared. She stumbled backward in shock, bringing her arms up to protect herself. I got in one good bite before she ripped my jaws away with a gripping force. I felt a few ribs crack; sharp pain laced up my side and I howled.

A flaming arrow cut through the sky and sank into the queen's shoulder. Her face took on a predatory look; she hissed. Then her strawberry-blonde hair caught on fire and singed, and Kai was suddenly free of his compulsion. He lunged at her abdomen. In one quick move, Layla yanked the silver-tipped flaming arrow out of her shoulder and rammed it into Kai's hind leg.

"No!" I screamed and involuntarily shifted into my human form. I could hear fighting behind me. Mist began to pour out of my hands—I couldn't stop it—swirling around my body like a funnel, like it was waiting for me to tell it what to do. Kai had retreated a few steps, limping and injured.

"Attack!" I screamed, and put all of my intention into the mist, like it was a living guard dog. The mist suddenly beaded, whirling before me and turned into thousands of bees. They covered Layla's body like a coat of black fur. The buzzing was deafening. The sky shuddered; lightning crackled as Layla fumbled backward, but the bees moved with her. I turned to Kai, who was dragging his hind leg, the arrow still in it. Kneeling down, I yanked the arrow out and we turned to the entrance of the water facility. There were five barrels of silver untouched. RAIDOS and our pack had taken care of most of the vampires, but a dozen or so remained. Seeing their queen covered in a blanket of magical bees, they began to advance on us.

"Shit," I breathed, and shifted into my wolf form again. The multiple shifts made me dizzy, and I was starving as well. My ribs were just a dull throb now, so at least that was good. I was guessing I needed a lot of calories to keep up with these body changes. Kai stood in front of me and growled. His back leg was quivering with the weight of him standing on it, but he held his position in front of me anyway. Then the bees began to dissipate. One of the people I mistook for a vampire was in fact the dark witch from LA. She raised her hands and black smoke leaked from her palms.

*'Don't breathe it in!'* I told Kai.

Just as the wave of black smoke came toward us, I felt a cool mist at my back, and turning, I saw Sylvia and her coven with their arms outstretched, white mist rolling on the ground making the black mist retreat. Yes! Glancing around frantically, I saw that Layla was nowhere to be seen.

"All alone, Prudence?" Sylvia shouted at the dark witch.

Prudence laughed sharply and it raised the fur on my back.

"I don't need a coven. I am more powerful by myself!" she roared, and sent a blast of hot air at us. Kai and I retreated to the side parking lot, while Sylvia and her coven threw spell after spell at Prudence. I could see Kai was hurt badly from the silver arrow. His damn wound wasn't closing.

We left the witches to deal with Prudence, and were snaking our way along the trees toward the front door of the facility when Layla and two vampires jumped out of nowhere. The two vampires pounced on Kai, while Layla grabbed my back fur and yanked hard. I yelped out in pain, helpless to do anything, hanging midair from her arm by my back skin, yapping with my teeth at nothing.

Shifting quickly to my human form, I grabbed Layla's arm and twisted, snapping it in half. She screamed in pain, but then quickly smiled evilly.

"Atta-girl." She pounced on me, taking hold of my hair in her hand and exposing my neck. I tried to wiggle out of her grasp, but she was fast, and too strong. Before I could register what was happening, I felt her teeth sink into my neck—I couldn't get free. Pleasure and disgust exploded simultaneously inside my belly and I cried out. It felt like I was eating the most delicious meal in the world; my mouth salivated. On the other hand, I was being bitten by a vampire, and I shuddered. These two feelings warred inside of me until, finally, I felt myself being torn away from her.

Dr. Tavern stood above us, holding a long sharp samurai sword in front of her. Layla's mouth was dripping with my blood. Oh God.

Dr. Tavern advanced on the vampire queen, but Layla just smiled. It was the creepiest, most blood-coated, sharp-toothed smile I'd ever seen. Then she fled fast into the woods, and my stomach dropped.

I looked at Dr. Tavern with wide eyes. "She drank my blood! That means she's fertile for the next few days! She can have a child."

Dr. Tavern nodded grimly and took off into the forest. I heard her say something over an earpiece, then helicopter blades whirred above me. Craning my neck, I saw two RAIDOS members hanging from ropes dangling from the helicopter.

I shifted for what felt like the fiftieth time and took off running as well. If Layla got away I was pretty sure that meant I was a dead woman. A major liability to the human race, the government would kill me for sure. Footsteps pounded behind me and I glanced back to see my mate. I grinned, happy that he was helping me. Together we could take her down, but just as I was turning to face forward again, his back leg gave out with a snap and he rolled hard, wiping out. Twigs and leaves scattered and I skidded to a halt.

'Kai!'

'I can't run that fast with a silver injury. Go!' he screamed.

Shit, he was pushing himself too hard in order to get Layla. I ignored his command for me to go, and ran back to him. I crouched over him, assessing his leg. The wound was about four inches long and still bleeding freely—it was bad; it had torn into the ligament and it wasn't healing. It gaped open, leaking a clear-ish fluid. Let RAIDOS handle Layla; my mate needed me. I shifted to human form and my ribs screamed in protest, I wasn't sure I could take any more shifts. My stomach was eating itself, and I think I had rebroken my ribs.

"I want to try something," I told him. Because ever since I had survived the accident and Sylvia had unleashed my witch magic, I had felt powerful, and right now I was feeling the strangest urge to try to heal him. I held my hands over his leg, the muscle twitching and bleeding freely. Breathing in, I focused on my magic and a warm sensation bloomed in my belly. Mist began to pour from my hands and Kai's nostrils flared.

'Magic,' he said, and I simply nodded. *Heal*, I told the mist, and closed my eyes, imagining all of the skin stitching together and becoming pink and then pale. I imagined his fur fluffy and thick. With my eyes still closed, I heard him panting. If I had this magic inside of me, then maybe I could do something good with it. After a few moments, I opened my eyes to see Kai standing and staring at me in fear. I looked at my hands and shook them, stopping the mist. His leg ... it was healed. No gash, no more weeping blood. I could hear his heart beating fast as his eyes bore into me.

"I'm a witch," I said as the helicopter blades whined off in the distance.

"You're a witch," he agreed. His yellow eyes appraised me. "A pretty sexy, and amazing witch."

I smiled, trying to cover up how completely freaked out and amazed I was that I had just healed his bleeding leg. But there was no time to dwell on it now. "Let's follow that helicopter."

My hand went to my neck and the two pinprick bite marks that were there pulsing and hurt like hell. I shook off the thought of what it had felt like when she bit me, the pleasure and disgust. Shifting to my wolf form for what was hopefully the final time that day, I took off after Kai. He ran easily now, with no sign of a limp, and for that I was grateful. The multiple shifts were starting to drain my energy and I was beyond hungry. The wind sailed past my nose, bringing the stench of a nearby rabbit, but I ignored it. Even my vegetarian human side thought a rabbit would taste good right about now.

*'Max is at the water treatment plant,'* Kai told me. *'He said the rest of the vampires have fled. One drum of silver made it into the water supply.'*

Shit. I ran faster. We had to catch Layla. We were approaching the sound of the helicopter. Peering up, I saw it hovering above us, two ropes dangling down and snaking across the ground. One of the RAIDOS agents was hunched over another.

"He's dead, and the vampires got away," the agent told us without looking up. His voice was hollow, angry. I inhaled deeply, trying to pick up Layla's scent, but I couldn't. I felt bad that one of their people had died for our cause. It wasn't fair. I was even more upset that Layla had gotten away ... with my blood in her veins. Footsteps behind me drew my attention; Dr. Tavern and another agent were approaching us, but they stopped when they saw the body.

"Brent," Dr. Tavern whispered, a tear falling from her cheek. It was then that I realized the RAIDOS humans were a pack. This was their family, united with one cause—to protect their kind. We weren't so different. I tipped my head back and howled in grief for this fallen soldier. Kai joined with me.

Dr. Tavern composed herself and spoke over her earpiece. Two men rappelled from the helicopter with a rescue basket and a bundle of clothes. They loaded Brent into the basket and Dr. Tavern nodded at Kai and me. "Can you become human? We need to talk." Then she turned her back. I wasn't sure I could do another shift but I had to try. It took me a lot longer to shift than normal. Kai was staring at me with his human eyes, concern marking his features. When I had finally taken on my human form, I shrugged on the black sweatpants and t-shirt. Kai put the pants on but left the shirt crumpled on the ground.

*'They smell like someone else,'* he told me. Typical alpha. Didn't want to smell like anyone else.

*'I'm not complaining.'* I winked. The man was some serious eye candy shirtless.

Dr. Tavern extended her hand to Kai and looked at his forehead, not quite meeting his eyes. Smart girl, she had done her homework.

"I'm Dr. Tavern. I have been authorized to be the communications expert between our two parties."

Kai shook her hand. "Do you do only what you are authorized to do?"

She smiled devilishly. "Not always. You don't exactly get chosen to join RAIDOS because you followed the rules all your life."

Kai's deep laughter cut the tension that had been mounting. Her two partners who stood just beyond her relaxed.

'*I like her,*' he told me.

'*Me too,*' I agreed.

"I'm Kai, the alpha of the Mount Hood and Portland, Oregon, territories. I have been authorized by the werewolf council to tell you what I deem necessary." There was no mistaking his subtle threat. Kai was in control of this conversation. Dr. Tavern nodded.

"The deputy director of the intelligence division has briefed the president of the United States on this situation tonight. I have received word that it is now our mission to gather intelligence on Queen Layla and any vampire spawn she may birth after having fed on Aurora."

My hand went to the bite marks on my neck. Kai glared at Dr. Tavern. "Do as you please in regards to the vampires."

Dr. Tavern leaned in and produced a small silver disc from her pocket. She clicked a button and it glowed red. Then her two agents began to walk away.

What the...? Kai grabbed my hand and creased his eyebrows in suspicion.

Dr. Tavern lowered her voice: "It has also been brought to my attention that if the vampire does in fact prove to have a successful birth, Aurora is too much of a threat to be allowed to roam freely. We are to take her into custody to run tests at that point."

Kai opened his mouth to shout something, but she placed a finger over her lips, then clicked the disc and the red light went away.

"We will be in contact with you," she said, all business-like. "If the vampires move to harm any humans, we may ask that you return the favor we gave you today."

What the hell had just happened? She warned us when she didn't have to. Kai was grinding his teeth as I stared into Dr. Tavern's eyes. There was something there ... kindness and fascination. She was intrigued with our species. If Layla gave birth, they would capture me? Run tests? She didn't have to warn us, which made me trust her, but not fully. Everyone had a motive.

*'You're mine. No one is taking you anywhere,'* Kai declared.

"Any final words, Mr. Krishna?" Dr. Tavern asked.

I saw Kai's face fall at the knowledge that they knew his last name.

"Yeah, tell your boss to keep his drones off my mountain." He shifted, tearing the sweatpants in two, and Dr. Tavern's staggered out of the way as his impressive wolf stood before her. Her eyes widened, yet she didn't look away. I was right. She was fascinated. She looked at me then.

"I'm a person," I said. "I have a family. I'm sure you know about my non-profit that helps hundreds of abused women and children every year?"

She grimaced. "Yes, we are aware of your philanthropic efforts."

"What does Layla do?" I prodded. I wanted her bosses to know that if they captured me, they were capturing a person.

Dr. Tavern chewed her lip. "She owns a few night clubs and an anti-aging skin cream line."

"Ahh, well, thank God for her." I laid the sarcasm on thick and took off running after Kai. It was important to me that the higher-ups at RAIDOS didn't lump vampires and werewolves together. We were nothing alike. If they thought they could just wipe me out because my blood could grow the vampire race, they had another thought coming. Did I have two enemies now? The vampires and the humans? I didn't want to think about it.

I ran alongside Kai, grateful for the easy pace he kept. We met Max and the others at the front of the water treatment plant. None of our wolves had died.

*'If RAIDOS hadn't helped us, this would have been a lot worse,'* I told Kai.

*'I know,'* he admitted.

*'Dr. Tavern didn't have to warn us about them taking me if Layla has a child.'*

*'I know,'* he said again.

I sighed. I didn't know why I was sticking up for them. Then I laughed out loud, as Sylvia and her clan joined our group.

"What's so funny?" she asked.

"We thought humans were a weak race." I gestured to the piles of ashes around us signifying dead vampires.

Max chuckled and nodded to Kai. "Guess we gotta up our game and buy a helicopter."

"Consider it done." Kai, now human, smiled.

## 25

## NEW FAMILY

A MONTH HAD PASSED ALREADY. It was a rough two weeks with no showering for everyone. We bathed in freezing cold creek water, and drank only bottled water. I wasn't affected by the silver, but I joined everyone in solidarity. When the running water tested negative for silver particles, we were finally given the all clear. Kai had ordered a device installed on every water tap in every pack members' house; it glowed blue if silver was present. This would prevent future attempts.

Packing my bags to accompany Kai to his sister's wedding in India, I couldn't believe how fast the time had gone by. Diya was dying to be mated already and join us in America.

We drove with Akash, Max, and Trent to the airport. I hadn't heard anything from RAIDOS. I didn't know how long it took for a vampire pregnancy to show, but I was anxiously waiting. I knew Kai was working on something. He had a plan A, B, and C in case certain things came about, but I didn't want to be involved. I focused on my spell casting nights with Sylvia and her coven, learning more about my witch powers. Diya had been video-chatting with Emma and me nonstop lately, to show us last-minute things for her wedding and to get our opinions. I was excited to have her and Jai join our pack. We had grown close.

Kai told Emma she couldn't travel pregnant, so we left most of the pack behind to protect her. Only the five of us were going. As we boarded the private plane and took our seats, the same stewardess that we had on our LA flight, the duff, was there to help us. Max appraised her body with his eyes and then caught me looking and blushed. Kai poked him with an elbow.

"Why not ask her on a date?" Kai challenged when she was out of earshot.

Max's face looked pained for a second and then it was gone. "I was just looking. I've had my great love. Anything else would taste like orange juice after brushing your teeth."

"I'll ask her on a date," Akash said, grinning. One stern look from Kai had him staring at his shoes.

I laughed at Akash, but what Max said had me totally confused.

*'What does Max mean?'* I asked Kai.

Kai looked at Max sadly. *'He was mated for four years. She died about twenty years ago during labor with their first child. Neither of them survived.'*

Kai's answer gutted me. I tried to control my

breathing and my face. I didn't want Max to know we were talking about him. I swallowed hard. *'That's horrible. What happened?'*

*'The baby shifted into wolf form during labor, while inside her belly. The placenta tore. They both bled out. She couldn't heal fast enough.'*

My hand went to my mouth. *'Could that happen to Emma?'*

*'I won't let it,'* he growled.

Oh my God. Why hadn't I thought about this before? Of course werewolf pregnancies would be hard. You were carrying a shape-shifting baby! Emma would be okay, I told myself, and closed my eyes, forcing myself to sleep. It took a long time but I finally drifted off and only awoke as the plane landed.

We were greeted at the airport by Jai, Diya, and the buffest man I had ever seen. He was seriously like Vin Diesel with hair. Kai embraced the large man, lifting him off of his feet. He ruffled Kai's hair and then turned to me. He placed his hands in prayer pose and bowed lightly. "*Namaste*, Aurora."

I grinned. "*Namaste*."

"I'm Nikhil. Welcome to India."

Kai punched him hard in the shoulder. "He is my middle brother and my father's second. He also has a weak right hook and makes horrible chai."

Jai leaned into my ear. "I'm his favorite brother though."

I laughed as Nikhil retorted something about working on his boxing.

Looking over Kai's shoulder, I saw Diya kissing Trent and I smiled. Weddings were fun. Kai cleared his throat loudly and they broke apart, red-faced.

"You aren't mated yet. Get over here," he scolded Trent and we all laughed.

I took in a deep breath. India. It had a distinct smell. Your clothes smelled of spices for weeks after you left, and I had missed it. After grabbing our bags, we made our way outside. The road was packed with cars, rickshaws, and motorbikes, but we all piled into two waiting taxis. I sat in back with Kai and Nikhil, squeezing myself between the two hulking males.

Nikhil turned to Kai. "We lost a few wolves protecting the water supply from the vampires, but thanks for warning us." He tipped his head to me and smiled. I suddenly felt uncomfortable. If I hadn't had that vision and warned everyone ... I shuddered at the thought.

"We didn't lose any wolves, but we had our own complications." Kai leaned into me, and it made me feel safe.

Nikhil reached over me and placed a hand on Kai's knee. "I've missed you, brother. The pack isn't the same without you."

Kai placed his hand over his brother's and gave a deep rumbling laugh. God, I loved that laugh. "I'm sure Father is glad I'm gone and you made second, so it all worked out."

Nikhil stared out the window. "Papa is becoming obsessed with the vampires attacking us. He doesn't want to sit idly and wait for another attack. I feel it fair to warn you, this trip isn't just about Diya's wedding. He will want to talk about the next step."

Kai sighed. "I figured. That's Papa. Can't sit still for a single moment. Always moving, never sleeping, always planning. In some ways it's good."

"Sounds exhausting," I said.

"It is," they said in tandem, and laughed.

We only booked a two-day trip to India, with two more days eaten up for travel. That was being away from the pack and Emma for four days total. I was hoping with us away that Emma would still be safe, but a lot of shit could happen in four days.

---

After settling into our hotel, I was quickly wrapped into a sari and taken to Diya's henna party. It was females only and I made small talk with some of the other girls, surprised to see a few white girls in the pack. I had assumed they would all be Indian. I was careful not to make eye contact. I could feel that my dominating and foreign wolf presence made a few of the more dominant wolves edgy, so I stuck to conversing with the submissives. I found my way to Diya, who had an artist working on her feet and another on her hands. An intricate elephant design was being drawn onto her palm.

Sitting down next to her, I held my hand still, careful not to smudge the small design I had gotten.

"Tomorrow we become sisters," she told me, and I smiled.

"I always wanted a sister," I shared with her.

"Me too! Instead I got a ton of brothers!"

I laughed and remembered Diya telling me over our video-chat once that she was a midwife in India. Now that Kai had told me about Max losing his mate and child, I was interested in werewolf birthing.

"Hey, Diya, is the werewolf birthing process more dangerous than human birthing...?"

Diya's face became serious. "Yes and no. Human births can have all sorts of defects. Heart defects, lung defects, limb abnormalities ... a werewolf pup is immune to these defects. They learn to shift at about thirty-five weeks' gestation. When they shift, they set off the uterus and most mothers go into early labor. Werewolf pups are bigger than normal babies but the mothers aren't. If the pups shift during labor, the cord can become compressed or the placenta can tear. There are a lot of complications."

Jesus. "Why don't you just do a Cesarean and cut them all out?" I didn't know much about birth, but I knew that a C-section would be better than placental tearing or cord compression due to a lengthy labor.

"We tried it back in the eighteenth century. The women kept healing too fast. The babies were stuck halfway out of their mothers' stomachs and the women's abdomens were starting to heal closed. The babies suffocated. Also, pain medication doesn't work on werewolves. We metabolize it too fast."

Oh God. My head was spinning. "Emma..." I breathed.

"Will be fine," she told me, holding my gaze. "I'm taking over her care when I get home with you guys. I have delivered thirty-six healthy pups, and Emma's baby will be my thirty-seventh."

I swallowed hard. I wanted to ask her how many she had lost, but this was a wedding. So I just smiled.

---

I WAS TRYING to battle my jet lag as I lay in the hotel room bed, when Kai entered the bathroom to get ready for the wedding. I heard the shower turn on; my eyelids began to droop. Kai poked his head out. "I feel like we should be good to the environment and shower together ... ya know, to save water."

A genuine laugh left my lips and I was suddenly awake. I gave him a smoldering look. "Well, if it's for the environment." I jumped off the bed and began undressing. I loved that I felt no pressure to go all the way with him. We hadn't talked about it, but I think we had decided to wait until our mating ceremony night before we did it. We were having more than enough fun doing other stuff.

After our shower I got ready and put on a bright teal sari. Kai stared me down in the elevator. I stared him down as well. His tight gray linen suit clung to his large biceps. Clean-shaven, with slicked back dark hair, he was totally yummy.

The elevator doors opened, bringing me out of my thoughts. The hotel lobby was decked-out in red and white flowers and a large sign read. "Diya weds Trent" in gold lettering. I whistled.

"This is fancy," I told Kai.

"My father has been waiting his entire life to marry off his only daughter. There will be no expense spared tonight."

Wow, I knew from Indian culture that the woman's family was expected to pay for the wedding. I couldn't afford a fancy wedding like this.

"What's bothering you?" he asked, reading my mental anxiety.

"Our wedding won't be this fancy—I can't afford much," I told him, tugging at a wrinkle in the sari and staring at the floor.

"I wouldn't want a wedding this big, but we could afford this, because my money is your money," Kai said casually. "We will have whatever wedding you want."

"No, I know the culture expects the woman to pay for the wedding, and I can assure you from my bank account, we cannot have this fancy of a wedding. Besides, I feel bad taking your money." He'd already funded the second location for Safe Haven. That was enough generosity to last me a lifetime.

"It's *our* money, not mine. I will add you to all of the accounts when we get home. Don't bother arguing this, I won't have it." He gave me a kiss that shut me up as we took our seats. How did I feel about him sharing his money with me? Weird.

*'Don't analyze this money thing. Pay attention. Our wedding will be similar.'* He patted my thigh and stood. "I need to enter with my family to show support for my sister."

I looked up then and saw Trent in the doorway. He looked handsome, wearing a bright orange Indian top that went to his knees. Max stood next to him.

"Hang on." I caught Kai's arm. "Trent has no living family? Who will walk in with him?"

Kai shrugged. "Max."

I shook my head. That wouldn't do. I walked over to two of the nicer girls from Diya's henna party. "Hey, girls, Trent doesn't have any family to walk in with him. Would you like to join me and stand with him?"

One of the girls, a submissive wolf named Tara, had a short black bob, and almond-colored eyes, with a big teal, jeweled bindi between her eyes. Her skin was a soft caramel color and she glanced at Max, who was standing with Trent.

"Sure." She stood and followed me with one other girl. We approached Trent, who looked nervous.

"Hey, Aurora, I think I'm going to faint," Trent told me. "They say the groom is supposed to come in first, with a big song and dance, and lots of cheering."

I looked at the girls. "I think we can manage that. We're here for you." We moved to step behind him, near Max.

"Thank you," Trent whispered as I passed, and I smiled. I put my arm on Max's shoulder to tell him how nicely he cleaned up, but my other hand brushed

Tara's finger, making my knees buckle as a vision took me.

My vision showed Max holding a beautiful woman with long red hair. Her body was limp in his arms and he was sobbing into her chest. Blood soaked the bed sheets he held her over; Kai stood frozen in the doorway.

*Oh God. Why am I being shown this? This was Max's wife. Their poor baby...*

The vision changed. Tara was smiling up at Max and had a crown of flowers on her head. It was in Kai's backyard on Mount Hood—their wedding day. Then it transformed and Max was screaming at Tara in the lobby of the hotel we were at today. He was telling her to go! To get out of his life. Once again it shifted, and they were kissing in a hotel room. A second later, a new scene played before my eyes and I saw myself waking away, and not telling Max anything. I was so confused. It was like the future kept fluctuating because it was undecided. I'd never had a vision like this one before.

I felt someone's arms around me and I was brought back to the present, peeling open my eyes. Max held me in his arms; Kai was running across the wedding hall toward me. Oh, great. What the hell should I do, tell Max or no?

'*I saw Max's mate die and you were there. Afterwards I saw him marry Tara, the girl standing next to me. Then they were fighting on this very night. Do I tell them?*' I mean, Max had already had his mate and she died, so it wasn't possible, right? Except it was. I *knew* that.

Kai's eyes opened wide and he stopped dead halfway to me. *'No, that isn't possible. We mate for life. Don't tell him, I'll handle it.'*

*'Right, we mate for life, and his mate died, so that's over. Tara isn't dead and neither is Max.'*

*'Drop this for now,'* Kai ordered me.

"Aurora? Are you okay?" Max helped me straighten myself. He looked nervous. Did he sense it? That I had a vision about him?

"I'm okay, Max. Thanks for catching me," I told him, my voice wavering.

Trent let out a long breath of air. "Okay, good, because it's our turn."

The music changed just as Kai reached me. He gave me a quick kiss and a stern look, then walked away. Max was looking at me accusingly. I looked into his eyes, unable to stop seeing him weeping over his late wife like that. It made my throat tighten; I would never be able to look at him the same. So instead, I looked ahead.

"What did you see?" he whispered.

Just then we were ushered out by the crowd, and I pretended I hadn't heard Max's question. A loud, upbeat Bollywood song played over the loud speaker. People shouted and clapped as we spun, and danced around Trent. I tried to smile and follow what Tara and her friend were doing, but I couldn't stop thinking about Max. Once we had escorted Trent to the stage, I sat down far away from Max.

The next three hours passed in a mix of fascination for the beautiful wedding, and arguing with Kai in my head. I felt I needed to at least tell Max what I had seen and let him decide. Kai said he knew Max better, and that I needed to let it be. In the end, I promised not to tell Max—for now. The most horrible part was that once dinner started, Max sat next to Tara and they seemed to be having a nice conversation. They were smiling and laughing and it was killing me.

The night ended well past three a.m. and we were beyond exhausted. I passed out the second my head reached the pillow, my thoughts a mix of werewolf labor, losing your mate, and what I would wear to my own wedding.

## 26

## SECRET

We woke up to the blaring of a phone call. Why were hotel phones so loud? It should be a crime.

"Yes?" Kai answered groggily. "You can have thirty minutes, Papa." Then he hung up.

Why did I feel like something was about to go down? We dressed quickly and waited for the car to pick us up. Kai's father stayed in a small compound in the nicer part of Delhi. As we drove through a guarded gate and into an open gravel parking lot, I saw his father and mother standing outside.

We exited the car and I wasn't sure if there would be hugs or small talk. We hadn't had a chance to talk much, since we had arrived in the middle of Diya's wedding preparations.

"Hello, thank you for coming. I want you to see something," was all his father said, and then he turned and walked inside.

So much for small talk. Kai and I shared a look as

Kai's mother approached me, and gave me a hug and a smile. His mother motioned for us to follow and we walked in after her. As we followed his father down a long hallway, his mother turned into a different room.

"I'll make some tea," she said, disappearing. She wasn't coming? We trailed down the winding hallway and my nerves went on edge as we approached a door with muffled hissing behind it. Oh no. This was not going to be good. We reached the dark wooden door, my heart in my throat with anticipation. Raj put his hand on the handle and turned to us.

"It's them or us. Choose a side." Then he opened it.

What I saw stole my breath. A sickly, skinny-looking vampire was shackled to a medical bed. Thick iron sheet cuffs bound his legs and hands, with another at his neck. His bed was tilted up so we could look right at his face. A large rag was stuffed in his mouth. He looked dehydrated and he was laboring for air. Everything about this felt wrong. Vampires wanted our kind dead, yes, but this was so messed up.

"You're torturing him?" I spat out.

Raj looked up at me. "It. I am gaining information from *it*."

I suddenly felt sick.

Kai looked only mildly uncomfortable. "How can you make it talk?"

*It?* He was clearly a male. My mate and I were going to have words after this.

Raj smiled. "One of my brightest wolves has designed a serum. If consumed in large quantities, it acts on the neuroreceptors. It's somewhat of a truth serum."

"So you starve him, he drinks it, and gives you information?" I asked scathingly.

His father nodded, looking proud.

"How long has he been here?" I looked to the desk in the corner, which held a silver stake.

"Since the water incident," his father said.

Almost A MONTH!

"We're better than this. Our kind—we're better." I spun and walked out. I couldn't take it. For just a second I had seen something human in the vampire's eye, some emotion. I couldn't be a part of this. I felt Kai follow me out.

*'This is why my father is a council member, an alpha of hundreds of wolves. He's ruthless. But if there is one thing I know about him, it's that he acts with honor. This vampire must be telling him things that are important to our kind. The second it stops talking or they don't need it, my father will cleanly kill it.'*

"After a month of torturing him!" I shouted back.

"Aurora, may we talk in private for a moment?" Raj had followed us into an open drawing room.

Kai stared his father in the eyes. "No."

I sighed. "Yes. It's fine." I placed a hand on Kai's arm. The veins were popping out of his neck. Not a good sign. But if Raj wanted to talk to me about my concerns with this, then I was happy to oblige.

"Your mother has made your favorite dish," Raj

told his son. "Why don't you go meet her in the kitchen. We will be right there."

Kai stared into his father's eyes for a good, long while. "Don't scare my mate."

His father stared back, not answering. Kai finally walked out, closing the door behind him.

Raj beamed at the closed drawing room door. "You know, he is my favorite son. Always has been. He's a leader, a lover, and a fighter. He is respectful, kind, and takes care of his pack."

The admission caught me completely off guard. "Why don't you tell him that?" I asked, aghast.

"Because to tell him would make me feel weak. I'm anything but weak, Aurora." His face looked stern, more like the man I had known for a short time.

"What did you want to talk to me about?" I rushed him along. I didn't want to be in the same building as that vampire.

His father rubbed the spot between his thumb and pointer finger and creased his brow. Did werewolves get headaches?

"There is no way to put this lightly," he said.

Oh God. I backed up slowly and found a couch that I half fell into.

"What is it?" I breathed.

"Don't marry my son. For the sake of yourself, of our entire race, don't you dare go through with the mating ceremony."

Nothing could have prepared me for his reply. My

hand immediately went to the engagement ring around my neck.

"Why would you say something like that to me? I thought you wanted this?" I couldn't help the emotion that rose in my throat.

His father looked pained. "I did want this for you. The council and I have been working on an intel project. We have a double agent inside of RAIDOS. We also have been questioning vampires, like you saw today. All of this has led to some pretty startling information."

A double agent inside RAIDOS? They *knew* about RAIDOS before I had met them? Who was it? I hadn't smelled a werewolf when I met them. Maybe I hadn't met that agent yet, or maybe they'd just now got one inside. I had more questions than answers, that was for sure.

His father stood over me, commanding attention. "The vampire, Layla, has not become pregnant, nor will she. As long as you stay infertile, so does your blood. If you take the mating ceremony with my son and Spirit blesses you with fertility, then any vampire that drinks your blood will have the ability to become pregnant."

Shock ripped through me at his declaration.

"NO! You can't know this for sure." I was in complete denial. This wasn't happening. On one hand it was good news if Layla wasn't pregnant, but on the other ... I couldn't marry Kai.

His hand rested on my shoulder. "I admit it's a

theory, but it's a strong one. The vampires have created a device, a bloodletting device, just for you. It will drain just enough blood to keep you alive. Then the blood is bottled and SOLD to the highest female vampire bidder. RAIDOS has the intel about your blood. They took a sample from the fight at the water treatment plant when you were injured. They tested it and the results say you're infertile."

He walked to a desk in the corner, retrieved a paper and handed it to me. They got a sample of my blood? I looked down at the paper and my heart leapt into my throat.

# 27
## CLASSIFIED

**Aurora**
    **Class:** Werewolf, Second-in-Command.
    **Pack:** Portland, Mount Hood, Oregon. (United States)
    **Mate:** Kai, Alpha (Indian Origin). Mating ceremony has not taken place yet.
    **Known Abilities:** Matefinder. Magic user. Silver Immunity. Extremely Fast Shifter.
    **Blood tested:** FSH, Prolactin, Luteinizing, Estradiol, Serum Progesterone.
    **Results:** Infertile.

I set the paper down. My hands were shaking. The only thing they didn't know about me was my shoe size. I wanted to be strong—I was sitting in front of the alpha of one of the biggest packs in the world—but a tear slid down my cheek.

Raj cleared his throat uncomfortably. "I'm sorry," he murmured.

I nodded slowly. I couldn't have a mating ceremony. I couldn't have children. Oh God. Now that I knew I might not be able to have children, it was the only thing I wanted. A son or a daughter, with Kai's dark hair and laugh, with my smile...

"So if I marry Kai..." I let that hang in the air.

"The ceremony will activate your fertility and your blood will change. We suspect that will then be the change needed to give female vampires fertility."

"You suspect. But you don't know."

He ran his hands through his hair. "We are ninety-nine percent certain."

I stood up and folded the paper, placing it inside my pocket. "I'm keeping this." I started toward the door.

He trailed behind me. "So what are you going to do?"

"If there's one thing I won't do, it's live in fear," I declared. "I've spent too much of my life doing that already."

"Then RAIDOS will kill you. That's their backup plan. You get married, they kill you!" he all but shouted.

My hand stilled on the doorknob and I leaned my head against the cool wood. What the hell was I supposed to do? Not marry the love of my life because I was scared of the vampires coming for me? It wasn't fair.

I could feel his father come up behind me. His voice was soft this time, understanding. "When the rogue werewolf burst into my house and attacked my family all those years ago, I felt helpless. I watched my wife writhe on the floor screaming in pain. Kai fought the werewolf hard—he nearly died of blood loss. My daughter didn't make it. I vowed that day to never feel helpless again. So I put myself in a place of power. I created a life for my family to ensure we would never be hurt like that again. You are my son's mate whether you have a mating ceremony or not. You are my daughter-in-law."

I knew deep down he was a good guy, I had a radar for that type of thing.

I turned to face him and tears swam in my eyes. I never had a father I respected, but I respected this man. He was hard around the edges, he was stubborn, and he was controlling, but he was a good man.

He placed both hands on my shoulders. "As a council member, I am telling you not to marry my son. You will bring danger to yourself, your pack, and our kind. As your father-in-law, I want you and my son to be happy. I want you to have children and experience every beautiful thing that life has to offer. Whatever you choose, you will have my blessing." The kiss he placed on my forehead was so quick I couldn't be sure it happened. Then the door opened behind me and Raj ushered me out.

I decided to hold off on telling Kai until we got back to the States. I needed to think, to process everything. He wasn't exactly easy to persuade. Asking for time to think before telling him something bought me about five minutes before he pestered me again. I finally had to snap at him.

"It's bad, okay! It's so goddamn bad I can't bear to tell you! Just give me time to figure it out. I will tell you when we get home to Portland," I screamed at him in the hotel while we packed our things.

He looked at me with an unreadable expression. "Are you in immediate danger?"

I lowered my head. "No." It was the truth.

"All right," he said reluctantly.

I zipped my bag. "I'm going to wait in the lobby for you," I told him, and left the room in a hurry. I needed time to think. I rolled my bag down the hall and was smashing buttons on the elevator when Tara spoke behind me.

"Hey, Aurora." The elevator opened and she followed me in with a duffle bag over one shoulder.

Of all the people to see. "Hey." I forced a smile.

"I wanted to ask you about your pack mate, Max. He's cute. What's his story?" She smiled shyly. I promised Kai I wouldn't tell Max I had found his mate. I said nothing about not telling Tara. I was feeling reckless—I thought I might regret this later.

I pulled the stop button on the elevator and pinned her with a dominant gaze.

"I'm going to tell you something and you cannot act on it. You cannot repeat it. Do you understand me?"

She swallowed hard and backed up a little, looking alarmed.

"Do you know what my gift is? That I find mates?"

She nodded.

"Max was mated to a woman who died during childbirth about twenty years ago. They lost the baby, too."

Her hand flew to her mouth. "Oh God, I'm so sorry. I didn't know. I mean, I thought he was nice and we had this intense connection … but I won't pursue him now, don't worry."

I placed a hand on hers. I stared into her eyes. "Max is your mate, Tara."

I could hear her heart pick up in speed from where I stood. "What? You just said he lost his mate." Her voice held so much confusion.

"He did. Werewolves mate for life, I know. But I'm telling you, I have visions of people's mates and you are Max's mate now." I drove the point home.

I released the stop button; the elevator dropped one floor and dinged open.

"I'm sorry," I told her, and walked into the lobby, leaving her there with her mouth open in shock.

---

THE FLIGHT HOME was long and I was stuck in my thoughts. Trent stayed behind to help Diya say goodbye and to tour more of India. They would be flying home in a week. I was excited and nervous to see

Emma. I wasn't sure I could look at her the same now that I knew werewolf pregnancy was so dangerous.

The second the plane landed on the tarmac in Portland, I powered up my phone. It beeped with a bunch of missed calls and texts. I was scrolled through them—Lexi, my mom, Dr. Tavern. I looked closer at that one—I didn't even have Dr. Tavern's number in this phone. This was my personal phone. She must have plugged it in when I wasn't looking. What the heck? I opened the text.

*No bun in the oven*, it read. I slipped the phone in my backpack. So everything Kai's father had told me was right. Layla wasn't pregnant; it didn't work. And Dr. Tavern was totally on our side.

We reached home and I was exhausted. I wanted nothing more than to sleep for a week.

Kai grabbed my arm lightly. "Are you going to tell me about what happened with my father?"

I sighed. "I'm so tired from the flight. Let me sleep and we will talk tomorrow. Okay?"

Kai looked into my eyes, then bent forward and kissed my nose. "Okay."

## 28

## DREAMS

That night, dreaming, I tossed and turned; a cold sweat broke out on my skin. This wasn't like a normal dream; I was half awake and aware of Kai breathing next to me. I also knew that I was dreaming, but I couldn't fully wake up. I felt trapped. Like I was out of my body somehow.

Suddenly, I was standing in my dream, in front of my childhood home. The front door was open and chills ran up my spine. Something felt wrong. I did NOT want to go inside, not ever again. I tried to back up but my traitorous legs began walking in.

"No!" I screamed in the dream.

I heard a whimper leave my throat as Kai woke up next to me. It felt like my soul was splitting in two. Part of me was now standing at the foot of the bed, staring at my sleeping body. Kai was awake now and looking curiously at my sleeping self. But, in the dream, I was walking into the house and heading right for the kitchen.

"No, no, no! Wake up!" I urged myself. A soft whimper left my throat again.

Kai nudged me this time. "Aurora, wake up. You're dreaming."

The dream continued, and I knew what I was going to see—somehow I knew. My father's body was crumpled on the kitchen floor, a pool of blood rapidly growing around him. I looked down at my shaking hands; they were covered in blood. The knife lay at my feet. He wasn't dead yet. I could hear his sputtering cough.

I didn't want to be here! Why was I here? Experiencing this once was enough. Tears streamed down my face and I tried to close my eyes, but they wouldn't. I was trapped. I knew what came next and I didn't want to hear it. His words would haunt me for the rest of my life.

"It should have been you," my dying drunken father wheezed. "Not my Drake." Then the blood became too much and the life left his eyes. A sob escaped me. The refrigerator door was open, and my mother's unconscious body lay on the floor, an open jug of orange juice pooled around her. To this day I couldn't eat two things: ketchup and orange juice.

---

"Aurora! Wake up this instant!" Kai's eyes had gone yellow. Fur was rippling down his arms but my body didn't move even as he shook me.

---

I looked again at my bloody hands and felt a presence at my back. Spinning quickly, I saw the dark witch that was working with Layla. Prudence. Inside my childhood home. In my dream.

"I always knew you had a dark side to you, Aurora. But imagine my surprise when I find out you're not just a murderer, but that you killed your own father!" She laughed, and clapped her hands together in glee. My stomach rolled.

"Kai! Sylvia!" I screamed frantically.

Prudence flung her hand out quickly, dousing me with mist, and suddenly, it felt like cement had been poured down my veins. I couldn't move.

---

Kai was shaking my body hard now, slapping my face. I watched, helpless, as Emma ran into the bedroom. Kai must have summoned her.

"Get Max and Sylvia!" Kai roared.

Emma paled when she saw my limp frame in Kai's hands.

---

I FELT SO HEAVY. Prudence walked back to my parents' old room and reappeared with a little girl. What the...? She looked scared. She must have been about four years old, and had long, inky-black hair. She clung to the witch in fear.

"Auntie, why am I here?" she asked Prudence.

The witch looked at the girl. "Because your mommy owes me a favor, little one."

I lifted my right leg up a few inches and stepped forward.

Prudence pulled a small knife out and pointed it at the little girl. "Don't push me!" she yelled at me. I stood still, my breath coming out in ragged gasps. "Do you have any idea what I am capable of? I can bring souls back from the dead! I can make a poor man rich with women and gold. I can even bleed a child to make a woman fertile..."

She smiled wickedly.

"No!" I screamed, trying to use my magic, but it was no use. I had a blanket over my powers. I was completely trapped.

---

Back with my body, I sensed Sylvia enter the room and grab her chest. "No! I should have taught her more. She should be learning protections spells. This is what happens when someone with her power doesn't know how to be a witch!" Sylvia was beside herself. I had never seen her this flustered.

Kai was barely holding on to his human form. "Fix it! What's happening?" he roared.

Sylvia pulled her shaking hand from her purse and began lining the room with salt. "Dark, dark magic. Old magic. I can't fix this. Her soul has been split. And I haven't taught her enough to fix it herself."*

The dream returned, I stared at Prudence in fear. "Let the child go!" I roared.

She smiled and put her dagger down. "Okay, would you rather I used Emma's baby?" The gleam in her eyes made me sick. There wasn't a scrap of humanity left in this woman. I couldn't reason with her.

"Be careful with your threats, witch. That's one I won't forget." I looked at the little girl. Her lip was quivering, her head down. Could you kill someone in the dream world? I didn't want to find out, but a thought struck me then.

I closed my eyes and concentrated. *'Nahuel, help! I need you.'*

Kai breathed in deeply through his nostrils just as there was a knock at the door. Max had stationed himself in the doorway, so he left to see who had arrived, and returned with Nahuel. Kai growled and hugged my body protectively. Nahuel creased his brow, looked at Sylvia, then again at Kai. "You're not doing a very good job at protecting her, are you?" he mused aloud.

Kai growled again. "Why are you here?"

Nahuel pulled a feather and a dried sage bundle from his satchel. "Your mate invited me. She woke me from a nice dream."

Kai didn't trust him. I could see that, but I could also see his desperation. Nahuel put the tip of the sage bundle to his bare palm and it ignited with flames.

"Showoff," Sylvia murmured.

He blew out the flame and a long stream of smoke rose up to the ceiling, then he began fanning the smoke with the large eagle feather.

"Listen to my words, Kai. *You* are Aurora's one true mate, her alpha, her pack leader, her soul mate. Like two drops in the ocean, I cannot tell where one begins and the other ends. You must use your link with Aurora to go into her mind. *Take* her mind into your power. Flood her with your presence. Saturate her being with your love. Free her from the binds that hold her. Remind her that nothing can hold power over her without her permission. Tell her that she is the creator of her destiny."

Nahuel came closer to Kai and grabbed his ankle with a firm grip. Kai flinched, glaring at the shaman's hand.

"Let yourself go," Nahuel said. "I will keep your spirit grounded to this world. I will keep your soul together. You have my word, I will protect you."

Kai swallowed hard. I could see his pride flaring up. He didn't think he needed the protection and he didn't want to seem weak, didn't want to trust an outsider. But he also didn't want to lose me.

Max stepped into the room. "Kai, do as he says. If he makes a move to harm you, I will kill him."

Nahuel tried to stifle a laugh. I wanted to tell Max that I had seen Nahuel stop time and so I was pretty sure he would be hard to kill.

Kai nodded and rested his forehead on mine. My skin was gray and sweat covered my face.

"*Meri pyari*, let me in," he whispered.

---

IN THE DREAM WORLD, Prudence was preparing an altar of some kind. She lit candles and began chanting. The little girl seemed frozen now too, unable to run. I needed to somehow get to Kai, so I closed my eyes and imagined myself in the woods behind our house. A large ball of light was floating toward me and I tried to run to it, but I couldn't. The light became brighter.

"Kai!" I looked down at my body. This was a dream. I didn't need a body, right? At that thought, I shed my body and I too became a ball of light. My ball of light raced toward Kai's light and the two crashed together, sending out sparks like fireworks. We became one.

I opened my eyes again. and Prudence was grabbing her dagger now. Looking down at my body, I gave a gasp of shock, because it wasn't my body, it was my wolf's, and it wasn't just me—Kai was with me, inside me.

*'It's a dream,'* Kai told my wolf.

*'I know,'* I replied.

I tried to move my paw but nothing happened. The witch was walking the little girl over to her altar and she hadn't noticed me yet.

*'Aurora, do you know why I love you so much?'* Kai spoke from inside of me.

*'Because you're my mate. You have to,'* I joked.

*'No, because you don't let anyone tell you what to do. I have never shared this with you, but I fear that you too may be an alpha. You may be more dominant than me. I sense that. I knew from that first day that you may actually have the power and strength to lead this pack, to be stronger than me. It terrifies me and excites me all at once. No one can make you do anything you don't want to do. You're a free spirit.'*

His confession knocked into me like a ton of bricks.

I felt his alpha power merge with mine, and a growl ripped from my throat. Prudence turned to look at me, and stumbled backward just as I leapt from where I had been cemented with fear. I landed on her chest, knocking her back into her altar. A candle fell onto her hair, which burst into flame and she began to scream. The little girl fell over, free from her spell, and I shifted instantly to my human form.

"Wake up! Go back to your body!" I screamed at the girl. "Tell your mother what happened here and run away!"

The little girl ran for the front door. The second she crossed the threshold she disappeared. Prudence was chanting now as her body burned. Screw this. I was out of here. I ran for the door, but a blast hit me from the back and I fell forward, knocking my chin on the hardwood floor. The door slammed shut then and smoke began building in the house.

Standing up, I turned and faced her. "One day I'm going to learn to fully use my magic, I'm going to find you, and I'm going to incinerate you out of existence."

With a leap, I jumped and slammed my body through the living room window. I felt Kai's power pushing me through the glass. The sound of shattering cut through the night, and as I was about to reach the ground, I slammed back into my body and out of my dream ...*

I opened my eyes to find Max, Emma, Sylvia, Nahuel, and Kai all staring at me.

"Well, I might have a hard time sleeping from now on," I told them.

Kai let out a sigh and grabbed me, holding me close in an iron-clad grip.

"Don't ever do that again," he breathed.

"Deal."

---

After promising Sylvia I would attend weekly Witch circles and spell castings, and promising Nahuel that I would wear a special protection amulet pouch he'd made me, they left.

I gazed at Kai. He had been patient. He had given me time to think things through. I owed him an explanation. I went to the dresser and slowly pulled out the paper I had taken from his father. Unfolding it, I handed it to him. It was sad to watch his features change as he read the paper.

"Okay, what the hell is this?" he grumbled.

"RAIDOS has figured out that I can't impregnate vampires so long as I stay unmated. I'm infertile. I love you, Kai ... but we can't marry. If we do, I become fertile and so does my blood."

I told him everything. About the device the vampires had to drain and sell my blood. About my fear and desire to have children. When I was done, he took my face in his hands.

"This doesn't mean we can't marry."

Hope sprang up inside my chest. "It doesn't?"

He shook his head, his eyes taking on a menacing shade of orange. "It only means we have to take out the vampires that want to hurt you first." The tone of his voice gave me chills.

Sometimes I wondered just how dangerous the man who shared my bed could be. I swallowed hard. "You have that look in your eye. The crazy, creepy look that says you want to go on a killing spree." I tried to make a joke but his face remained sinister.

"Vampires are like bees," he told me, as I saw a plan hatching in his mind.

"Bees?"

He nodded. "Bees. They spend their whole life obsessed with their hive and honey. Money and blood for vampires."

"Okay." I could kind of see where he was going. Sure, vampires and bees had some similarities. "And this helps us how?"

"They are also obsessed with their queen. Their pathetic little lives revolve around one bitch. Take out the queen, take out the hive."

Oh, shit. Kai was going to go after Layla.

"What are you going to do?" My heart was pounding.

Kai smiled. "Don't worry. You just plan our wedding. We will be mated, Aurora. No one is taking that from me."

In that moment I didn't care. About any of it. I was loved. I smiled and folded myself into his arms and he kissed me long and deep. After everything that had happened in my life—my broken childhood, my car accident, my newfound abilities—it was all a part of a greater outcome. This was where I was meant to wind up. I belonged in Kai's arms. Kai and I were made for each other, and no one was taking from us what we deserved. We deserved it all. We would have everything we wanted in life, and God have mercy on whoever got in our way.

A growl left my throat and Kai nodded.

"Yes, *meri pyari*. We will fight for what we want in life. Let no creature stand in our way."

Mist began to rise off of my skin and I felt patches of fur break out on my arms. If the vampires wanted a war, then that's what they would get.

Read Book Two here now! My Book

## ACKNOWLEDGMENTS

This book literally wouldn't have been possible without the help of my mother and father-in-law. I sat at the dining room table in our kitchen dreaming up Kai and Aurora while they ran after my twins and made sure everyone was clean and fed. Thank you, Amma and Appa. To my husband, my biggest supporter and fan, I love you so much. Thank you for pushing me to follow this dream, and for helping Kai's fight scenes be a little more badass. To my mother, who allowed me to be free-spirited and creative as a child. This is all because of the person you raised me to be. To my editors Patti Geesey, and Lee of Ocean's Edge Editing, big thanks for polishing this up! And to my other editor, Sara Meadows, for ironing out the kinks. Lastly, I want to thank Earl Chessher and the awesome authors at Fiction Writers Group. I love our 2 A.M discussions over comma usage and the best place to hide a body.

## NEWS!

This series has been optioned for film! Stay tuned and like my author page on Facebook to follow the latest news.
www.facebook.com/leia.stone/

**ALSO BY LEIA STONE:**

MATEFINDER SERIES

Matefinder - Book 1

Devi - Book 2

Balance - Book 3

Matefinder Next Generation Series

Keeper - Book 1

Walker - Book 2

USA TODAY bestselling Hive Series

Ash - Book 1

Anarchy - Book 2

Annihilate - Book 3

NYC Mecca Series

Queen Heir - Book 1

Queen Alpha - Book 2

Queen Fae - Book 3

Queen Mecca - Book 3

Dark War Saga

Protector - Book 1

Defender - Book 2

Redeemer - Book 3

Dragons and Druids Series

Skyborn

Earthbound

Magic Torn

Sign up for my monthly newsletter! Get inside details and win free stuff. No spam. Can leave at any time.

Visit **http://goo.gl/Jk3Slm**